in the
silences

Praise for the works of Rachel Gold

Being Emily

"Engrossed...Enchanted... Rachel Gold has crafted an extraordinarily poignant novel in Being Emily... The unique mechanism of depicting Emily's speech as computer code is striking, defining the character distinctively. The careful and deliberate spacing of Claire's chapters are extraordinary; resulting is a pacing of action that is gripping. There is definitely gold to be found in this well-constructed novel."

- *Lambda Literary Review*

Speaking as a teen librarian, Miss Ingrid writes, "Gold, however, is incredibly adept at making the reader understand what life is like for Emily, who is navigating the world in a body that just doesn't feel like it's hers. She's got some allies, like her girlfriend, but has so many more obstacles preventing her from being comfortable, let alone happy and fulfilled."

- *The Magpie Librarian*

"It's rare to read a novel that's involving, tender, thought-provoking and informative... What's impressive is Gold's delicacy in handling the physicality of Emily's story. She smoothly navigates the more intimate parts of Emily's transformation. And the author can bring you to tears as you read about Emily's struggle with gender identity."

- *TwinCities.com*

"I couldn't put it down... It's not a sad or angst-ridden story at all. Instead it feels incredibly honest, and there are moments of joy, anger, and sorrow, laced together in a way that will make you cry and laugh along with the characters. It doesn't shy away from the hardship but it also doesn't make the claim that this hard stuff is all a trans person's life is ever... All in all, I think this is an excellent book that captures an honest, painful, but ultimately hopeful and joyful story of a young trans teen."

- YAPride.org

Being Emily 2013 Collection Recommendation

- Young Adult Services Library Association

Just Girls

"The novel covers all manner of sex, sexuality and gender identities and is an excellent educational tool, as well as a very good read... This book sits particularly well in the teen / young adult audience category, but can be enjoyed and appreciated by a much older audience as well, especially those who are keen to expand their knowledge and try to understand a little more about what it means to be trans*."

- Curve Magazine

"Brilliant, brilliant, and all kinds of brilliant... Written with a sure-footed and almost magical lightness... Like a great wine: a beautiful blend of different emotions and different people told with depth, and complexity. It is a richly layered novel, which leaves the reader enthralled and wanting more of this exquisite concoction."

- Lambda Literary Review

"As I said for Being Emily, this is an excellent book for any young person to read as it is a story about people like them and unlike them, which is always the basis for a good tale... What comes across strongly is that, to use my favourite quote from that great woman philosopher Marge Simpson, "our differences are only skin deep but our sames go down to the bone." This is also another fine read for any age – we were all young once and as I always maintain, still changing, still evolving."

- Glasgow Women's Library

My Year Zero

Gold has skillfully written a story with timely topics for
navigating the slippery approach to adulthood, ranging from
sex and sexuality, relationships, self-discovery, overcoming
difficulties with authority figures, parental bullying and neglect,
and bipolar disorder. My Year Zero...will appeal to both young
and more experienced adults, meeting difficult topics head-on
with a compelling story (and a masterful story-within-a-story)
written to both inform and entertain.

- *Lambda Literary Review*

Other Bella Books by Rachel Gold

Being Emily
Just Girls
My Year Zero
Nico & Tucker

About the Author

Rachel Gold is the award-winning author of five queer and trans young adult novels—including *Being Emily*, the first young adult novel to tell the story of a trans girl from her perspective. Despite having a B.A. in English and Religious Studies and an MFA in Writing, Rachel is better known as a nonbinary lesbian, all around geek and avid gamer. She teaches classes (that are also games) for teens at the Loft Literary Center. As a marketing strategist, Rachel has developed brands and messaging for businesses across the U.S. and has won awards for her writing, ideas and "genius marketing." For more information visit: www.rachelgold.com.

in the silences

rachel gold

BELLA
BOOKS
2019

Acknowledgments

This novel would not exist without the friendship and help of Ha'Londra Dismond, who beta read multiple drafts, consulted about Aisha's family, and helped with dialogue for Aisha's mom. And this novel would not be nearly as sweet without Patrice James, who brainstormed scenes and geeked out about comic books with me, in addition to beta reading. Many thanks to both of you for your dedication, brain power and humor!

I am always grateful to have Katherine V. Forrest as my editor, but even more so with this novel. Thank you Katherine for your many insights, for always pushing me to be my best, and for doing it in such a clear, generous, caring way.

Also many thanks to:

• Stephanie Burt who read multiple drafts, also geeked out about comic books, and researched the Science Bowl questions

• Vee Signorelli for creating the phrase "two kinds of gay" and letting me borrow it (and so much more!)

• My mother, Sarah Lee Gold, for all her support and many conversations about race and social justice. Thank you!

• My dad, Robert Gold, for asking for a book with a nonbinary character!

• Alia Whipple for teaching me how to speak to and understand dogs

• Qamar Saadiq Saoud for initial brainstorming about Aisha's family, especially her Yoga dad

• And my crew of amazing beta readers: Jessie Chandler, Cheryl A. Head, JJ Khale, and Jane Wisdom

As always, so much love and gratitude for my household: the people and animals who love me and take care of me every day. You're an essential part of my superhero team!

If you see yourself in Kaz or Aisha, or both,
I wrote this book for you.

CHAPTER ONE

August 2015

There was nobody else in the world I wanted to kiss—not even famous people or superheroes—only Aisha. I'd been thinking about kissing her since the end of eighth grade, not even three months. Summer meant more reading together, more of her telling me stories about our favorite books, comic books, movies. She saw parts of the characters I missed and explained them in startling, genius ways.

I wanted to put my lips on hers and inhale her words into my brain.

I should've asked Aisha out on the anniversary of the day we met. I wish I could've kissed her then.

* * *

I met Aisha because I got roped into setting up our block's annual shindig. Due to my grandmom Milo's unofficial standing as Queen-Emperor of the block, the party happened in front of our house. My job included carrying a ton of folding chairs from our open garage to the street and setting them in big circles.

Wolverine—"Wolvie" to her friends—my big, silly loveball of a dog walked with me, her leash looped over my belt. That reminded her to stick close, except when she saw other dogs and squirrels. It was early for squirrel season and we didn't have a lot of dogs on our block, plus the street had already been blocked off for the party.

Behind me, I heard a car pull around the "street closed" signs and stop a few houses down. I didn't realize the leash had come loose and Wolvie wasn't beside me until I heard a man yell, "Get your dog away from me!"

Wolvie is seventy pounds of black-and-brown fuzzy love, half German Shepherd, half Lab. Her size can scare people who don't know her—especially when she body-checks them out of joy.

She'd backed this man against his car, but only because he wasn't petting her. Square-faced, graying brown hair, peach skin, he looked older than my mom but not as old as my grandpop. He held his hands out, trying to ward off Wolvie, who pushed into his thighs, wriggling.

He glared past me, down the street, yelling, "Dammit, girl, get over here and get this dog off me!"

A girl's resonant voice called back, "That's not my dog."

I turned one-eighty to see who he was yelling at. A brown-skinned girl held a puffy white Bichon Frise in her skinny arms. Even with her curly black hair piled up on her head, she wasn't taller than me. Couldn't have been older than thirteen or fourteen. Anger narrowed her eyes and set creases at the edges of her mouth.

She had to be from the new family that'd moved in across the alley weeks ago. Our town was about ninety-five percent white and less than two percent black; a black family moving in was hard to miss. From my treehouse, I'd seen an older boy and his dad in the yard across the alley. I didn't know they had a girl my age.

"Of course this is your dog!" The man was spitting mad at the girl. "Don't play dumb with me. You get over here right now."

I was half the distance away from this guy and standing in plain sight. Why would he think Wolvie belonged to her?

"Wolverine, down!" I yelled.

Wolvie dropped to her belly, tail wagging, watching me. She opened her mouth in a happy, befuddled pant, the edge of her tongue over her black lips.

"Come. Sit." Wolvie jogged to my side and sat. "This is my dog," I told the guy, though it was blazingly obvious at that point.

From behind me, the girl said, "I told you."

"Don't mouth off to me," he snarled. "Bitch." He stormed up his front steps and slammed the door.

The girl's mouth scrunched up. More anger or trying not to cry? I couldn't tell. She turned away, still holding the fluffy white dog to her chest. They must've been on a walk and she'd picked up her dog when Wolvie got loose. I didn't want her to be scared of Wolvie.

"Hey, I'm really sorry," I called to her. "My dog wouldn't hurt your dog, I promise. She's real sweet, loves people."

The girl half turned back, then glanced down the street like she was going to walk off without saying anything. I picked up Wolvie's leash, tapped my thigh with the command for "heel" and took a few steps closer to her. Wolvie paced with me. She knew how to behave when she had to. Wolvie sat when I stopped, just the way I'd trained her, two houses away from the girl and her dog, in case she was scared of Wolvie too.

"I'm sorry," I said again. "I'm Kaz, this is Wolverine, but you can call her Wolvie."

The girl's eyes focused on me, face set serious like this was going to be the most important question in the history of the world.

In a way, it was.

"Logan or Laura?" she asked.

Warm sunny joy burst open in me. Those were the names of classic Wolverine from the *X-Men* and the new, awesome, All-New Wolverine. I thought I was the only girl for twenty miles who read comics.

"Laura!" I told her, bouncing on my toes from excitement while staying in place so Wolvie wouldn't get up.

A grin took over her face, dimpling her cheeks, warming her eyes. "I'm Aisha, this is Mr. Pickles."

"You want to come into my back yard and let Mr. Pickles and Wolvie play? Wolvie's gentle with small dogs."

She set Mr. Pickles down and he ran out to the length of his leash but couldn't reach Wolvie, who was thumping her tail hard but knew better than to break a sit.

Aisha asked, "Are you the house with the treehouse?"

"Sure am. Come on, I'll show you. Did you move in to that house behind us? You probably met my grandmom, Milo."

"She brought us brownies."

Aisha followed me to the side gate and I held it open for her. She wore a white T-shirt with a cute row of buttons at the top, plus blue jeans. Garage dust streaked my blue shirt, making it match my crappy gray jeans and the old tennies with no laces that I used for chores.

I closed the gate. "Wolvie might try to tackle you with love, but she won't hurt you."

"I'm not afraid of dogs," she said, eyes cutting toward the house where the jerk had gone. "But let Pickles go first. You can call him Pickles; he likes you."

"Sure," I said. Did her dropping Mr. Pickles' formal title mean we were on our way to being friends?

As soon as she put Pickles down, he ran up the stairs to the back patio and declared himself king of the hill with his ears up and tail high. I let Pickles sniff a bit before unclipping Wolvie's leash. She butted against Aisha's legs, so Aisha bent down to rub her with both hands.

Pickles came back to sniff Wolvie and they did the whole dance of butt-sniffing. Aisha peered up at the treehouse. It was six feet up the big oak in our yard, with a wrap-around staircase so Wolvie could get up there. Four walls, but one opened for good weather.

"You want to see it?" I asked.

"I have to get home soon. Do you want help with those chairs before I go?"

"Yeah, thanks. My brother bailed on me."

"Older or younger?" she asked as we put the dogs back on their leashes.

"Older," I said.

"Same here. Two of them, but one's at college."

We walked around to the front of the garage and I picked up a folding chair from the stack inside the open door.

"We should have a support group for younger siblings," I told her. "What comics are you reading?"

As we carried the chairs into the street, Aisha listed her comics and I listed mine. When I brought up *Ms. Marvel*, her eyes lit up. "That Wolverine crossover in the sewer with the giant alligator? So epic!"

She faced the army of empty chairs. I only saw half of her smile, but it was the best smile, broad and open, but also like she knew a secret, her dimpled cheeks bunching up, crinkling the skin by her eyes. And she smiled like that about comics, about Wolverines and giant alligators. I thought: *I am going to be her friend forever.*

"Do you want to come to the cookout?" I asked.

"Let me take Pickles home and ask my parents if it's okay."

She set the last chair into place in a big oblong that took up the middle of the street. Getting Pickles' leash from where she'd looped it around another chair, she waved and walked off down the block.

I wondered how we'd look together: a white girl walking a mostly black dog and a black girl walking a white dog. Did that look like a commercial for world peace or fabric softener?

* * *

I wanted Aisha to come to the block party cookout so much! If she didn't, how weird would it be to show up at her house with a stack of comic books?

I'd invited my best friend Jon to the cookout, even though he would diss everything about it, so I had to stay. If Aisha didn't return, maybe tomorrow I could walk over to her house. Or I could hang a sign on my treehouse that said, "Come over! Read comics!" Would she see that from her yard?

After carrying out cutlery and napkins and condiments, I went inside to change. If Mom didn't drive around the signs, like that jerk guy had, she'd have to park in the alley, by the big, heated shed that held Milo's woodworking equipment. I didn't see Mom's current favorite purse on the hooks by the garage door, or thrown on the dining room table, which was more likely. I stopped in the kitchen to drink half a glass of water and poured the other half into Wolvie's bowl to cool it down.

A quick check out the back window showed no car. Maybe I'd get lucky and Mom would be stuck at work. She did a lot of evening shifts because she assistant-managed a Maurice's, a chain women's clothing store that also sold shoes and accessories, but not any that I'd wear. Mom didn't like me bringing Wolvie to neighborhood events, but it wasn't fair to leave Wolvie in the house with so many people right out front.

My grandpop, who we all called Pops, stood in the back yard, cleaning the surface of a grille that was already cleaner than any other grille in our town. Like always, he wore khakis and a blue short-sleeved button-down shirt. In winter he switched to long sleeved. Milo bought his shirts a dozen at a time. He wore them buttoned all the way up, an uncannily hip old guy, but I think he was being hip on accident.

Hearing rustling from the basement, I yelled down to Milo, "Need help?"

"Nope," she called back. "Go wash up."

I headed for my room. My brother Brock must've come and gone because our bathroom stank of his acrid body spray. I could smell it from the top of the stairs, even though my bedroom comes before the bathroom. Brock's room is in the basement, but he shares this bathroom with me because Mom, Milo and Pops kicked him out of the other two bathrooms. He left his socks, underwear and shirts in every corner and they reeked like thousand-year-old cabbage.

Pops and Milo have lived here for way longer than I've been alive, like since the eighties, when my mom was a teenager. She used to have my room, or I had hers, however that worked. Now she slept in the first floor den that Milo converted into a bedroom when we moved in. Milo and Pops slept in the big bedroom on the second floor and I had the little one, which was still plenty big for me.

After a quick shower, I changed into my blue Wolverine T-shirt, the one with Laura on it rather than Logan, and less-torn jeans. I switched the dog treats from the pocket of the other jeans to these. When I got back to the street with Wolvie on her leash, Pops had the grille rolled out and fired up. The smell of pork fat and spices rested heavy in the warm summer air. I gave Wolvie a treat since she wasn't allowed to eat bratwurst—though she'd steal part of one off the ground later and then have gas that made everything Brock smell like air freshener.

Milo sat in a folding chair with people all around her since she was the official/unofficial royalty of our neighborhood. Adults had taken up most of the chairs, but I saw a blanket on our front lawn with Jon and Brock on it. Jon had biked over from the fancy housing development on the other side of the river. This used to be a small town when Milo and Pops first moved here, but then people noticed it was a pleasant twenty-five minute drive from Saint Paul, so new houses kept getting built for the corporate folks who wanted big yards. And the small, old houses in my neighborhood got built onto or torn down and replaced with big, new ones, like the one across the alley, where Aisha lived.

I'd been taller than Jon when we first met and he'd started to catch up. Plus he'd discovered fashion. I didn't like either of those trends. He had on dark blue skinny jeans and a short-sleeved button-up, black with pink flamingos, ironic and stylish. Jon's jeans looked like they wouldn't be caught dead in the same store as mine. He'd been growing out his very black hair, now past his ears, and it made him even more handsome-pretty.

Brock wore his usual sleeveless T-shirt and baggy jeans. He'd been allergic to sleeves since last spring when some girl at school talked up his arm muscles. They were bigger than Jon's arms, but Brock had a ways to go to catch up to Pops in muscles, size and height. Brock got the freckles in the family and with the acne and sad attempts at shaving, most days it looked like his brush of red hair had launched a partially successful missile attack on his face.

I dropped onto my butt on the blanket and bent my knees up so I could rest my arms on them. Wolvie sighed because she knew she so wasn't getting at a brat anytime soon and flopped on her side against my hip.

"Kaz, just in time," Jon said. "Pick a hero."

Jon had more interests than having superheroes fight each other, but this was the one that crossed over to Brocks' interests, or at least his old interests. Now that Brock was starting tenth grade and had approximately seven hairs on his face, he was trying to give up that kid stuff.

Jon had another version of this game in which you described the heroes going on dates, but no way Brock would play that.

"I'll be Wolverine," I said. Because it was a very Wolverine day, in the best ways.

"X-23, Laura Kinney?" he asked.

"No, Logan."

"You can't be Logan," Brock said. "You're a girl. You're Laura."

My brother the traitor. He hadn't cared when we were little if I was guys as often as I was girls. The whole idea of tenth grade had corrupted him.

"It's a game," I insisted, loudly. "I can be whoever I want. I can be a guy."

"You're Laura!" Brock came back louder.

"Why can't Kaz be whoever she wants?" asked a newly familiar voice from behind and above my left shoulder.

I hopped up and pressed my arms to my sides because I already wanted to hug Aisha and that would be so weird when we'd only met today. Jon and Brock also got up, Brock with a more WTF stance: legs wide, arms crossed.

"Aisha moved in across the alley," I told them. "This is Jon and my brother Brock."

Everybody said "hey," with varying levels of enthusiasm. Brock picked up his pop bottle and didn't quite turn back to face her.

To me, Aisha said, "Laura does have more cutting force per claw, so bear that in mind."

"What? How?" Jon asked. He ran a hand through his hair and it sifted down ending up looking as great as when it had started. My hair was only an inch longer than Jon's, light brown instead of black, about as straight, but it never did that—only got frizzy if I touched it, sometimes even when I didn't.

Aisha rocked back and shrugged in a no-big-deal, this-is-obvious way. She'd put a light jacket over her delicate shirt, a patchwork of orange fabrics, different colors and patterns. It fit close to her shoulders and made them look tiny.

She said, "Two claws instead of three means the total force of the strike is split fifty-fifty, rather than into thirds, so even if her striking power is less than Logan's, he'd have to hit significantly harder to match her. Plus a lot of their strikes aren't based in muscle force, they're based in momentum, so she basically owns."

"Cool, okay then I am Laura," I said and sat back down on the blanket because Wolvie had been gazing up at me like: *For real? Are you going to keep standing and make me get up for nothing?*

Aisha sat on the other side of Wolvie and ruffled the thick fur by her ears. Wolvie huffed and rested her head on Aisha's thigh.

Brock sprawled out on a whole third of the blanket, and Jon took the remaining edge. He said, "You're still never going to win because Quentin will just mind control you." These days, he aways picked Quentin, who was queer and a super powerful telepath.

"Not with Jean Grey on her team," Aisha said.

"You're not Storm?" Jon asked.

"Why would I be Storm?" Aisha pitched the question with full curiosity.

"'Cause she's African American," Brock told her, sounding both like he was talking to a little kid and like African American was *not* a great thing.

"Oh, you're going with the obvious reason," Aisha said. "Yeah, we're both black, but as someone wise once said, 'It's a game. I can be whoever I want.' I'm Jean Grey. Who are you?"

"Apocalypse," he declared.

"Shoulda picked Franklin Richards," Aisha told him with a dramatic sigh and a single shake of her head. "Well, that was a short fight. I'm going to get a burger."

"Try the brats, they're better," I said, unable to stop grinning.

"Who the hell is Franklin Richards?" Jon sputtered.

"No way," Brock insisted. "If I empower Quentin, you two are fucked."

Aisha tipped her face down and looked up at Brock out of the tops of her eyes, like she was staring over glasses even though she wasn't wearing any. She raised her eyebrows and kept them up.

"Let me break this down for you. I shield Kaz's mind and she goes in as a distraction. Sure you can defeat her in a minute, but it'll take you a minute. And any damage you do, she can heal from. Meanwhile, I use the Phoenix Force to reach back in time and push around a few minor details in the universe, step on a butterfly, whatever. Now Apocalypse is born as a normal human and Quentin is much less of a jerk. Fight's over before it even started. Should *not* have messed with the Phoenix."

"No, what? No!" Jon sputtered.

"Why are you being like this?" Brock asked me.

"I thought the point of the game was to win," I replied. But I could see the point of the game, today at least, was for them to win. They didn't think they could lose to me and Aisha. And somehow this was worse than losing to me alone.

"Show me to the brats?" Aisha asked and I pointed to Pops' grille. She got up and offered me her hand. I let her pull me up because of how her fingers tightened around mine.

As we walked over, Wolvie heeling next to me, I said, "That's only the third time I've won against Jon. You're amazing."

"Phoenix is pretty much always the answer," she said, grinning. "Are you usually Wolverine?"

"In the fights, yeah. But by myself, Beast. He's super smart but he's also funny, goofy, especially in the earlier stuff. Are you always Jean?"

"Yep. You know, people underestimate Beast," Aisha said. "Maybe 'cause he doesn't look like they think a genius should."

I introduced Aisha to Pops and we got two brats, lightly charred on one side, perfection. We heaped them with relish, mustard and ketchup. Aisha bit into hers and widened her eyes.

"Oh this is good. It's like a hotdog that got bitten by a radioactive spice truck."

"You were going to let me feed you something bad?"

She shrugged and smirked, all cute. I just dug into my brat, radiating inside because she trusted me enough to take my recommendation.

Jon and Brock pounced on us before we even got back to the blanket, coming around either side of the cooler as we got drinks.

"If you didn't have the Phoenix, we'd totally win," Jon said to Aisha.

"Yeah, you're not shit without that," Brock added. "So we win. We just wait for a time when you don't have it."

"You know Jean can call the Phoenix, right?" Aisha said. "I mean, that's literally how she got it in the first place. She used her powers to draw it to her and save her own life. So, no. You still lose."

Brock faced me, his cheeks ruddy with anger. "Have fun cleaning up by yourself. Your new pal's not going to win a lot of friends around here with that attitude." He stomped off toward the house and Jon headed back to the blanket.

"I'm sorry, my brother's a pretty bad loser," I told Aisha.

"Yeah." From her tone, she didn't buy that. "Or the obvious reason."

She'd turned away from me, as if she could see through my house to hers. In this one day, she'd had to deal with the mean neighbor calling her a bitch, Brock and Jon being hyper-aggressive and me clueless about all that.

It took almost a year for me to see how much of the time when Aisha held her ground with a white person, even with as small and smart and funny as she was, they'd come back at her hard. I didn't understand how in my town, and not only mine, blackness acted as a lightning rod for white people's anger.

Took me a lot longer to figure out what to do about it.

CHAPTER TWO

August 2016

Flash forward one year of as many hours and minutes as possible with Aisha. School mornings, I'd run over to her house so we could walk to the bus together. Summer mornings we walked the dogs. Aisha lit up telling stories. I made up questions so she'd keep talking. Her bright, melodic voice had a depth that made me feel I could wrap myself up in her words.

Now in two weeks, we'd start ninth grade and I'd been worrying that she'd find someone else she wanted to spend her time with. I had massive questions about how people dated, about my body and what to do with it. But I knew one thing: I wanted Aisha to be my girlfriend.

Being from L.A., she'd been out about liking girls since she was eleven. She'd even had a girlfriend for part of seventh grade. She insisted everyone from California wasn't automatically cool and that homophobia was still a huge problem in the black community, but looking at her family, I'd never have known. Aisha had spent a month this summer in California with her lesbian aunts—her mom's sister and her partner—and I'd missed her so much and envied her. I wished for more queer and trans people in my family. Or, like, any.

I decided that the perfect day to ask Aisha to be my girlfriend would be the anniversary of the day we'd met. That morning, I texted her to see when she wanted to walk the dogs. We walked them in the morning all summer because it was cooler for Wolvie and then they weren't jumpy all day.

She texted back: *Can we walk the dogs to downtown? I need coconut water and candy?*

Coconut water?

Dad.

Her dad had hooked us on coconut water with much more success than his smoothies. More than half the time his smoothies came out like murky swamp water. Aisha kept telling him to stop putting kale in them, but he wouldn't listen.

Aisha didn't wake up as early as I did, especially in the summer when she didn't have to, so by the time she was up, dressed and eating breakfast, it was nine. Wolvie and I went across the alley and hung out in the back yard, texting Aisha to let Pickles out.

Pickles chased Wolvie around their backyard tree. When they'd run each other out a bit, I put them on their leashes and went inside to see if Aisha was done with breakfast.

Aisha's mom sat at the kitchen table reading *The Plays of Georgia Douglas Jackson*, looking like a taller, heavier version of Aisha without the grin. She had a thoughtful face and her hair was in two French braids close to the sides her head, tucked in at the back. That gave her a level of seriousness that couldn't be cracked, even by her faded blue T-shirt saying: "Books, because reality is overrated."

"Are you excited for ninth grade to start?" she asked.

Her question reminded me that I had to ask Aisha out soon, like today, and I got sweaty despite the air conditioning.

"I like that we're the oldest students," I told her. "But you know I'm still going to study, like, two-thirds of how much Aisha does."

She chuckled. "Who knows, this year it might be three-quarters."

Aisha ran down the stairs and stopped at the bottom to put on the blue sneakers that went with most of her sundresses. She took Pickles' leash and went out the front door, me and Wolvie following.

The whole walk there, I tried to figure out the best way to ask. I got her talking about whether sorcery or telepathy was stronger in the Marvel comic book universe, hoping that would give me cover to figure it out. "Do you want to go out?" seemed too blunt. "We're really good friends, maybe we should date," sounded more tentative than I felt. I'd about settled on, "Do you want to be my girlfriend?" when I got pulled in to her argument. As with most of our comic book debates, it ended at, "It depends on whether large-scale telepathy can disrupt sorcerous artifacts; we need more research!"

We reached the CVS before I was ready. Anyway, it would be better if we had drinks and chocolate—better yet if we went to the ice cream place after CVS and I could ask her there. I stayed outside with the dogs while Aisha went in to get our candy and coconut water. I watched people go in: a guy older than Pops, bent forward in the shoulders; a girl about my age but way taller; Mrs. Branch from the local library who sometimes ordered graphic novels for us. I said hi to her.

And I watched people come out: two kids, maybe ten, jostling each other and admiring their handfuls of candy bars; a woman with dirty blond hair, wearing cool cargo pants who walked off down the street.

A police car pulled up. Last year I'd have smiled or waved at them. Now I got a thick dread in the center of my chest.

Six weeks ago, in early July, a Saint Paul cop had fatally shot a black man driving home with his girlfriend. Aisha had sent me the link to the news story the day after it happened. I'd scanned the headline fast, registering the words "black man" and "police shooting" and then—a dizzy, sick vortex inside me—"Falcon Heights." I'd been there. That was near the Minnesota State

Fairgrounds. It was less than thirty miles from where we lived, where Aisha lived.

I'd scanned down the article fast. Philando Castile was driving home with his girlfriend and her kid. The police had pulled him over for a broken taillight. He was doing what they said. He had a gun that he was registered to carry and he told them that. When he reached for his license, the cop started shooting. His girlfriend took video of it as she was praying that he wasn't dying, but he was. He died at the hospital.

I'd searched for the video, but Facebook had already taken it down, so I found a transcript. When I got to his girlfriend saying, "Please don't tell me my boyfriend just went like that," tears dripped down my face.

I'd thought stuff like that only happened on the coasts, maybe in the South, for sure not in Minnesota. We had to be careful, sure, but Aisha was supposed to be safe here.

I'd stared at a photo of Philando for a long time. He had a sweet smile and big nerd glasses. His skin wasn't any darker than Aisha's.

She wasn't safe here.

Everyone who'd gone into or come out of the drugstore was white. The cops were white. One got out of the car and took three steps toward the drugstore, then paused, waiting for his partner.

I got my phone out and texted Aisha: *Where are you!!*

Checking out now, she wrote back.

The air was nearly eighty, Wolvie's tongue lolling out from the walk over, but I went freezing cold. I tied Wolvie and Pickles' leashes to the bike rack in front of the store, but to be safe, I put Wolvie in a down-stay. Then I sprinted into the drugstore ahead of the cops. What could I do? All I knew was to put my body between Aisha and them.

She stood at the counter with a small mountain of candy and four bottles of coconut water, because we had to get two for her dad. Her headband matched the purple in her purple and white sundress and the laces of her blue sneakers. She was basically the cutest human on the planet; my paranoia couldn't be real.

Her gaze flicked to me, forehead wrinkling with confusion, and then seeing past me, her eyes went wide. I watched her body freeze like a deer on the highway in front of a semi's headlights.

One cop was the size of Pops, not quite six feet, bulky in his uniform. The other was taller and thinner, and he looked so big with that massive belt and his gun.

"We got a call about a woman shoplifting," the tall cop said.

"My manager asked me to call," the cashier told him. "Should I get her?"

I couldn't remember ever being this scared, not this shock of immediate terror. I knew about being scared of the kids at elementary school, being scared of my mom the years after dad left, but those were slow fears over days. This was being hit in the gut by ten pounds of ice.

I'd never felt like this around cops. Our great-grandfather had been a police officer and the whole family had a deep respect bordering on awe.

But I hadn't been around cops since I'd met Aisha.

I forced words out of my mouth. "I saw someone suspicious," I said. "I was outside with my dogs. Dishwater blond with a fake tan. Gray cargo pants with big pockets." I looked at the cashier, "Right?"

"Uh, I don't know, another employee heard someone putting things into a bag or, I guess, maybe, pockets."

"Miss," the shorter cop said to Aisha. "Can we check your bag?"

She nodded slowly. Her voice quavering, she said, "I'm going to put it on the counter and take a step back from it, okay?"

"That'd be fine."

She moved like underwater, slow motion horror movie, pulling the strap over her head. The buckle caught her headband and pulled it loose. It fell to the floor and she didn't reach for it. She put her bag on the counter and stepped back.

I fumbled my phone out of my pocket and opened the camera app. I moved to where I could have Aisha and both cops in the frame and started recording even though I was shaking so hard the video wasn't going to come out well.

"Put that away," the shorter cop told me and I felt like I was going to pee myself, but I shook my head at him. He sighed and rolled his eyes at me.

The tall one shrugged and opened Aisha's bag. It wasn't big, just enough for her wallet, phone, keys and a few necessities. He pawed through it, flinching when he came across a tampon and dropping that on the counter like it was a mouse.

Mrs. Branch had come to the end of an aisle and stood there, staring at all of us, staring at the cop dropping that tampon like it had bit him. I heard the sharp rustle of someone putting a hand on a chip bag and pulling it back fast. I knew the tall girl was behind me, watching. Probably the other employee had come up too and the manager. Everybody in the store except Aisha was white.

The old guy stood behind Aisha in line and he'd started clicking his tongue, like "shame, shame, shame."

The tall cop opened Aisha's wallet and pulled out her school ID, looked from it to her and back.

"We're fourteen," I said. "We're both fourteen."

The guy's tongue clicking got louder, a metronome of recrimination. Like being kids made it worse, like here we were, criminals already, when we hadn't done anything. But not "we," just Aisha.

"Mrs. Branch knows us." I jerked my chin in her direction. "She sees us at the library all the time. We didn't take anything. We wouldn't."

I looked to Mrs. Branch for help and she took a step back. She stepped away from us, even though she'd seen us at least twice a week all summer. Even though she ordered books for us and talked about what we'd read. Now she turned her face away and down, lips pressed together. Disapproving, not of these cops, not of their pristine authority, but of us.

The tall cop looked Aisha up and down in the sundress. There wasn't any place she could've hidden more than a pack of gum.

"You can go," that cop said, pushing her bag toward her.

Aisha took it by reflex. Hands shaking, she got her phone and keys back inside it. She stared at the candy on the counter like it was a puzzle.

"Hey," I said softly. "The dogs are outside alone. Please, check on them?"

"Yeah."

She went out through the door. I put my phone in my pocket, stepped to the counter, and picked up the errant tampon and the twenty she'd gotten out to pay for the candy. I didn't touch the candy. I shoved the cash and tampon into my pocket, bent down and got Aisha's hairband. We'd buy our snacks somewhere else from now on.

"You said you saw someone leaving?" the tall cop asked me.

"Yeah I did, but you went through my friend's bag anyway, why?"

"Procedure. Can you describe the person you saw?"

I spun on my heel and confirmed that the lanky white girl was hiding behind the end of the chip aisle. "Why didn't you check *her* bag?"

"Um, could you move?" the cashier asked, pointing at the old guy now behind me.

He'd stopped clicking his tongue now that Aisha was outside, and had moved on to sighs of increasing volume. I leaned back against the counter and crossed my arms.

"Who did you see?" the cop asked.

"A *white* woman. Five-seven, closer to my mom's age, blond-brown hair, skinny, wearing tan cargo pants. The pockets looked really full. She had her head down but looking around fast, arms close to her body, defensive."

"You noticed all that?" the cop asked, doubtful, like I was making up stuff to protect Aisha.

I raised my chin, pulled my shoulders back. "I train dogs. I see what people's bodies are saying." Like I'd seen the eight adults here stand around Aisha in a circle of blame, seen how their eyes and hands and shoulders said how easy it would be for them to hurt her or turn away while someone else did.

"Did you recognize this woman?" the cop asked.

"No. Haven't seen her around here before. Is that all?"

He nodded and I fled through the double doors into the hot air. My shirt was soaked with sweat despite the air conditioning of the store.

Aisha stood near the corner, holding Wolvie and Pickles' leashes, staring into the distance. Wolvie had backed into her legs, facing the police car, a ridge of fur standing up on her back. She had one ear flat to her head, one to the side, listening for danger because she could feel how upset Aisha was.

Aisha held the leashes out to me and, as soon as I took them, walked across the street, away from the drugstore. I ran to catch up and offered my hand. She took it and didn't let go.

We walked along the downtown storefronts. Past the fancy salon where mom always wanted me to get my hair done—Aisha's mom drove herself and Aisha into Saint Paul to get theirs done—past the Perkins and the German place and the Chinese place, past the butcher shop where Pops got his brats. We crossed a street and walked by the building for sale that used to be a local bank, its parking lot currently the site for Thursdays' farmer's markets, and then the big, new vape store.

I'd keep going as long as Aisha wanted, but she stopped in front of the ice cream store across from the Great Clips where I got my hair cut.

"Chocolate chip and pistachio," she said, her voice catching but making it through the words.

"Okay, you stay with the dogs and I'll get us pints?"

She nodded.

I got in and out with ice cream in under a minute. On the walk home, she took my hand again.

I said, "I'm sorry. I was so scared, you...?"

She nodded, took in a long breath and let it out. "We're okay."

"Yeah. We're better than okay."

But she didn't let go of my hand.

At her house, her mom was still reading at the kitchen table. It felt like we'd been gone for days, but the clock told me we'd left fifty-two minutes ago.

"It's too early for—" Her mom stopped mid-sentence and focused on Aisha's face. "What happened?"

"We're okay," she said. "Cops checked my bag because someone reported a shoplifter. I didn't move. I kept my hands where they could see. I did what you said. And we're okay."

Her mom surged up and opened her arms. Aisha folded herself against her mom's body. I put the ice cream in the freezer, then stood with my hand on the refrigerator handle because we hadn't gotten the coconut water and I wanted to cry. When I turned around, Aisha's mom held a hand out to me and drew me into the hug.

She said, "I'm so proud of both of you."

Nobody had been arrested or shot, but that wasn't the only way to do harm to a person. How long would it be before Aisha went back to the library? Would she ever? From now on, every time she saw Mrs. Branch she'd remember cops with their gun belts and all those accusing eyes on her. She'd hear that awful man behind her clicking his tongue, shaming her.

Every time I saw Mrs. Branch, I'd remember that too.

I knew what to do for cops: get badge numbers, take video, call an adult. But they weren't the whole problem, not even most of it. What could I do about everyone else? How could I fight something that vast and invisible and embedded in the brains of people around me? People I'd grown up with and liked and needed on my and Aisha's side?

CHAPTER THREE

Mid September 2016

After the drugstore, my plan for asking Aisha out was cursed by association. I'd wanted to ask while we sat outside the ice cream place with the dogs at our feet. Now I stalled out until the second week of school.

Our junior high included ninth grade, so we didn't have to deal with a new school until next year. Start of the year still put me in a daze—like when I'd take Wolvie to the dog park at a busy time and she'd run back and forth because she couldn't figure out which humans to greet and which dogs to play with. I had to figure out my schedule, plus what each teacher wanted, which homework was going to be easy, what was going to suck, what I probably wouldn't get done and how to avoid the worst consequences of that.

Ask-Aisha-out plan B slowly formed in my mind: comic books. Last spring, Aisha had started saying how certain people in our comic books were cute, and I'd agree. Unless it was Kate Bishop, the new Hawkeye. I could not get into her. But then I got to thinking that Kate Bishop kind of looked like me. Not exactly, but if you needed to pick a not-yet-tall, skinny white girl with some boobs and more hip than I wanted, Kate Bishop was your go-to.

I could ask Aisha why she liked Kate Bishop, point out how I had those characteristics too, and then ask if she'd be my girlfriend.

Of course on the day I picked for this super smooth girlfriend conversation, we came in the back door of Aisha's house and nearly walked into her dad's butt. He was all downward dog on the back porch.

Aisha yelped, "Oh Dad!" and threw her hands over her eyes.

I should've expected this. Truth was, I kind of loved Aisha's dad, even though he was awkward as anything. He had no idea that dads do not wear yoga pants and stick their butts up in the air because nobody ever wants to see that much detail about their dad's butt. That said, his downward dog *was* impressive for a guy the shape of a thick bookcase with a belly.

Aisha held her hands over her eyes, fingers spread so she could rush into the living room without running into the door frame. I kept my eyes on the taupe, all-weather carpet and muttered, "Hey Mr. Warren."

His job was super technical, engineering for 3M; this was not my mental picture of an engineer. Aisha's mom was a pharmacist and she actually looked like someone you'd trust to dispense prescriptions. I'd never seen her with her butt up in the air.

"Do they teach yoga at your school?" Mr. Warren asked over his shoulder, flashing me a grin. "They should."

Mr. Warren had a big, effortless grin, but no dimples unless they were hiding under his close-cropped beard. He had more hair on his face than on his head. When Mrs. Warren tried to grin like her husband, she appeared to be clenching her teeth. But when I'd seen her just smiling, not trying, she had this thoughtful, "I know something" joyful half-smile. Aisha had gotten her mom's dimples and her dad's grin, but she could also do her mom's smile: lips parted, corners of her mouth turning up and in.

"Uh yeah, we should definitely have Yoga in PE," I told Mr. Warren and followed Aisha, smirking hard.

We hung out at Aisha's house most of the time. A bigger house meant she had a bigger bedroom. Plus Tariq was more fun than my brother.

As we stepped into the living room, Tariq paused his Xbox game to laugh at Aisha's look of horror and asked, "Is Dad being all yin-yang again?"

Tariq lived in sweatshirts and baggy board shorts. He was a few inches taller than Aisha, broader in the shoulders, a warmer brown color. His smile echoed her grin, even though he didn't have the dimples. His broad nose balanced his round face. He kept his hair in tight curls on top and a high fade that I'd heard Aisha call "so nineties."

When he wasn't working—off saving the world as an EMT—he planted himself in front of the Xbox, headphones on, yelling commands to people scattered around the world as they got fragged in *Destiny* or *Call of Duty*.

From the back porch, Mr. Warren yelled, "It's yin in the yang, yang in the yin. It's complex."

"I'm getting a complex all right," Aisha groaned.

"Hey, at least it's yoga and not camping," Tariq told her.

"Camping?" I asked.

"That was Dad's thing the year before we moved here," Aisha said.

"Black people do *not* camp," Tariq told me.

"Hush you, don't give Kaz tired stereotypes. Some do, just we don't. And I mean we really do not. Riq went to pee in the woods, came back screaming."

"Did not," he grumbled. "Darius punked me." Darius was their older brother, off at Berkeley. I'd met him last winter break when he came to visit for two weeks; he'd gotten their dad's height and weight, like he'd used up the family's allotment, so Tariq and Aisha both ended up shorter and thinner.

"You're contradicting yourself," Aisha pointed out. "Either he punked you and you did scream, or you did not scream, in which case what's that punking assertion about?"

"Why did I get you for a sister? Can I trade you? Kaz, how's your current brother working out?"

"Honestly, you're more fun and nicer, but, I mean, if I had to switch families, that would be my dad out there in yoga pants, so…"

"Oooh burn," Aisha declared and we ran up to her room.

Aisha had scored the bigger of the kids' rooms in her house; she had a desk wide enough to put a computer on and still have space for two open books and a notebook. To the left of the door, her bed stretched along the wall with a bookcase headboard. The big desk was across from that, with her dresser and closet on the right. Desk, headboard and dresser all matched: cream-colored and modern, bright against the light brown walls. She kept her comics in a storage trunk by her closet. A robin's egg blue cushion on top matched her pillows and comforter.

Nothing in my room matched anything else. My three pillows all had cases from different sheet sets. My top sheet didn't match my bottom sheet. I'd started that way out of necessity, but it had become my style. Mom kept wanting to "do my colors" and update the room. Last month, I'd made sure to get a burgundy-and-gold dog bed for Wolvie that clashed with everything else in my room.

Aisha's room smelled like her, coconut and sweet almond and girl—which reminded me how much I wanted her to say "yes" to dating—but also reminded me how people always saw me as a girl. Today, once again, I'd forgotten how my body should feel. A few days ago, I'd been fine having soft skin and slight curves but now I only felt angles and bones and not enough muscle.

Aisha put her school backpack by her desk and leaned against it to take off her sneakers. I kicked mine off and settled in the middle of her bed, leaning back against the wall. Mr. Pickles jumped onto the bed and dove head-first into my lap. Propping one blue pillow against her headboard, Aisha sat and tapped my knee with her toes.

I rubbed Mr. Pickles' silky ear fur and said, "That's actually cool, yin in the yang. It's not, like, two separate things; they mix. Like gender." I almost said, "like my gender," but I wasn't quite there. I knew I was some kind of non-conforming or trans or shapeshifter, but not what.

"But we agree my dad is weird," Aisha insisted.

"Your dad is so weird," I told her.

Aisha had her hair up, tight and neat around her face with a mass of tiny, soft curls on top. The deep V-neck of her light green and navy striped sweater showed off the slenderness of her neck and breadth of her smile. Definitely time to get on with the girlfriend conversation.

"Hey, what's it about Kate Bishop you like?" I asked. "I mean, cute-wise?"

Aisha pulled her stack of to-read comics and graphic novels off the headboard bookcase and thumbed through them. Half her headboard hosted the weirdest, best beanie baby collection ever. Her rules for the collection included: one, it couldn't be a currently existing animal and two, the stranger the better. She had a pterodactyl, a mammoth, a dodo bird, a triceratops, a T-Rex, some dragons (blue, green and hot pink), a Pegasus unicorn, a brachiosaur, a hummingbird she insisted was a phoenix, and a wolf-dog that had to be a chupacabra.

"Kate's a badass," Aisha said. "She's super brave because she doesn't have all the powers in the world but she goes up against the big baddies, same as all the heroes who do."

"But, physically?"

"She's kind of long but curvy, but also the sweatshirts and stuff, she's not all about showing off. And truth, it's her jaw. The way she sets it when stuff gets real."

"Oh, cool," I said and sat on my hand so I wouldn't touch the side of my jaw and see if I could set it like that.

I snagged the latest Kate Bishop comic from Aisha's to-read pile, rested it on Mr. Pickles' butt and opened it. But I ended up just listening to Aisha's quiet breathing and the soft sound of pages turning.

Aisha scooted from her headboard to sit against the wall next to me and opened an issue of *Black Panther*, pointing at two women characters, Ayo and Aneka, who were very in love with each other.

"Who do you think is cuter?" she asked.

I pointed and said, "Ayo. Her hair."

"Hey!"

"Your hair's great too, you know that."

"Mmhm, you don't like the girl with the nappy hair, I see how you are," she said, scrunching her lips around her grin but failing to hide it.

"Oh shut up, Aneka's hair is common compared to Ayo's," I protested. "You know shaved-head ponytail is my number one hairstyle, but then it's all nappy, kinky and curly down to number twelve."

"What's twelve?"

"That side-braid fishtail thing."

"Oh yeah. What's number two?"

"Natural curl, loose or with a headband," I said. "And number three is natural messy updo."

Those were how she usually wore her hair. She pretended to go back to her comic, but I saw her dimples. I'd cued up the dating question.

But then she asked, "Seriously, across all our comics, who do you like?"

That threw me. I should've known she'd ask and prepped an answer, someone like Aisha. I should say "Jean Grey," since that was her character, except I had less than zero interest in the actual Jean Grey. Would she know what I meant? Should I pick someone black, like Aneka? Except I'd just said I liked Ayo's hair better and that wasn't Aisha's hair… crap.

Plus, I had too many real answers to this question because who I'd date in the comic books depended on who I got to be.

"As me?" I asked.

"Yeah. Or not. It's okay if you're ace. I know you don't like talking about who's cute. I'm not pushing you. I'm just asking. We don't have to be the same, you know?"

What I really wanted to ask her: *If I'm not exactly a girl, would you be my girlfriend anyway?*

"I'm not ace," I mumbled. "I had a dream the other night that I kissed Wiccan."

That was meant to prove the not-asexual point, but as soon as I said it, I realized how far it was from what I'd meant to say. Now was the *exact wrong time* to talk about kissing boys.

"So you think Wiccan's cute?" she asked.

"I don't know. I'm not into him right now. In the dream I was Hulkling." She hadn't read much *Young Avengers* yet, so I added, "They're boyfriends in the comic, or I guess fiancés? Hulkling proposed to Wiccan, it was super cute. But maybe I was only dreaming the comic book, you know."

I'd woken up from that dream half on fire and rolled onto my belly and rubbed against my mattress until the fire rose and flared and died down. I wasn't going to say that. But I blushed like mad and Aisha saw, then glanced away toward the beanie collection.

My problem with the "who do you think is cute?" question was that my answer changed based on who I was. If I thought of myself as Hulkling, a cute, shapeshifter, muscle guy with a mop of blond hair and a goofy smile, then of course I was perfect for Wiccan with all his emo damage and his black-haired, waify, white-guy handsomeness.

And if I was like America Chavez—an ultra-confident Latina-from-another-dimension girl superhero in short shorts and kickass boots—then I'd absolutely have asked Aisha out weeks ago.

Still, I could do this!

The comic book angle wasn't working. I lifted Mr. Pickles out of my lap. He grumbled and went to his dog bed beside Aisha's desk. Climbing over Aisha's legs to the headboard, I grabbed the phoenix and the green dragon. Sitting where she'd been when we started talking, I bent my legs over hers. I walked the two beanies up to my knee and wiggled the head of the dragon as it asked the phoenix, "Do you want to go out? Like date?"

Aisha looked from the beanies to my face and back, her forehead wrinkled, a slight shake to her head. "That's not one of the gay dragons," she said. "Wait, are you...?"

"I *am not* the hot pink dragon," I told her.

"I know! Blue?" She leaned past my shoulder to snag the blue dragon off the headboard.

"Give it," I said.

Smirking, she rolled halfway back to where she'd been, bracing on her elbow, back against the wall, holding the dragon up, away from me. I stretched for it leaning forward, across her. My skin turned to flowing energy except where my fingers wrapped around hers. I barely breathed. I didn't want to break this moment. Her dimples deepened, the corners of her mouth quirking, her eyes crinkling. That perfect secret smile.

I got my fingers around her wrist, inching up to snag the dragon, but I didn't take it. I wrapped my fingers all the way around her hand and the dragon. I wanted to put my hand around all of her.

Her eyes shone bright and dark, like the night sky. It was too much to look in her eyes or at her curving lips. I stared at the slope of her cheek up to where her ear got cute, hoped I'd aimed my lips close enough to hers, and kissed her.

Her elbow slipped out from under her. I fell forward. Lips brushing down her cheek. Her chest under mine moved fast with her breath and suppressed laughter. Her breasts pressed against my body. Against my chest.

Against my... breasts? I didn't have. I had. I couldn't. My breath stuttered. My body cracked and broke apart like ice hit by a ship. I floated away from myself, fought, drowning, against these feelings.

I did not begin or end where I thought I did.

I sat back, arms wrapped around myself, shaking. Aisha propped up on an elbow. "What happened?"

"My body," I said, because those were all the words I had.

"Hurts?"

I shook my head.

"Scared?"

I shrugged.

"Of what?"

Looking up through the drowning deep gray water inside me, I saw her face getting hard, jaw set, eyes going narrow: the look she got when someone hurt her.

"Me," I crammed the words to the front of my mouth and kicked them out with my tongue. "This body. You're perfect."

"Oh," she said. "Can I...?" She held her arms open. I slumped sideways, arms still around my chest, falling half into her lap and she leaned over me, hugging gently.

"It's okay," she said, and again, a whole bunch. And repeated other things about how we had time to figure out who we were. I heard some of that through how much I was trying not to cry and be a baby.

The blue dragon had fallen toward the edge of the bed. She leaned forward and tugged its tail until she could pick it up. Then she rested the blue dragon on her knee, saying, "However you are is okay. We're friends no matter what."

I took the dragon from her and pressed it over my heart, trying to force that trapped drumming to slow.

Aisha sighed and rested back against the wall. She kept one arm over my shoulder, fingers rubbing slow circles. I tried to relax with my head in her lap, the back of my head almost touching her belly.

She picked up the green dragon and had it hop over and kiss my forehead. Wiggling the dragon's head, like it was talking, Aisha asked, "Do you think I should date the brachiosaur?"

"Do dragons even date dinosaurs?"

"Where do you think pterodactyls come from?"

I snorted and curled my hand around her knee. She stroked her fingers over my hair.

"I should stick to Wolvie and trees," I grumbled.

"You're going to date a tree?" Her voice got rough and she stopped to clear her throat. "What, like your treehouse tree?"

"She's like part of the family. It would be weird."

"She?"

"Trees aren't really gendered like that. Milo says 'she,' but the treehouse tree is an oak and they're all—I mean almost all plants are—both male and female. So I guess that tree's pronouns are they/them. I wish I could ask what pronouns they use with each other, but trees talk to each other with chemicals, so the pronoun would be a chemical signal, not a sound."

"What chemical?" she asked.

"Maybe carbon since it's a building block of life? I feel like it would mean all the pronouns at the same time: I, you, us, them."

"I like that. Like there's a pronoun that's just for life. I think maybe that's what pronouns were supposed to be for."

"I hope so," I said.

"Kaz, carbon pronouns. Works for me."

It worked for me too, but I had no idea how to get from there to being able to kiss her.

CHAPTER FOUR

Early October 2016

After the kiss, the next few mornings, while Aisha slept, I took Wolverine on long walks and told her what had happened. She trotted ahead of me, glancing back like: *You should tell all this to Aisha; she's cool about carbon atom pronouns, what more do you want?*

"I don't know what to say," I explained. "I don't even a hundred percent know what's wrong."

She wagged her tail to say: *I don't know why you bother to bark all that. You should use your ears and bodies for the important stuff. And tails. Where is your tail?*

"Trust me," I told Wolvie. "Trying to explain everything to Aisha without talking would be a thousand times worse."

She said: *squirrel!* And ran to the limit of her leash, so that was all the help I'd get from her.

I wanted to tell Aisha everything, but I'd have to include the dreams I kept having about two guys from the comics, the super cute boyfriends Hulkling and Wiccan. I was always Hulkling, the shapeshifter with sandy hair and muscles. Sometimes I thought about those dreams when I was awake. And I mean: I *thought* about them—in detail, alone in bed, late at night after Mom was asleep. And not just thinking.

Milo and Pops went to bed at nine p.m., before Mom. Not to sleep right away, but that's when they went into their bedroom and didn't come out again. Probably they read and talked about the rest of us. Brock went to bed whenever he wanted, but his room was in the basement and he wasn't going to bust in on me anyway.

Once Mom had said good night, I was alone to think about two really cute boys together. Or two cute girls, America Chavez and Kate Bishop, or maybe—since I wasn't that into being Kate—Ayo and Aneka, even though they were older. I always imagined being a girl with girl or a guy with a guy.

Maybe whatever gender I turned out to be, I'd like the same. Or some flavor of the same. Hulkling was hunky and Wiccan was more the emo, goth boy, so they were two different kind of boys, but they were both boys—so if I was a boy, then I liked boys.

But if I was a girl, I liked girls.

Did that make me bi or two kinds of gay?

Or if I was a shape-shifting alien…? I should stick to trees.

Except that was *not* my body's agenda. If I tried not to think about it, I'd have those dreams where I was a boy kissing a boy, or a girl kissing a girl—and more than kissing. I'd wake up shivering and hot and not sure what to do about it since my door didn't lock.

Smarter to get ahead of the process and imagine that stuff at night when I was awake and I could handle how it made me feel, without worrying that my door would go flying open in the middle of it all.

Maybe, a few times, I got to thinking about what would happen some morning if Aisha opened my door. I made up ridiculous scenarios to justify her coming over at six-thirty a.m. and having to burst into my room. Like her dad having a yoga accident while the cell network was down and she needed Wolverine to run for help. But once I thought about

Aisha opening my door—and getting into my bed with me, just holding each other—I couldn't look her in the eyes for two days, so I had to go back to the other scenarios.

It was safest to think about being Hulkling and kissing Wiccan. Imagining the two of us rubbing together, how cool that would be to rub against someone if you both had your business mostly on the outside of your bodies. Plus it would be so easy to know that he was into me. And really easy to let him know I was into him.

And yeah, sometimes I'd roll up a pair of thick socks and put them in front of me, down there, between me and the mattress. It made sense to have a thick presence there. I'd imagine kissing a cute guy who was a bit smaller than me, how his body fit against mine, the feel of his hands. That never lasted long because I'd flare up inside and end up flushed with good feelings and sweaty and scared.

How could I be a lesbian girl and a queer guy and some trees and a nebula all at the same time?

* * *

October came in warm. Yeah, October, because it took me three more weeks to get up the courage to talk to Aisha.

Plus she got busy with school and I still had most of the dog walking jobs I'd picked up that summer. She walked with me a lot in September, but by October she wanted to use that time for homework so we'd have a good amount of TV-watching time after. Evenings when we didn't have family dinners or homework, I watched TV at her house or we texted about what we were going to watch and started shows at the same time in both our houses.

Saturday afternoon, after I'd done my dog-walking job, cleaned my room, done my chores and half of Brock's because he offered to legit pay me to do them, I texted Aisha from the treehouse.

Pops is grilling, want to come over and stay for dinner?

Yeah! she wrote back, *Mom's at work, Dad's at Yoga and Riq's still married to the Xbox. They're going to have little robot babies.*

I thought they already had & that's what the controllers are.
Aisha sent back a laughing emoji.

A few minutes later, she opened the door and crawled in. The treehouse roof wasn't quite high enough to stand up unless you were in the middle by the tree trunk. Aisha had her hair in two soft buns on top of her head, making her look half grown up and half kid. She wore the super soft, girly denim shirt that had been washed half to death, a shirt I loved, over an old pair of orange knee-length shorts that might've been Tariq's when he was a kid. They made her knees look bony in an adorable way, like I should cover her kneecaps with my palms.

We'd stocked the treehouse with old pillows. I had cushions from some lawn furniture Milo and Pops got rid of a few years ago and Aisha contributed a bunch of throw pillows her mom had decided to replace. Two weeks ago, a few days after the failed kiss, Aisha had moved both of the big lawn chair pillows to the wall, so we could sit side by side, really close.

I sat there now, but I'd made Wolvie lie down by the open window because she was chewing a rawhide and that always gave her the swamp farts. Aisha knew the deal with rawhide and sat on the far side of me from Wolvie. She picked up a comic book and started reading. And she leaned into me, so I leaned back.

Pops and Milo came into the yard talking about the election. I heard Pops rolling out the grille and the rustle of Milo settling into a deck chair. Our yard had a weathered gray cedar deck overlooking a lighter gray cement patio. One of the deck chairs stayed on the patio so Milo could sit near Pops while he grilled.

The back door opened and closed a few more times as Pops got his burger-making things. I wanted to talk to Aisha about the kiss and kissing in general and maybe even some of the dreams. If I whispered, Pops and Milo wouldn't hear me. But where to even start?

Aisha caught me looking at her *Patsy Walker A.K.A. Hellcat* comic and slid it over both our knees. I opened my mouth, but she put her finger to her lips and pointed through the treehouse wall in the direction of Pops and Milo's voices.

I tuned in to Milo saying, "In California a person had her gender legally changed to nonbinary. How does sexism operate then? Does the third gender come in at the bottom or does it break the system?"

Pops chuckled and said, "Depends if they put you in charge."

"Should," she replied.

"Amen to that. Does it say how it works? Did they add a third sex when I wasn't looking?"

"You know sex and gender aren't the same," Milo told him. "Cultures have all sorts of genders."

"Nonbinary?" Pops asked.

The screen door whooshed open and shut. Aisha scooted to the treehouse's open wall, eyes going wide as she peered down. I crawled over to where I could join her, hopefully without being seen. As expected, Pops stood at the grille in a light blue, short sleeved button up shirt, buttoned all the way up. Milo reclined in the patio's one deck chair, in a faded red flannel shirt and loose gray pants. Reading glasses perched on her nose as her finger slowly tapped letters on her tablet.

Brock and Mom had come onto the back deck and stood by its railing. Mom wore a heavy sweater, like the calendar date was more real than the weather, and had her hair back in a messy bun. Brock's gray tank top with the skinny straps was supposed to show off his muscles and make it seem like he didn't give a crap about fashion. He asked Mom or Milo to buy them for him by the dozen, just like Pops' button-downs.

"Let's see," Milo said. "Nonbinary can be used for anyone whose gender isn't exclusively male or female."

Brock sneered with his lips and his voice as he asked, "How do they know if a person's male *and* female? Do they have only one boob? Or is it like two boobs and a wang?"

That got him laughing so hard he had to catch himself with his palms on the deck railing. And Mom laughed too, resting one hand on Brock's shoulder for support. Pops turned away, tinkering with the propane tank, so I couldn't see his face. Milo's was in profile, facing the deck, lips pressed tight. Did they wonder how they'd ended up with my mom as their kid? Because I sure wondered how she got me as hers.

Mom said, "We've been talking about that nonbinary trend at work because they're making a unisex restroom. It's the new thing. I don't understand why people can't be happy the way God made them. It's so complicated. It's like people will do anything to be special."

Yeah, because gender was totally a fashion trend. I *so* wanted to spend half my life trying to figure out how my body felt and what that meant. And I *super* wanted to talk about my boobs with everyone, like, all the time.

I wished everyone would stop looking at my body as if it meant so much about me because it didn't. And I very badly wanted to stop feeling wrong so I could kiss Aisha again.

Mom went on, saying, "Kids come in and it's like everyone has to be their own special snowflake and make up a word that's just for them. Demigirl? What *is* that?"

Milo frowned thoughtfully. "At a guess, a person who feels somewhat like a girl but not entirely. I knew Greek and Latin prefixes would come in handy someday." She tapped on her tablet. "Yep, I'm on track: someone who identifies partly as a girl or woman."

"You can't be part woman," Mom insisted.

"Sure you can. Hell, I had my ovaries out a few years ago, I'm not even sure how much woman I am at this point," Milo said.

"Pops!" Mom yelped and looked to him for help. "You can't agree!"

He shrugged. "Same Milo, that's all I care about. Not like we were going to use those ovaries again. Did a good enough job the first few times, I'd say."

I was somewhere between "I love my grandparents so much" and "Oh holy crap why are my grandparents talking about ovaries?" I tried to focus on that first one.

"If I date a girl, I want to *know* she's a girl," Brock said.

I gave Aisha the "I'm dying here" look, wondering if we could make a run for her house. Aisha shook her head and motioned for me to stay back from the visible part of the treehouse with the open wall.

She snorted, loud enough for Brock to look and see her. "You in no danger," she called. "No nonbinary person's gonna ask you out. Your loss."

"Oh yeah, California," he called back up to her. "Your home state's crawling with hot nonbinary people?"

"Matter of fact it is, Hometown. That's why we got one of the country's first legally nonbinary folks."

Milo did that thing where she leaned back in her seat and the room, or yard, settled around her. She said, "A woman I used to work with told me that in her tribe, and she was Shoshone from out west, there were five genders."

"How can you have five?" Mom asked.

"I'm going to guess same way you have two. Gender is a social construct."

"Nah, that makes no sense," Brock said. "There's only two kinds of people. It's obvious. Me and Pops are men, the rest of you are all women. That's just how it is. Some people can, like, carry babies, that's a real thing."

"And some people are left-handed, that's a real thing, but there are cultures who made left-handed people worse than right-handed, and some where left-handed people are wise or special. The fact that some people can carry babies only means they can carry babies, not that they're great parents or super nurturing or even want to carry babies. Plus women who don't have kids, and women who don't have ovaries, we still consider women—because woman is a social role with less of a foundation in biology than you might think."

"You can't argue that biology isn't real," Mom declared. "Animals are male and female and that's that."

Milo laughed. "Remember that time your brother Joey's clownfish turned female and we had to decide if her name was still Nemo?"

"So what if a few kinds of fish are weird," Mom argued, voice going sharp. From my spot in the shadows, I saw her glance up at the treehouse. She had to know I was up here because she said, "Humans are men and women and we're born that way and I don't want kids getting these ideas that they can make up whatever they want. If Kaz decided she was a dog, we'd never go along with that."

I crossed my arms over my chest and hunched around them. Like I didn't know the difference between being a dog or a person. How my body felt wasn't up to me, or I'd have picked a body that went easily with Aisha's.

"People and cultures are very diverse and now the law is catching up," Milo said. "That's not idle fantasy."

I scooted farther into the depths of the treehouse and uncurled my arms long enough to put them around Wolvie, even though she smelled like a rawhide sewer.

My brain kept replaying Brocks words: "… only one boob? Or is it like two boobs and a wang?"

What I wanted wasn't real. People could transition from one gender to another, but there were two, or maybe three, except those third people were weird. I had ovaries and boobs and to most people that meant "woman" and I could invent some fancy third gender and they'd maybe humor me, but I couldn't have *this* body in the world, not the one I woke up with and dreamed with.

I couldn't have a body that felt like more than one body, that shifted and changed and didn't settle into a gender for more than a few days. I must be making it up, wanting attention like Mom said.

Aisha curled her fingers around my arm, holding on to me, but I pulled away.

"Don't," I whispered. No one should touch me. I felt monstrous.

"They're wrong," she told me.

I pressed my face into Wolvie's thick neck fur, too sad to cry, wanting to believe her.

Maybe I could focus on getting Aisha what she needed. Maybe I wasn't the hero of this story or even the sidekick, just one of those nameless, red-shirt extras. If Aisha got her dreams, at least me not having mine wouldn't suck as much.

CHAPTER FIVE

October 2016

We didn't talk about gender again. Not that night at dinner. Not the next days or weeks. I stayed out of the house by walking a lot of dogs; Wolvie always calmed down the hyper ones, me included (not that I was a dog, just sometimes I wished).

In my room late one night, I asked Wolvie, "Do you guys have binary gender? Most of you are spayed and neutered, so how does that even work?"

Sitting, she cocked her head, one ear flopping over, and contemplated me for a long time with her deep brown eyes, probably wondering if the Great Dog Consortium could trust a human with its deepest secrets.

"It's scent-based, isn't it?" I asked. "And super complicated but also quite flexible?"

She sighed and hopped onto my bed, putting her head on her paws, like: *Dammit, cat's in the bag now.*

"It's out of the bag," I said.

A light snort from her suggested that I should not lecture her about cat metaphors. The cat was definitely *in* the bag, because a cat out of a bag wasn't nearly as interesting or potentially dangerous. Probably three or four cats were in that metaphorical bag, but she knew better than to go anywhere near it. I didn't.

* * *

When we were kids, me and Brock played together a ton, being less than two years apart. I snagged his old clothes as often as Mom would let me. Kids thought I was his little brother. Even when he started junior high and I was in fifth grade, he didn't blow me off. After Dad left when I was six and Mom lost it for a while—working all the time, too tired to cook or clean or sometimes talk when she got home—it had been me and Brock against the world.

I couldn't figure out the exact point in time when that had changed. Back when he was a string bean of an eleven year old and I was nine, Brock's favorite game had been pretending we were a rock band. He'd do dramatic makeup and put on a cape because he was our over-the-top lead singer, and I'd put on nail polish and pantomime drums. I still think nail polish looks badass on anyone regardless of gender.

He'd always known I wasn't exactly a girl, so his comment on the deck bit deep and kept biting. I finally volunteered to run errands with him, planning to ask him what he really thought about gender and trans people and me.

We borrowed Milo and Pops' car, which we could use for school or errands now that Brock was seventeen and had a year of practice driving. Brock got into the driver's side with an annoyed sigh. Compared to Mom's Mazda, the Toyota was an energy-efficient turtle. And pristine! You could lose an entire outfit in Mom's back seat, but if we left even a gum wrapper in here, Milo would be on us.

Brock drove us to the bike store and the pet store and the gaming store in South Saint Paul that was twenty minutes away but still the closest place with comic books. The whole time, I didn't ask him anything serious. I wanted to hang out like we used to.

Plus I'd been thinking about how maybe we'd been closer before I'd started eighth grade, maybe the distance was because I'd been spending all my time with Aisha. That gave me two questions I didn't want to ask him: "Why are you being an ass about gender?" And, "Do you have a problem with Aisha?"

Way too many cats in those bags.

I left the rock station playing loud and figured I'd talk to Milo about this first. But in the neighborhood by the gaming store, pulling up to a stop sign, there was a black family on bikes: mom, dad, three kids, the littlest on the back of the dad's bike in one of those booster seats.

They stopped on the corner and watched us. Brock sat there, waved impatiently, said, "Go already! What's the hold up?"

The dad watched Brock. He was a lot skinnier than Aisha's dad and had more hair. When he glanced at me, I gave him a nod. He looked at Brock and back at me, not moving.

"Just drive," I told Brock.

He grumbled and hit the accelerator too hard. I put my fingers on the window, wishing I could turn around, go back and apologize.

"They take up so much space all the time," Brock was saying. "Walking in the street, going slow, making us wait like that, why?"

He wasn't honestly asking, but I answered anyway. "He was afraid."

"I've had my license for over a year." He said it fast, huffing.

"Because we're white."

"That's stupid."

"No, it's real. Most white people here don't look out for black people like they do for other whites. He's got to protect his kids extra because we're the ones who are being stupid."

"Aisha tell you that?" He said it with a sneer.

"I read it, fuckwit. Some of it. And figured it out. I have eyes. She doesn't have to tell me everything, I can see for myself."

Like when I went out with Mom or Brock, or both of them, they barely looked at people of color. Mom would glance up and smile if we passed a white person and maybe also if they were

Asian. We had a big Hmong population in our neighborhood and Mom was always super polite to them. But walk by a stranger with medium brown skin or darker and Mom looked away or down, at her phone, at her purse, anyplace else.

And Mom got startled when I didn't. Last spring in the grocery store parking lot, a young woman let her cart get away from her on the down slope. She ran a few steps to catch it, smirking to herself. I'd been watching, because the moving cart caught my eye, so I grinned. She grinned back.

I told her, "Nice catch."

She said, "Thanks."

That was it, but Mom stared at me all big-eyed, as if I didn't say hi to strangers pretty often. I did, especially if they had a dog.

But this woman had deep brown skin so I'd broken the code. I'd say it was a code nobody clued me into, but I knew exactly what it was. I'd been absorbing it without thinking since I was tiny: *Don't look at black people, don't talk to them, definitely don't joke with them. There's something wrong and shameful and you need to keep quiet and look away.*

Part of that was true: wrong and shameful things had been done. But they'd been done by people who looked like me, so maybe it was on me to close the gap, make things better as best I could.

How to tell all this to Brock? We were on the highway back home and I had about fifteen minutes for all the thoughts and questions in my brain.

"What? You think I'm racist?" Brock asked, all up in himself.

"Yeah," I said. "So am I. It's in our brains and in the world around us. Racism doesn't have to be on purpose. We grew up in it. It's like speaking English. Nobody gave us a choice when we were little, but now we've got a choice."

"Right," he snorted. "They have a lot of choices too and they don't make good ones. They have the same chance anybody has, they just don't work as hard because of their cultures."

I wanted to yell at him. Instead I clenched my teeth. I wanted him to understand how this whole thing worked and sometimes I still didn't understand enough myself.

"Brock, what do you think we'd have done without Milo and Pops?"

He drove silently for miles. He didn't have to answer; we'd talked about this when we were smaller. During the two years after Dad left, we were always one step away from losing our home. Dad used to have money, but he and Mom spent a lot of it on a house near the city. Milo declared it "too much house." After he left, Mom refused to sell it. The first year, we thought he was coming back. The second year, Mom stayed locked in a fight with everyone, trying to prove she could manage on her own.

Brock even told me that when he was ten, he'd walked by the homeless shelter a few times, checking it out in case we had to go there. When I'd been eight and trying not to get beat up at school, he was thinking about where we'd sleep if we didn't have a home.

Part of the reason we hadn't lost the house was that Milo had been giving Mom money the whole time. I found that out after we moved in with Milo and Pops, just before I turned nine, because Milo talked to Mom about being able to spend some of that money on better clothes now that they weren't keeping two houses going.

So Brock didn't have to answer about what we'd have done without Milo's money. We both knew life would've been immensely harder.

I turned down the radio and asked, "What'd Milo's dad do for work?"

"Cop," he answered.

"And his dad?"

"Iron Range," he said, back to huffy and impatient, because this was not family trivia night.

"How'd he get there from Poland?" I asked and then answered my own question. "The family came over together because they could pay for passage."

We'd heard the story often, how my great-great-grandfather's little brother almost didn't make it on the ship because they didn't have enough to pay his way, but his mother had given up some jewelry so they could come across together.

Brock said, "But that's my point, our family worked for everything we have."

"Across generations. What if Milo's grandfather had been taken away from the family, made into a slave, brought to the States with no one, and then, when the slaves were free, couldn't get any decent work because no one was hiring blacks? What if he only made enough to get by, didn't have enough to pass on to his kids? And then those kids grew up and still couldn't make as much as white people?"

He grumbled, but I turned half toward him, seatbelt tugging at my shoulder.

I asked, "What if Milo didn't have enough money in the family to finish high school and had to take jobs? If she hadn't gone to college? She might not have gotten a good post office job. Plus her dad left her some money and that's money that's taking care of us today. What we did with slavery, we took people away from home and family, from their resources and support. And even after slavery, we kept them poor."

"I didn't do that. Our family didn't."

"We benefitted from it," I said.

"We didn't take anything from them. And that was a long time ago."

"We didn't have to live out of a shelter because of money and opportunities passed down in our family," I said. "*Not* because we work hard. You can't take that away from a whole group of people and act like it's their fault."

"You're not going to make me feel guilty," he said and launched into a rant about immigrants taking jobs away from Americans.

"Asshole," I said and turned up the radio.

We said a few more things to each other after that—loudly, over the rock music—the kind we'd never dare say around Milo. By the time we got home, we weren't talking.

I'd seen Aisha's family photo album, including where her family tree got ragged and bare. On her mom's side of the family, it ended at six generations. It just ended.

Milo's sister was super into genealogy and had done that side of the family back to the late 1700s and knew exactly what town in Poland they were from. And honestly, I didn't care that much about it, but it was there if I ever did care.

No matter whether Aisha wanted to or not, she couldn't trace that part of her family tree back any farther than "John," a name he hadn't even been born with. How did Brock *not* get how awful that was?

Probably because I'd said "we."

And in truth I was still getting my head around that. Seeing that family at the crosswalk having the right of way but afraid to take it, watching us like we were dangerous, because we were. We didn't have to be openly racist assholes who wanted to smash through them on their bikes, only ignorant white people who could look away, hurt them with our carelessness and call it an accident.

I knew how it felt to be scared and watching the people around you, from wearing Brock's old clothes to school and feeling the threats that no one had to say aloud. I'd been the one staring with wide eyes, waiting to see signs that someone was going to hurt me.

I didn't know what to do when I was the person who had to be watched. How were you supposed to behave if you're the one who's dangerous?

CHAPTER SIX

October 2016

I'd gotten a late start on my education about race in America. At least, according to me. Brock probably thought I shouldn't even be reading the books Aisha's mom recommended.

I'd been seven when our first black president took office so of course racism was over. And Aisha didn't talk to me about race the first eight months of our friendship, which I'd figured meant everything was okay. I hadn't realized it was like me talking about gender: I didn't do it if I thought the other person wouldn't get it.

While I'd been testing Aisha with comments like Beast being the hero I saw myself as, even though he was a guy, she'd been suggesting comics, books and movies with mostly black characters and watching how I responded. Slowly my brain started to see race in new ways.

I didn't manage to bring up race as a topic in any reasonable way, just blurted stuff out. The first hot, sunny day in April of our eighth-grade year—four months before the cops at the CVS—Brock got a blazing sunburn from riding his bike out to see the girl he'd started dating.

Sitting in Aisha's backyard with Pickles in my lap, tossing a ball for Wolvie, who kept taking breaks to chew the fuzz off it with her little front teeth, I said, "Both our brothers are redder than we are." As soon as I said it, I thought that I shouldn't have.

"What?" Aisha glanced up from our history textbook, nose crinkled in confusion and concern. She'd been reading me the important bits, fingers toying with her curls. An orange headband held her hair back and she caught the lower curls and tugged at them while thinking.

I said, "You know, how Riq's a redder brown and Brock's pink, even when he's not burned all lobster."

She shook her head. "He looks white to me."

The feeling that we shouldn't talk about this started to dissipate. Did that feeling come from the same place as the message that I wasn't supposed to smile at people of color in public?

"Seriously?" I asked. "But I'm pasty white and he's pink white. You don't see that?"

Aisha's hand rested on the textbook while she studied my face. "You both just look white."

I was too busy thinking to close my half-open mouth. Mom had the same pinkish complexion as Brock and always fussed about how hard it was for her to tan and how easily she blushed. How many kinds of white did I know? At least four, not counting sunburns and fake tans.

How many kinds of brown? Until I'd gotten to thinking about how Tariq was redder than Aisha, I'd have lumped them together. So maybe two? Just light and dark. Were we all light white to Aisha?

I grinned about the idea of my mom not looking pinkish and Aisha asked, "Why's that funny?"

"Because my mom would freak with joy if she knew you don't see how pink she is."

"She's pink too?" Aisha said like she didn't quite believe this many pink people existed just across the alley from her.

"Pink-white. She's Maple, you know, on the wood stain chart in Milo's workshop."

"What are you?" Aisha asked.

"Oak."

Her eyes narrowed without any smile lines around them. "What am I?"

"Walnut."

"What kind of tree is that? Is it good?"

"It's extra good," I told her. "First off, actual walnuts, which are delicious, but also the wood is great to work with, at least according to Milo. Plus walnut trees look awesome."

"Cool." She flashed me a grin that settled into a slight upturn of her lips.

"How many colors of brown are there? I only see light and dark."

Closing the history book, she put it next to her knee. "Depends how you're asking because it's not only about the shade of somcone's skin. They might be light tan but also a black girl and that's different from a light tan Asian girl. So if you mean just black girls, I'd say about six to nine. How many kinds of whitc are there?"

"Four. Or six if you count tanning and burning."

"For real? I thought there was just white and people who pass."

"Hang on," I told her and ran across the alley to Milo's workshop.

Wolvie came with me, but I tossed the ball over the tall wooden fence so she ran back into Aisha's yard. I got the stain chart from Milo's workshop wall and took it back to Aisha's yard, putting it on the ground in front of us.

"See here, what they're calling Autumn Oak and Natural Maple, that's me and Brock and I tan to this Golden Oak color and he just burns pink. They don't have a stain for white-person sunburn because no one would buy it. And Pops is Golden Hickory, so he starts out tan and then he can tan darker to this Country Pine color. That's six kinds of white."

Aisha placed her hand like a karate chop diagonally across the chart, separating the top third from the bottom two thirds. "And the rest of these are everyone else."

"That's a lot!"

"Yeah but you don't need to know all that unless you're doing makeup. Your two-color system works fine. Just know that all the people who are lighter—Cherry and Pine and Cinnamon—usually get treated better than the rest of us. That's all these colors: Walnut, Black Walnut, Mission Oak, Mahogany, Midnight."

She took her hand away from the chart and I put a finger on Autumn Oak and one on Country Pine, my other hand connecting Cherry and Walnut. "These two don't get treated differently, they're just white," I said, indicating the first two colors. "Why are these other two different?"

"Because colorism is real," she said.

Wolvie dropped her ball by me and I threw it, then shook my head because I hadn't figured out what that meant.

"Oh, sometimes I forget how white you are. So okay racism hits everyone, but then darker people get it worse because colorism, because—hey, Mom."

Aisha's mom, who'd passed the open back door, came back and stood inside the screen door. She looked at the wood stain chart and the two of us and shook her head.

"Would you define colorism for Kaz?" Aisha asked.

Aisha's mom sat on the back porch steps. Even though it was warm for spring, she had on her big slippers with the leather bottoms and fluffy lining, plus jeans and a gray "USC" sweatshirt over a red thermal shirt.

Mrs. Warren said, "It's a bias that arises alongside anti-Blackness and considers everything white and light to be better than black and dark. On a practical level, it's what's happening when people are considerate with white or light-skinned kids and rough to darker-skinned kids." She met my eyes and held them before saying, "People are going to treat you better than Aisha. Or they're going to treat you worse for being with her."

"But it's twenty-sixteen—isn't that all way past?"

Mrs. Warren's eyebrows lifted slowly toward her scalp and stayed in two very dubious arches. "Sweetie, we're black and a lot of people are going to see our blackness before they see anything else about us. Even in twenty-sixteen. Aisha might be the most brilliant person in the world and some people are only going to see that she's black and a girl and they're going to think all manner of negative things. It's best if you don't forget that."

"Mom," Aisha said in a half-exasperated sigh.

"I'm not telling Kaz to watch out for you, you know what to do. But she's got to know to watch out for herself and she's got to understand why there's a different standard. Summer's coming, it's about time she got the talk."

"What's the talk?" I asked.

"How to behave around cops," Aisha said quietly. "And white people with power, or who think they have power or are trying to take power. And white guys in general."

"Have you seen the two of you get treated differently?" Mrs. Warren asked me.

"Sometimes, but not right away. More often I get it afterward, at least the times when Aisha changes."

"I what?"

"Like this." I set my jaw, lips pressed together, eyes up but hard, shoulders a set in a line but the left one rolled in, hands clasped, palms pressing, knuckles tight with the pressure.

"Well," Mrs. Warren said and it was a full sentence.

"Is that what I look like?" Aisha asked.

I relaxed the pose and nodded. "When you're mad but you're not saying anything, yeah. And then I try to figure out what happened."

"What about you when you're mad?"

I ducked my head so my hair fell half across my face and crossed my arms over my chest, shoulders curled forward. Aisha put one hand on my shoulder, the other on my elbow and gently tugged me out of that closed-off position. I brushed my fingers down her hand to say thanks, but didn't take her hand like I would've if we were alone.

"So what do I do?" I asked Mrs. Warren.

"You're used to people giving you the benefit of the doubt," she said. "If you mess up, they assume you're having a bad day. When you're with Aisha and it's just the two of you, your family isn't there, most of the time you'll lose that. Some people will assume you two are up to trouble, and not cute little kid trouble, dangerous trouble. So here's the talk I gave Aisha, short version: stay away from the police if you can. If they do talk to you, be on your best behavior. Always have your hands in view. Do what they tell you. If you have to move, first tell them what you're going to do and then move slowly. Do not argue with them but do not give them any more information than is necessary. Start asking 'may I call my mom?' and ask that as many times as you need until they let you call or let you go."

"Really?" The word slipped out of my mouth.

Aisha stared at her feet, moving the toes of her sneakers back and forth. She muttered, "There are four times more white people than black people in the U.S., but last year twice as many black people were killed by police as white. Plus black people are more likely to be killed while unarmed."

My breath caught at the base of my throat and in my chest, pushing my ribs out painfully.

"But not here, right?"

"You have to be careful everywhere," Mrs. Warren said. "And Kaz, if an accident happens, God forbid, and Aisha needs medical care, people are more likely to think she's not in pain, more likely not to give her the help she needs, so you need to call me or her father right away and tell us exactly where you are."

"I will," I said.

Aisha had one hand on her leg, the other rested on the cover of her textbook. The first few times we hung out, I'd been super aware that she was black. I didn't mean for it to be that way, but that's what my brain was all about. And then that faded and she'd just been Aisha for most of a year. But a year in which I'd seen her take her quiet-angry stance how many times? Fifty? A hundred?

Aisha snagged my hand with hers, squeezed my fingers, saying, "We'll watch out for each other, Mom."

Mrs. Warren looked at us for a long time, then nodded. "I think that's enough of the talk for today. Come to me if you have questions, Kaz. And Aisha can give you some books to read."

Aisha squeezed my fingers again, dropped my hand and opened the textbook. "Back to history?"

"You okay?" I asked her.

"Kaz, I have brothers and a lot of cousins, I've heard that talk at least three times, the first time when I was eight. Are *you* okay?"

I wanted to curl up and shake, like Wolvie when a thunderstorm is coming.

I said, "When I was ten, there were these two guys in my grade, white kids, and I knew if they ever caught me by myself, they were going to beat me up. There was a playground fight I wasn't even in and one of them dragged me into it, but I kicked him good and Brock saw."

"I'm sorry."

"No, that's not my point. They were fourth graders too, they weren't much bigger than me. Getting beat up would suck, but I'd get through it. Cops are big. They're not only adults, they're adults with uniforms and guns. They're supposed to protect you. You've been scared of them since you were eight?"

"At least. More scared they'd kill Darius or Tariq or Dad or Mom." She scooted closer to me, our arms almost touching, lowered her voice. "You know what I really hate? Always making sure Mom and Dad know where I am. Always being home on time. Having to be good all the time, even when it's not enough."

Four months after that conversation, we'd been standing in the drugstore with the tall cop searching Aisha's tiny purse, with Mrs. Branch the librarian pursing her lips and turning away, like being suspected of a crime was the crime itself.

* * *

I'd been afraid to talk about race because in those first months of knowing Aisha I'd been nauseously aware of a horrible voice in my head. It must've been there the whole time, only I hadn't heard it clearly because it sounded like my other thoughts. As if some evil supervillain had gotten into my brain and mimicked my voice, to keep me from questioning.

In those first weeks, Aisha would be telling me stories we'd read, or ones that she loved that I hadn't read yet, or fan stories about our favorite characters. I first caught the evil voice when we were walking the dogs. Aisha was telling me about the greatness of America Chavez, the new generation version of Captain America. We'd turned down that long stretch with no trees, where I'd complain that it was too hot and she'd roll her eyes at me because, being from California, nothing here got too hot for her. Prairie flowers and tall grass stretched away from both sides of the path, ending in trees on the park side and houses on the other.

In the middle of Aisha explaining the university that America attended, this voice in my head said, "She's too loud, shouldn't be that loud, drawing attention."

I glanced at the houses. They were way far away and even if that old guy in his backyard could hear her, would I care? Why worry about that?

And then the evil voice said, "She should know her place."

I stopped.

Aisha took a step, turned. "You okay?"

"Sec," I said and knelt to fix Wolvie's collar that didn't need fixing. I unbuckled and buckled it anyway.

That voice in my head was *not* me.

But what the shit? How did I have an evil voice in my brain that I hadn't heard before?

"Sorry." I stood up and joined her. "I missed what you said. Who's Prodigy again?"

I listened to her words but also the sound of them. If Jon was walking next to me, would I think he was too loud? No way. And Aisha had a better voice than Jon.

I pushed it down under other thoughts, ignored the flashes of shame and the fear of what this voice could do. But after the talk with Aisha and her mom, about colorism and police and how much I did not know, after the cops in the drugstore, I realized I had to stop turning down the volume on that voice.

Disgusting as it was, I had to turn it up, to hear it first before it could poison my thoughts the way it poisoned Brock's.

Mrs. Warren was right, it did tell me that Aisha didn't feel pain like I did. Not in those words, but I remembered her crying during a movie and a flash of surprise that she felt that deeply, that she had the same emotions as me.

I remembered being startled at how smart she was, how fast she thought, how she could get to answers before I did.

I'd grown up with this parasite in me, disguising itself as me. And in people I loved, but how could I tell them?

* * *

In the months after the cops in the drugstore, I'd been reading everything Aisha's mom recommended. Once I got settled into the ninth grade routine, I read faster. My plan for ninth grade had been to coast, read books, play with Wolvie, hang out under as many radars as I could, especially my mom's. She was on rails about this whole "young woman" thing, like that backyard conversation about a third gender inspired her to shove me hard into the "girl" box.

Aisha had other ideas. Next year, in high school, we could get into an advanced academic program and start earning college credit. She wanted this as much as anything. Like: new computer, more comics, college credit. While I was all: be left alone, more comics, Wolvie and other dogs, Aisha.

The first few months of ninth grade, this meant that she spent way more time on school homework than I did, which was good 'cause I had a whole lot of real world homework to catch up on. Every time I saw a news story about the election that scared me, I'd curl up in bed with Wolvie and read about the real history of my country, and racism, and how to fight it. And every time I got shocked by a story or a statistic, I'd tell Milo, who usually ended up reading each book as I got done with it.

Milo was an easy audience. Mom wouldn't be and Brock for sure not.

After running errands with Brock devolved into the two of us yelling at each other, I knew I couldn't simply tell him facts. I couldn't walk him through the same steps as me, because my steps rested on Aisha being my best friend.

As October turned cold and rolled into November, I kept getting up early, walking Wolvie and thinking of ways to talk to Brock, none of which would work.

Saturday morning in the pre-dawn deep blue of the world, I stared at myself in the bathroom mirror. How could I see this parasite in a way that helped me defeat it?

All the times I'd seen black people around the neighborhood, the parasite-voice had said "lazy" or "rude" or "dangerous." Not loud enough or clear enough for me to catch it, just laying back there whispering that evil shit to me. About Aisha, who was the best person in the world! But even if she hadn't been. Even all the people who weren't as amazing. Nobody deserved that.

Nothing had forced me to stop and think about this. Someone should've already told me! But everyone close to me had been white. Did they all have this same voice inside? Even Milo and Pops?

And maybe there was another voice that spoke to guys, to Brock and Jon and told them not to listen to women, said words like "trivial" and "shallow" and "weak," and they thought this voice was them.

Like most of us had been infected or influenced by some massive villain who could mind control people. But it only worked if you didn't notice, so he had to make sure he sounded like you. He had to make sure you didn't question.

I had to see this evil. I'd left the bathroom light off and my face in the mirror looked blue-purple, reminding me of Apocalypse from the X-Men movie. He imbued his followers with power, but he could also control their minds. He even had a creepy old dude voice.

In the movie preview, Professor X says, "Oh God, he can control all of us." And then when they fight, Professor X takes Apocalypse into the house of his mind, Apocalypse gets super big and starts crushing him in *his* house.

Evil had come into the house of my mind like Apocalypse—a parasite that promised to empower me if I listened to it. But listening didn't give me power, it made me destructive.

If I didn't pay attention to this voice, it would gain power, it would overtake me when I wasn't aware. It would use me to hurt Aisha. It would hurt me in order to hurt Aisha.

Still staring in the mirror, at the blackness in the center of my eyes, I tried to see him in there, to fix him in my mind so I'd always hear him, always fight him. I said, "Not in my house, fucker."

From the hall, Milo cleared her throat and I jumped, spinning a half circle to face her.

"Talking to myself," I said. "You know, like usual. Do you sometimes have thoughts that aren't yours except you didn't realize that before?"

Her bushy eyebrows drew closer together. I figured I had to say more about it. I didn't want to say what the thoughts were because maybe she didn't have the voice, maybe when she read the books about racism she was all, "Oh yeah, the struggle," and I was worse than average.

I went on talking. "Like maybe there are things that other people think, but you've been thinking it too... Like how a lot of people think it's gross when two guys kiss but it isn't. But I thought that too when I was a kid."

Milo gave me a look that said I was clearly still a kid, but she knew what I was driving at.

I did not add, out loud, that I'd thought it until I realized that if I was a guy—or when I was a guy—I'd want to be kissing Jon. Suddenly this idea that naturally men only kiss women became ridiculous. The belief that two guys kissing was gross now seemed so fake.

If it was all that unnatural, people wouldn't have to keep saying it was unnatural. But people had to keep saying that two men kissing was unnatural and wrong—because it wasn't. It only seemed that way because I hadn't seen it on TV and because kids, and sometimes adults, made jokes about it. There was this whole structure in place to make sure we believed it was unnatural and apparently we needed a heck of a lot of persuading.

Milo folded her arms and leaned against the wall. She'd rolled up the arms of her faded blue flannel and her crossed forearms looked thicker, more powerful stacked like that.

"Do you mean social conditioning?" she asked.

"Maybe. If I knew what that was."

She snorted. "You and me, but more me, we both grew up being told and shown that men *are* only certain ways and that includes not kissing other men."

"Yeah," I said, hopeful because that's what was in my head, that black people were certain ways. Like, *all* of them. Which, when I thought about it, was so obviously untrue. "What do you do about it?"

"Keep taking it apart," she said. "That's what feminism has been doing for decades: taking apart the idea that women can only do some things and not others, that a woman's place is in the home, women can't be leaders. Look for examples outside of the socially approved roles."

"How do I get it out of my head?" I asked. "I don't want to think those things."

"You can't do it all at once. Think about how many TV shows you've seen that reinforce it, how many books, magazines, ads. You have to keep fighting it. Talk back to it. Prove it wrong, over and over. Collect examples that are outside your conditioning. Keep looking at the real world, not all those fake ones on TV."

"Thanks," I said. "You're kind of a superhero, you know."

"Glad you think so. Should I go use the downstairs bathroom or are you done talking to yourself for now?"

I laughed and scooted into the hall and then my room. Milo said to collect examples. That seemed like a great place to start for myself but also for Brock, to have so many examples that he'd have to hear me.

That voice, Apocalypse's evil mind control, had to keep telling me that black people were dangerous—the same way it told me women were less than men and that gay was unnatural—to keep reinforcing those ideas.

I knew that women were as powerful as men, Milo made sure of that. I knew that gay guys were beautiful together, my body made sure of that. But what was the truth of the situation with black people? It took me a long time to work through because there were a lot of truths, but the one that hit me hardest was this: in America, black people were *in danger*.

That was a truth the voice wanted to hide.

CHAPTER SEVEN

November–December 2016

I told Wolvie, "A diabolical force has taken over Western Civilization. I don't know how to fight it, but I'm going to figure it out."

She thumped her tail and perked up her ears, like: *Thank goodness you've realized this! We've needed to have a talk for some time now about the vacuum cleaner.*

* * *

Then the elections ate November.

* * *

The days after the election got hazy. Any time I tried to sleep, I couldn't settle, but walking around I felt only half-awake.

"We need something good," Aisha said, looking as dazed as I felt.

She started with more books and comic books, and by December, she'd found our school's very unofficial Gender &

Sexuality Alliance. Our junior high didn't have a GSA because the grown-ups all thought we were too young for that. (So not.) Aisha was in the prep classes for the high school's International Baccalaureate program and two years ago one of those classes had been almost all queer and trans kids, so they'd started going out afterward, on Thursdays, to the Chinese buffet in our town's Main St. strip.

A lot of those kids still went, though they were at the high school, and they brought other high school kids and passed the word around the junior high that we were all welcome. Aisha told Jon and me, and that's how we all ended up in the back of Jon's cousin's pickup truck in early December. The open bed of a pickup was cold, but at least it was a quick, bracing cold compared to the bone-deep cold of walking from our junior high to the restaurant.

I told Mom I'd be home late because I was going to a study group. I'm sure Aisha told her folks it was a queer & trans student group and they cheered.

Five Star Chinese restaurant had a narrow front but went back a long way, filled with booths, dark wood, red paint, gold highlights. Walking in, I got hugged by the heavy scents of egg rolls, tangy soy sauce, hot sugar, pork and ginger. I relaxed a bit. Pops loved this place so much that Milo brought him here for monthly brunch dates where he could spend a few hours indulging in the buffet. The whole family ate here every few months and more often got their takeout.

Way in the back, the restaurant had a party room with a single, oval table. Kids sat around it in clumps. It was only three p.m., so the place was glad to have us, even if only half of us ordered (and the other half stole fried, round donuts off the plates of the first half). I saw a few other kids from our school and some who looked older and taller, from the high school.

One pretty, frenetic girl called us to order and had people say their names and anything they wanted people to know about them.

There were three gay guys from our junior high and one tough-looking girl with them. Then it came to our group. Jon went first, waving cheerfully and saying, "Jon, totally gay!"

I wanted to grab Aisha's hand under the table, but that felt extra meaningful here—like I should have her permission—so I just said, "Uh, I'm Kaz and I'm some kind of queer and trans, nonbinary, genderqueer or probably all of the above."

Aisha was super smooth. "Aisha Warren, moved here from Cali almost three years ago and haven't warmed up yet. I'm bi—the kind of bi that covers girls and nonbinary people but not cis guys. Not into that kind of emotional labor."

"Is that even bi?" one of the guys asked.

"Girls plus people equals two," Aisha told him. "Bi doesn't have to mean girls and guys and it doesn't have to mean you're into everyone. Nobody I know is into everyone. So bi covers all the genders and bi-erasure is a thing and I'm going with bi until there are so many out bi black folks that it gets boring."

After us came a group from the high school: a curvy, pretty trans girl and two trans guys—one heavy, white, shortish, brown-haired; the other was maybe an inch shorter than me, tan-skinned, stocky, and growing a pretty great goatee for a high schooler. The second guy introduced himself as Zack and said, "I hope it's cool if we hang with you all even though we're seniors. The GSA at the high school is trans-skittish and straight-up no fun. But you tell us if you need us out of your space, cool?"

Nobody said anything for a minute and then Aisha straightened up and said, "I want you here. It's not like you're that much older than us. You belong."

Nods and murmurs of agreement went around the table, mine being the loudest. I missed the next introductions, including the group leader, because I was checking out the trans guys, especially Zack. He had a mop of black hair emphasized by shaved sides, and big, square, black-rimmed glasses.

The girl leading the group tried to get us talking about how to get through the December holidays with family if you weren't out. Only a few people here were out to their parents: Aisha, of course, Zack, Jon and the organizer girl, whose name I'd forgotten. Of course every single person turned this into complaints about the election, how many of their family members were gloating about it, not realizing the pain this delivered to their queer and trans kids, cousins, nieces and nephews.

When we ended the formal part of the meeting for general chatting, Aisha's intro about being from Cali and not having warmed up led to her getting the most cheeseball pickup line, "Maybe you need someone to help you warm up" from the most beautiful girl in the room, Dani Mehta. And she made Aisha giggle, which pissed me off.

I had a twenty-sided die out on the table, rolling it between my hands, deciding if I got a twenty, I'd break into the conversation between Aisha and Meta.

"Working on your saving throws?" a guy asked me, sitting in the chair next to me.

A quick glance showed the grin and neatly-trimmed goatee of Zack.

"I need a twenty," I told him.

"No modifiers?"

"Not in the real world."

He held out his hand and I put the die in it. He rolled four times, getting a 20 on the fourth. "There you go."

I peeked over at Aisha who was laughing at whatever Dani Mehta had said.

"You came in with her," Zack said. "Is Meta moving on your girl?"

I raised my eyebrows at him because he'd said her name like the prefix "meta" not Mehta.

He explained, "Her nickname's Meta-Mehta, because she's both meta-meta and too meta, which is, itself, meta in a way that makes my brain warp. So... Aisha?"

I shrugged. "We're friends, for now."

Jon had been talking rapidly with two of the other guys from our school, but he could do this and eavesdrop at the same time, because he leaned back into my conversation and said, to Zack, "Kaz is totally into her but scared to ask her out."

"Ass," I said. "Get back to your group."

He did, but not before giving Zack a meaningful look and saying, "Kaz likes guys too."

"Double ass, get out!"

He went back to his conversation and damn if I didn't still think he was so cute with his dark hair curling on his pale forehead and his wide mouth laughing. But then I looked across the room and Meta had her hand over Aisha's on the table. Not holding Aisha's hand, but touching her in a way that only I was supposed to.

Zack turned his chair toward mine, our knees touching, shutting us off from the room. "You want to talk or ask?"

"Ask," I said. "But I don't know what to ask."

"You said trans, nonbinary, genderqueer." He put a finger on the twenty-sided die and rolled it back and forth on top of the Chinese Zodiac placemat, from Tiger to Dragon.

"How do you know what you are? I mean, really *know*?"

"At the gender clinic they ask 'if you were alone on an island, what gender would you be?' or the one I like better, 'if you had a magic wand and could be any way you wanted, how would you be?'"

"Is this a one-use wand or do I get to keep it?" I asked.

"Whatever you want."

"What if some days I'd be a girl and some days I'd be a boy?"

"Sounds like genderfluid."

"And some days I'm not either and sometimes I'm maybe… an alien." It was easier to say "alien" than to say "tree" or "dog." Especially that last made me sound like a really little kid. Plus I didn't honestly want to be a tree or a dog, I just wanted to live in their super-straightforward world for a while. But that would put a serious dent in my dating capabilities so not a real option.

"Most of us feel like aliens at some point," he said. "Look, for me, when my breasts started growing, they felt wrong, like malignant. And getting a period, like my body had decided to attack me." He spread his hands and looked at them. "This feels right, like being home. You'll find that place."

I wanted to, but it was a moving target. I shrugged.

"Nonbinary covers a lot of identities," he suggested.

"But I don't feel like I'm non-something. I feel like a whole lot of something. Too much of it."

"The way I see it—and this is me, so you do you—everyone is made up of patterns, in your soul. The energy of the Almighty, your higher power, nature if that's your thing, this energy shines through the patterns that make up you. And some of those patterns give your gender. So my pattern's a guy. And when the One made humans, some of us got made trans or genderqueer as a way to point to the mysteries of the world. Maybe you got extra patterns, extra blessings."

"Doesn't feel that way. I don't understand how to do this. How does your body know what patterns you are?"

"What does your body feel like to you?" he asked.

I knew the answer—beyond trees and dogs and aliens—but I couldn't say it, because as soon as I thought it, I heard Brock laughing and saying, "Do they have only one boob? Or is it like two boobs and a wang?"

"Impossible," I told Zack. "My body feels impossible."

"Give it some time and space, a lot of space," he said.

Did I have time? I peeked across the room at Dani Mehta with her long, straight black hair and light brown skin, dark eyes outlined with a hint of shimmery eyeshadow. She and Aisha were beautiful together. Dani played with Aisha's index finger and Aisha's smile turned deep and dimpled.

That was supposed to be *my* smile.

How did genderfluid work anyway? Was I able to kiss Aisha on some days and not others because I was a girl only some of the time?

And anyway, if I was attracted to girls when I was more a girl, and if Aisha liked girls, the obvious next step was to be more girl. If I was genderfluid, I should get to pick, right?

CHAPTER EIGHT

December 2016-January 2017

So...girl research?

I went at it so hard Mom thought it was a homework assignment. I cut photos out of catalogues—Mom's girly ones and Milo's practical outdoor gear ones—and stuck them to the magnet board in my room, previously used only for dog training and dog walking schedules.

I asked Aisha what I'd look good in and she sent me a photo of Ellen Page with her tall, blond girlfriend and their new dog.

Am I supposed to be the girlfriend? I texted her. *I think I already own that shirt. I'm looking for something more girly, but not too girly.*

She sent an image of Wanda Sykes and her wife Alex, a tall, blond Frenchwoman.

Yeah I could maybe wear that suit in twenty years, I said.

She replied, *I meant the overall style, not that exact suit.*

I'm going to need exact examples, I told her.

Another photo buzzed into my phone: Angel Haze and her ex-girlfriend, Ireland Baldwin—but before they'd broken up—laughing together.

I said, *Okay that's a cool T-shirt, but do I also get Angel's boots?*

Aisha asked, *Is that all you see in that photo?*

I studied it: Ireland gazed up at Angel with a total love-face, while Angel laughed super hard.

One of us needs to get better jokes? I asked.

No.

I looked harder, but all I saw was an awesome black rapper with a white model in a pristine apartment.

Everyone's girlfriend is a tall, blond, white woman?

No.

Their place is way cleaner than my room?

Kaz.... Yes, that T-shirt with those boots and just wear jeans.

She didn't text me again that night. The next few days, I couldn't tell why she was frustrated with me. If she saw me looking, she made herself smile, but I caught the tight press of her lips a few times. Usually she told me what upset her, though it could take a few days. When she didn't, I figured it was finals pressure.

I squeezed through finals with mostly Bs, but I got an A+ in identifying women's clothing that would look great on people other than me. I ended up watching Demi Lovato's video for "Confident" about a hundred times. Both Demi and Michelle Rodriguez were amazing in it. And hot. Demi especially. I loved how she wasn't all stick-skinny.

I looked more like Michelle Rodriguez, including the boobs. I even had a halter top kind of like hers, but when I put it on, there was a kind of wrongness.

The person in the mirror looked good, but she didn't look like *me*.

How do you know what you're supposed to be? How could I have a sense of myself that I was trying to match when I couldn't find a match anywhere around me? How could I know what I was—because I knew this wasn't it—and yet not be able to name it?

I knew that I liked being in groups of girls. I liked being with girls when they told me secrets and trusted me, which seemed easier if I was also a girl. But I didn't feel like a girl, or not *just* like a girl. Did I even know how "like a girl" felt? How did I know I didn't feel that?

I tried to find outfits that Demi Lovato wore that weren't wildly girly, and failed. Michelle Rodriguez wore tank tops, scoop necks, V-necks, slender but not skinny jeans and some wicked good combat boots, but those were for a movie. I copied some of the more doable pics to my phone and asked Mom if we could go shopping.

Tragically, this aligned with Mom's plans for me. Mom's whole "young woman" campaign had started about a year ago, around the time I had to swap the training bras I never wore for an actual bra (that I hated). It itched. But I could never figure out where it itched. It wasn't a tag or seam. It was the fact that it touched my boobs all the time and made me think about having boobs all the time.

As part of Mom's plan, she always asked me to go shopping with her. Used to be every week. Since I kept saying no, she'd toned it down to every other, but sometimes she pulled Mom rank and made me. Any time I told her to take Brock, she'd roll her eyes at me. Super unfair that every time she needed something I was the kid she picked. Like she couldn't even tell I didn't want to go. Like it was this stupid default: because I have boobs and Brock doesn't he gets to stay home and watch TV and I have to go shopping.

When I asked if she was going shopping the Friday before Christmas, and if I could come with her, she said some crap including, "Oh my little girl's finally growing up. I'm so glad you're starting to take an interest in how you look. We can stop at the makeup counter and get makeovers together. They'll do your colors."

"Can we just start with clothes?"

"You'll see," she said. "We'll look so great together."

I profoundly doubted that.

* * *

Aisha and her family were spending Christmas in L.A., which gave me breathing room on the asking her out situation. When she got back, I'd ask. They flew out on Wednesday. The next two days, I spent a lot of time staring at myself in my mirror.

I was nearly fifteen. I'd been kissed by a boy once because I'd failed to duck. And I'd dated a girl for six weeks in seventh grade as part of a roleplaying game. We were elves. All the elves were bi. She didn't talk to me now.

And I'd kissed one girl. The one girl I loved more than anybody. And screwed it up.

I didn't feel like a young woman.

From in front of the mirror, I could see the height marks on the frame of my door. There wasn't one for age nearly-fifteen, but I knew where it would be: more than two inches higher than twelve. Not an inch a year, either. Most of that had been since last winter. I liked everything about being almost-tall, except how it made me stand out.

I wasn't the tallest of the girls. I wasn't even basketball tall. I'd just started shorter so it seemed like a big difference. I was about 5'6", but up wasn't the only direction I'd grown. I had really good boobs, according to everything about boobs ever. I looked the way women superheroes looked in their skin-tight uniforms, except less skinny.

My feelings in order of frequency:

1. These are wasted on me. They should've gone to someone who wanted to look like this.

2. Oh good now I can attract...who? (Please let the answer be: Aisha.)

3. Wow, I'd look great in a thousand things I don't want to wear.

4. Huh, cool, boobs.

5. Wait...what am I supposed to do with these?

* * *

Friday morning our expedition set out early, well-provisioned with water and protein bars. Holiday sales were Mom's sport.

I'd put on a girly-top thingy from the back of my closet, with a loose shirt open over it, and Mom gave me the approving smile-nod. She asked, "Why don't you take off that overshirt?"

"I'll get cold."

She let that pass, even though I had a great winter jacket, and we got in the car.

Chaos ruled at the mall. Mom cut through the crowds and pulled things off racks. I couldn't focus beyond the noise and all the people rushing from one rack to another. I kept thinking how Wolvie would be freaked out by this, but she'd also be thrilled because she loved people.

Mom pushed a bunch of clothes on hangers into my hands and steered us to a dressing room. I hated everything once it was on me.

I could see a shirt, see that it was cute, but not on me. Like it changed from the rack to my body. Mom would hold up a shirt and I'd think, *okay, maybe*, but in the changing room, I ended up staring at an alien in the mirror.

Like being a shapeshifter with no control over my powers and every time I put on girl clothes, my body changed to whatever did not match. This was not the vision of being a badass genderfluid person that I had in mind. My body changed whether or not I wanted it to.

But this time I had a mission. I studied the photos on my phone and ignored what I saw in the mirror. I came home with two new pairs of not-quite-skinny jeans, ankle boots, two sweaters and a jacket I kind of loved. Plus I got blue streaks in my hair, the color of the superhero Beast. Having some of Beast's color on me helped me not mind the girl-clothes.

In this jean-sweater-jacket-blue-streak combo, I could be a girl asking another girl to date her. Sure I could!

I put on the jeans, the best sweater and the jacket and sent a pic of the outfit to Aisha.

She wrote back: *That looks amazing!! You survived shopping with your Mom!*

Yeah, I had to pretend I was a shapeshifter being Wolvie being a superhero, but I made it. How's Cali?

So much warmer than MN. And there's so much food. It's so good!!
I wish I could bring you some.

When do you get home? I asked.

Wednesday afternoon.

You want to come over?

There was a long pause, weird. Maybe her family was talking to her or she had to do something. I changed from the new sweater into a sweatshirt, figuring I'd layer up and take Wolvie for a walk in the snow.

My phone buzzed with a text. Aisha said, *I don't know if you're going to be mad.*

What could I be mad about? Was she going to stay in Cali longer? Had she read ahead a bunch of issues of the comics we'd agreed to read together?

She wrote: *I was going to tell you when I got back but maybe this is better.... Meta asked me out and I said yes and I'm going to see her on Wednesday when I get back. But we can hang out on Thursday.*

I threw my phone on my bed and got Wolvie. We stomped through the snow, played fetch, lost a tennis ball, found it, lost it again, left it somewhere in the snowdrifts around the frozen marsh.

When I got home, Aisha had left a bunch more texts for me:

You there?

Are you mad?

Should I have asked you first? I don't know where you're at. I didn't want to push you.

Are you okay?

K, just tell me you're okay. We don't have to talk. Don't make me worry.

I brushed my thumb over her words, moving them up and down the screen, always ending with her question "Should I have asked you first?" in the middle. What did she mean? Asking me if she should date Meta or asking me out?

Probably too much to think she'd been considering asking me out when I was some kind of shapeshifting alien who'd freaked out just trying to kiss her.

I wrote back: *Yeah, I'm fine. Congrats, I guess.*

She said, *You're mad.*

I felt like we'd broken up, like I'd been dumped, when we hadn't even been together in the first place. That made it worse.

I wrote: *This might be an asshole question, but is it because I'm white?*

What? No!! How can you think that?

Because I'm white and she isn't.

Well she also asked me out, Aisha said.

I'd…tried to. And I could see how, that having been over three months ago, Aisha might've gotten sick of waiting for me to get my shit together and try again.

Because I hadn't the first idea how to keep things from Aisha, I said, *I was going to ask you when you got back. I hadn't figured out how, with everything. But I've wanted to, for months.*

Oh, she typed and then nothing for long enough that I had to go down to dinner.

In the middle of dinner my phone buzzed. Mom and Milo were deep in one of those conversations about all our relatives that's like family ping-pong with news flying back and forth so fast I couldn't keep up.

I snuck my phone out of my pocket and peeked at the screen. Aisha had sent: *I would've said yes.*

I typed furiously under the table: *why didn't you ask me?!?!*

Trees. Carbon atoms. I didn't want to hurt you or scare you or push you into saying no when you hadn't had enough time to figure things out. You kept pulling away.

A pause and then another message from Aisha: *I hadn't figured out how to ask so you'd know it was okay if you said no…I didn't know if I'd be okay if you said no. I can't have you not be there every day.*

"Put your phone away," Milo said and I had to tuck it back into my pocket, which was good since looking at it made me feel like crying.

Later, in my bedroom, I did cry for a while and threw my new jacket into the back of the closet. Stared at my phone, read back through all the messages, still crying some.

When did she ask you? I typed.

Sunday.

That was over a week after Aisha had left for Cali, which meant Meta had asked over the phone or by text.

She long-distance asked you out? Wasn't it weird?

I hated that I hadn't thought of that. Except I would've been weird. But if I didn't have to be there in person, asking, I could've maybe sent comic book panels.

Aisha answered: *Meta said she'd been thinking about the new year and resolutions, what she wanted this year, and I was high on that list and did I want to go out. It was sweet. I'm sorry, I would've... you...damn.*

Yeah. You can't really break up with her a few days after you said yes.

K, are you even ready for that if I did?

I don't know. Have fun with her. I guess I'll grow up someday.

I threw the phone under my bed and curled up with my arms around Wolvie. I ignored the phone buzzing. Wolvie sighed, stretched out and kicked me in the crotch.

I laughed myself into crying again. Eventually I went to find a tissue and got my phone. It must've buzzed a few more times after I'd tossed it under the bed because Aisha had called, twice, but not left a message. I didn't call back.

CHAPTER NINE

Winter to Spring 2017

Aisha got home five days before school started again. I considered not going over to see her—for fifty-seven seconds—then I went over on Thursday, trying not to wonder what she and Meta had done the evening before. Had Meta already kissed her? Had it gone a thousand times better than when I'd tried?

I failed at not wondering, and at not asking. As soon as we were alone in her room, me sitting carefully at the foot of the bed with Mr. Pickles wriggling in my lap, I asked, "What'd you guys do last night?"

"You'll laugh," she said. "We looked at some of my algebra."

"No."

"My last test scores sucked. Hey, guess what my cousin got me." Aisha dug through her backpack and pulled out an orange and brown speckled dinosaur with a crest arching up from its head. "It's a parasaurolophus, can you believe that?"

"Um, no. Are they doing velociraptors next?"

"Is that the only dinosaur name you can think of or are you mad?"

"Both," I said.

She held the dinosaur out to me. "Do you want to decide where the parasaurolophus goes on the shelf?"

I sighed and took it. "Can it be a nonbinary parasaurolophus?"

"Of course."

"Is the trans dragon going to not like dating a dinosaur that doesn't have their gender all figured out?"

"No, she'd like that," Aisha said and looked away fast, digging in her bag again.

I put the parasaurolophus on the shelf by the pink dragon and went to use the bathroom—well, to use it for sitting on the closed toilet lid with my face in my hands.

When I got back, we silently agreed to not talk about who'd been crying or for how long.

Aisha showed me her new iPhone and re-enacted her grandmom in the Apple store asking the most regular questions over and over again. By the time her mom called us down to dinner, we'd settled into hanging out in a fairly casual way, except without the touching or most of the laughing.

* * *

So, just, fuck spring. Especially early spring in Minnesota, when everyone is cheerful and in shorts in March and shit if Meta didn't look great in shorts, but not as good as Aisha.

I walked a lot of dogs and wore girl sweaters and steadily read my way through my comics, going backwards in time because there were some of my dad's from the 80s that I wanted to save for last.

I got pissed off at Jon for cracking a joke about the Aisha & Meta situation and didn't talk to him for a week. I walked more dogs. I moved around in the world, but mostly I was off-planet somewhere with Captain Marvel or Moondragon, having a long adventure where all anybody cared about was my superpowers and how good I was at using them.

I came back to Earth when Aisha and Meta started having loud enough fights that I overheard them. The first was about

Aisha canceling one of their dates so she could study, then Meta cancelled one the next week to get her back. They argued about that in Aisha's back yard, not yelling but loud enough that I kept hearing phrases of it from the treehouse.

When I was sure Meta had gone, I messaged Aisha: *want to come over?*

She did. We didn't talk about the fight. She sat on the lawn chair cushion next to me, not leaning into me, but close.

I put the stack of *America* comics by her knees and she started again from issue #1. It was one of her go-to, feel-good series. Everybody had that, as far as I could tell: the handful of things that could make them feel better no matter what. For Aisha it was certain comics, rearranging her beanie babies, and geeking out about great medical discoveries (especially by black women). With me, in addition to comics, it was dogs, mostly Wolvie, and trees, especially walking through them. For Milo it was woodworking and reading things to Pops, and for Pops it was cooking and painting historical replicas.

I wondered if Meta knew Aisha's go-tos.

* * *

Their next fight happened because Aisha always wanted to do things with other people but Meta thought they should have more time alone. The fight started outside of Five Star Chinese after one of the GSA meetings, so a bunch of us heard it. Jon pulled me aside, part way down the block and said, "Look serious."

"Don't I?"

"More serious," he insisted. "Frown like I'm telling you something really important."

"Are you?"

"No," he said. "I'm listening to Meta delicately rip into Aisha about not spending enough alone time with her. Shhh."

"Jon, should we—"

He put a hand on my shoulder and leaned close, but didn't say anything. The grip of his fingers on my shoulder shut me up for a minute or two.

Then he said, "Okay, here's what I've got so far: Aisha thinks the two of them need to spend more time with Meta's family and Meta's pissed about it. Like her family is off-limits or something. And now Aisha's getting pissed, like is Meta ashamed of her because… no… oh shit, she *did* go there. And now Meta doubled down on the alone-time thing, saying Aisha's afraid of intimacy and is using all this schoolwork as an excuse, like a shield."

"That's shit," I said. "That stuff really matters to her."

"Yeah, she's getting more mad at Meta, just said something about Meta trying to sabotage her because she's threatened. Ooh, score, Meta's stomping away. Go collect your girl."

He gave me a shove toward Aisha.

I went down the sidewalk, not sure what to do, but my feet kept moving toward Aisha. She'd already started walking home, so I fell in next to her. "You okay?"

"Please don't," she said.

"Can I walk with you?"

"Yeah, of course."

"You walking all the way? Riq's not coming to get you?" The day was chilly and Aisha froze quickly, as if every time she went to Cali her body's thermostat reset itself. It was over a mile to our houses and I'd be warm when we got there, but she'd still be cold.

"He went to the airport to get Day. He's coming in for the weekend and half his spring break," she said.

Day was Darius, her older brother who went to Berkeley for materials sciences; I didn't know what that was, but it sounded cool like material + science, and I pictured him learning to make the perfect bullet-proof dress. I'd met him a few times in the last two years, guiltily liking him, since my brother-loyalty should be with Tariq. Well, after Brock, technically, but Brock was never at home these days and he'd turned into an ass in the last few months—like the election had unlocked his full-douche level.

I texted Milo that we were walking back from the meeting and she drove out to get us and take us the last mile to our houses.

"You coming over?" Aisha asked me as we got out of the car. "Family dinner with Day."

I looked to Milo, who nodded. I told her, "Thanks" and gave her a hug before darting over to Aisha's.

Darius got the tallness and the breadth of both parents, Tariq got neither. Darius had pushed Tariq around lots when they were kids, according to every family story, so I'd expected him to be a jerk in person, but his wry sarcasm had won me over. He had a wide smile and dimples, like Aisha's but less cute. With his super short hair, clean-shaven face and rectangular, nerdy glasses, I'd have thought Darius was the middle kid, not the oldest.

For most of dinner, Darius updated all of us about his academic career, sprinkled with anecdotes about eccentric professors and wild students. Materials sciences classes included experiments in a lab. About every week somebody caused an explosion or a fire. The lab tested the strength and flammability of different materials, so breaking things, blowing them up, lighting them on fire was often a legit part of Darius's schoolwork. But from the way he told it, the students went above and beyond in the breaking, burning and exploding department.

If I ever decided I didn't want to be a vet, materials sciences could be a fun route to go.

After dinner, Darius and Tariq shoved each other to the couch and grabbed the Xbox controllers.

"Come play," Tariq called over his shoulder.

Aisha dropped onto the couch next to them. Beside Darius, she seemed extra short. I curled my feet up in the armchair and Pickles jumped into my lap because I'd pet him longer than anyone else.

"Day, can you look at my Algebra test with me while you're home?" Aisha asked.

"If I remember Algebra," he said, chuckling. He offered her the game controller but she shook her head. He held it out to me.

"Thanks but I'm holding out for *Lego Star Wars*," I said.

He riffled through the pile of games and pulled out the box for *Lego Star Wars: The Force Awakens.*

"Is it good?"

"It's funny," Aisha said. "We're playing as Finn and Poe gay boyfriends."

Darius grinned. "I want to take you to Berkeley with me. They'd love you out there. You've got to come west when you graduate. What's up with Algebra?"

"I got a C on the test. I studied my butt off."

"By yourself?"

"Mostly. I asked Meta some things, but she's sick of answering my math questions."

"You need a study group," he said.

"I can do it," Aisha insisted.

"I know you can. But it's more efficient in a group. I made that mistake first year of college. But out at Berkeley they've figured out there's this factor that can drag on you when you're working at something hard. It's called stereotype threat. You're afraid of being a stereotype, like we're not as smart as everyone else, and that fear gets in the way of you doing your work. So then you push harder, all on your own, because you don't want anyone to see that you're having trouble, that'd confirm the stereotype, right?"

"Right." Aisha had a wide-eyed, you've-been-reading-my-mind look.

Was that the same as when I panicked that I'd say something stupid or awful about race and prove that I was just another ignorant white person? Sounded like it.

Darius slung his arm across the back of the couch, behind Aisha's shoulders. He said, "Thing is, you're all kinds of smart. You're just in a setting that wants to prove you stupid, wants to make you stupid. You react to that. You freeze up or you spend so much energy worried about how they're going to see you that you don't have it for what's important to you."

"Yeah both," Aisha said. "Like freezing up and my brain gets all cloudy."

If the supervillain Apocalypse was the voice of racism in all our brains, was stereotype threat one of his main weapons? Did it keep me so freaked out about addressing racism that I hadn't dared? Did it drag on Aisha's concentration and her energy, keep her from using her full power?

I leaned forward, listening to what Darius said we should do about it.

"Get in a group," he said. "You get to be smart in front of others, so when you get to test-taking time, that stereotype threat doesn't feel as big. The group will move at the speed of its smartest members; you learn more, faster. And, if you really want to ace your tests, you look at all the black women doctors, scientists, mathematicians right before the test. You prime your brain with all that. You get right up on their shoulders and you kill that shit, Aisha."

"Language!" their mom yelled from the kitchen.

Darius called back, "Sorry, Mom!"

He side-hugged Aisha, then thumbed on his control and joined Tariq in a fight game in which Tariq was about to slaughter him.

Did that group advice apply to me too about talking about race with other white people? I felt more effective when I could talk to Milo. But who else could I include?

* * *

Aisha was kind of popular in our Algebra class—because she was a person who liked math and also had boobs. My boobs didn't count as much because I wore a lot of baggy tops while she wore things with necklines.

She asked Tommy, one of the top guys in the class, if we could study with his group. The boobs worked their magic and he said yes. I deeply felt like the sidekick as I tagged along to the weekly study sessions. At least when they found out that we read comic books we had something to talk about.

And it was time together when she still spent way more time than I wanted her to with Meta. I hung out with Zack and the trans kids from the high school when I missed Aisha too much.

Within a few weeks, Aisha was slaying in Algebra. Studying in the group took a ton of pressure off. Someone always had the answer and could explain it. That was never me, but it was as often Aisha as it was Tommy. The guys got over her boobs and began asking her to explain things to them. Even my grade came up because I couldn't help but listen when she explained the formulas.

We both got on track to be in the advanced pre-college math class for tenth grade. That was exactly what Aisha wanted and something that had never occurred to me to go for. I was perplexed, but I wasn't going to mess with my good luck. No school subject sucked if Aisha was there. Plus I'd need math for Vet school.

I wanted the future where we were both doctors, except I got to work with animals because they're nicer.

CHAPTER TEN

April 2017

In April, the weather got freaky hot for Minnesota. Hot enough that Wolvie complained about it. With her thick, black fur, she loved snow and resented summer heat. After school, she'd stand by the back door like: *I'm waiting, just turn down the temp a bit, okay?*

"I can't, it's the weather," I told her.

She stared at my face, dog eyebrows slanting together like she didn't know why she had to explain this to me: *You know what I mean, turn on the cold blowing air thing.*

"I can't air condition the whole outdoors," I explained, but she didn't believe me.

I didn't believe me either every time I tried to tell myself I was okay seeing Aisha with Meta.

* * *

Every spring as soon as it got really warm, students from the high school would bring games and set up on the grass across from the junior high. Like a ritual welcoming the graduating ninth graders. This year they rolled out a slip-n-slide on the grass between the high school and the stout office building on its east side. Someone got a hose hooked up to the office building so kids could sprint and slide down the water-filled plastic.

It couldn't have been above seventy degrees, but half the guys had their shirts off. They wrestled, jostled each other in line, sprinted and leapt, seeing who could go farthest on the slide. The afternoon sun gleamed on their lean shoulders, their flat chests, wet from sliding. One guy I'd known since seventh grade must've grown four inches and his shoulders were wider than Brock's, his hands big and strong as he wrestled some guy I didn't know.

I flexed my hand and wrapped it around my forearm, a pale imitation of his grip.

Girls were sliding too, but of course this got their shirts wet. In no time all slide activity centered on girls in wet shirts, which girls the guys could persuade to go down the slide, and how much they could all show off for each other.

Boobs and shoulders, chests and hips. Everyone made it look so easy to be in their bodies. How?

Aisha sat next to me. "Penny for your thoughts."

"I think they made me in a lab."

She reached across my lap and pried my hand off my forearm. I'd been digging my fingernails into my skin unawares. She closed one hand over the red crescents on my arm, her other hand lacing fingers with mine.

"I just can't figure out who I'm cloned from," I said. "Because it's not Wolverine."

"K, this isn't your scene. Let's go somewhere."

"Yeah okay."

I let her help me up and hoisted my bag over my shoulder, but I kept watching the guys at the slide: the easy way they got to carry their bodies, their shoulders, their muscles. How could I feel the muscles I didn't have? How could a lack of something be so present?

Could I be one of them?

Aisha pulled another step and stopped. Meta stalked across the grass toward us, hands in fists. She had an ironically floral beanie over her long, sleek black hair and looked like she didn't know how to sweat.

"Here you are with her again!" she yelled at Aisha.

"Do *not* start this," Aisha said.

One word rang in my head, "her." Was that right? I glanced back at the guys. Thought about Brock, about wearing his shirts, how much I loved them. What happened if I said I wasn't "her?" Did that mean I'd be "him?"

I tried it in my head: *here you are with him again?*

Not bad. Not at all.

Except a lot of yelling was happening a few feet from my face. I tuned in again as Meta hollered, "Oh so you're not totally into the girl whose hand you're holding right now in front of me?! Stop playing me."

I thought:... *totally into the guy whose hand you're holding*... and it made me want to hold Aisha's hand a lot more, a lot stronger, to pull her close to me.

Aisha waved our joined hands in Meta's direction. "I have friends. I've known Kaz a lot longer than you, so back off and don't be trying to police this."

"I wouldn't care if you weren't super crushed on her. I'm supposed to be the important person in your life. I don't care how long you've been friends."

...super crushed on him...

Wait, Aisha was crushed on me? Even now, after I'd screwed up kissing her and failed to ask her out so many times?

I wanted her to be. I wanted it so much I was shaking. All the moments of the last few years, all the seconds together in the treehouse, all the times she touched me, leaned into me, caught my hand when I reached out to her—all those moments came in on me at the same time, into my body. My tall, broad-shouldered, guy-shirt-wearing body that wanted to put an arm around her, hold her close, kiss her.

"I can have more than one important person," Aisha insisted.

"Well the one you're dating is supposed to be *more* important!" Meta shot back.

Aisha dropped my hand. I couldn't move one way or the other. The shock of my feelings pinned me.

"You are," she told Meta. "Of course you're important to me."

"And you're not hopelessly in love with Kaz?"

"No," Aisha said, but even she didn't sound sure of that. She turned to me and froze with her mouth open.

Could she see what I was feeling?

I felt massive and powerful. World-destroyingly giant. Reality-warping magical. Heroic. Time to use my powers for good. I forced my hands up, palms out, gesture of denial, warding, refusal, maybe harmlessness, though I felt the least harmless I ever had in my life.

"We're just friends," I said, voice coming out low and rough.

"Then why don't you date someone?" Meta asked.

I squared my shoulders and stepped to her. I wasn't tall, but I was taller than Meta. I held her glare and said, even and calm, "Because I'm barely fifteen and I'm not ready. You have a problem with that? Some kind of timetable we're all supposed to be on?"

"Whoa, sorry, back off white-girl thug."

I dug in my memory for her first name and said, "Dani, don't call me a girl."

Shock flashed in her eyes. Then they set into something like respect. "What should I call you?" she asked.

"Kaz works just fine." I moved toward the sidewalk. "You two have fun. I'm out."

Heading up the sidewalk, I heard Meta say, "What is her deal?"

"Leave Kaz alone," Aisha said. "You want to talk about us, let's talk about us."

"Why are you always protecting her?"

I didn't hear Aisha's answer because I'd turned the corner of the school and took off running. I ran four blocks, paused to catch my breath and check my bearings, ran another four and ended up panting on the front porch of Zack's house.

He waved me into his living room. "What's your emergency?" he asked, heavy black eyebrows lowering toward the big, square frames of his glasses.

"What if I'm a guy," I said. "Or want to be a guy or partly a guy. Can you teach me?"

"My friend, I was born for this. One sec." He yelled into the other room, "Mom, I'm going to take a friend upstairs and teach him how to dress, okay?"

Him. Said out loud the word settled into my skin like sunlight. Yeah, maybe this could work.

An answer echoed from the back of the house. "No funny business."

"All serious business, I swear," he called.

Zack's bedroom shouted full-on mythology, geekery and masculinity. One poster showed the genealogy of all the Egyptian gods. Another was a detailed study of dragons. His bedspread was dark gray, the walls a silver gray. I counted four shades of gray total.

"You're not going to get this all in one afternoon," he said. "And you have to practice."

"What do I practice?"

"Standing, sitting, taking up space, not curling your shoulders. Hang on."

He dove into his closet and went through boxes. "Here, I have an old binder. It'll be too big on you. And my shirts are going to be too short, but we'll give it a shot, right? My pants aren't going to fit you but those jeans look fine and the boots are great."

"Binder?" I asked.

"Chest binder—makes your chest flat."

"Yeah, I read that online but...for real?"

"Just try it," he insisted. "Shirt or sweater?"

"Shirt."

"You like any of these?" He waved at the left side of his closet. I pointed to an olive green military surplus style shirt.

He tossed it on his bed with something that looked like a brown half tank-top.

"Try it, I'll be in the hall. Let me know when you're decent."

He went out and shut the bedroom door.

Taking off my sweater and shirt in his bedroom didn't feel nearly as weird as I expected; we were just guys together. But pulling on the binder took ages. It resembled an innocent half-tank but it had been made out of super-reinforced spandex. (Superhero outfit? Yeah, totally.)

When I wrestled it over my head and tugged it down, it squashed my boobs against my body, but not uncomfortably. Zack was right about it being too big to flatten my chest completely, so at first it looked like I was wearing a tight sports bra. But when I pulled my T-shirt back on, the difference was obvious: I might have boobs, but definitely an A size if that.

Then I pulled on the military shirt and buttoned it. Any hint of boobs disappeared under the shirt's chest pockets.

I stared at myself in the mirror.

No boobs.

I looked amazing: powerful, sleek, capable.

Zack knocked on the door. "You okay in there?"

"Oh yeah, come on in. I'm dressed."

He shut the door again behind him. I went back to staring at the mirror. I ran a hand across my chest, feeling the slight rise that was so different from what I'd had the last three years. I wanted to make up words to express these feelings I'd never had before.

"You like it?" he asked.

"I love this." I half-laughed the words out.

"Welcome to Team Trans. You can keep the binder and the shirt. I've been meaning to donate the binder and that shirt's not my color."

"Thank you."

So much relief and gratitude that I could cry, except I figured crying about being a guy—probably not a guy thing.

"I'm going to get us some chips," Zack said. "You'll be standing there a while."

When he got back with a bag of chips and two pops, I was still in front of the mirror, turning side to side and staring at my chest. It was the longest I'd been happy in front of mirror since...ever.

Zack sat on the foot of his bed. I rolled out his desk chair and sat where I could reach the chips. "So was it like this for you?"

"I hated my breasts," he said. "Like growths. Just no point to them and they bounced around and they hurt."

"I don't hate mine," I told him. "But I hate how people treat me because of them."

"Huh, yeah. That too. It's obnoxious how people let me talk now. I used to think people talked over me because I was the youngest kid. But no, turns out because they saw me as a girl. Last semester I started counting how many times I had to say 'she had her hand up first' and point to some girl in the room. Sixteen times, and not in the same classes."

"Damn," I said. "I never noticed, but I don't raise my hand all that much. Also I don't listen that much, so that's what gets me, that people think because I have boobs I'm going to listen to them. I'd rather be reading or thinking or whatever."

He laughed. "Yeah, big, round ears on your chest, right? Like boob tissue makes you give a crap about people."

He fished chips out of the bag and crunched while I turned back to the mirror.

"If I love this, does that make me a guy?" I asked.

"Wear it around and see," he suggested.

I spent the rest of the afternoon in Zack's room and went home with the binder and two of his shirts. If I felt this comfortable being a guy, maybe that solved all my problems. Maybe I wouldn't even mind seeing Aisha with Meta.

Yeah and maybe I'd figure out how to turn on the outdoor air conditioning for Wolvie.

CHAPTER ELEVEN

April-May 2017

Was I a guy? I liked roughhousing, goofing off, running around, stupid jokes, but did guys have a lock on that? I wasn't wild about the idea of a beard or having to shave my face. I liked guys, but did I want to have to be like that all the time? I watched a bunch of YouTube videos of trans guys talking about transition, trying to figure it out.

Of course Mom walked in and I didn't even have my headphones on. She walked in during the part where the guy talks about telling his mom he wanted to be a boy. I hit pause super fast.

"What are you watching?" she asked.

She wore brown leggings and a peach sweatshirt with rectangular holes cut out down the arms. Who needed a ventilated sweatshirt? If it was hot, just don't wear a sweatshirt. Or was it one of those girl things that's supposed to look delicate?

I couldn't tell how much she'd heard, so I said, "Just stuff. What do you need?"

"What does FTM mean?"

On the screen, under the video, of course it said, "FTM interview."

"Mom."

"Don't 'mom' me." She put her hands on her hips in the Wonder Woman pose which only worked because I knew it meant she thought she shouldn't give up. I couldn't think fast enough to come up with something else for FTM to mean. Obviously the "M" should stand for "math," but what about the first two letters? I floundered.

"Who is he?" Mom asked.

"Just some YouTuber, you know. Everyone makes videos."

"Do we need to have a talk about boys?"

"No, please, no."

The "t" could be "teaching?" Finally teaching math? Finally triumph at math? Would she buy that? If she asked me to play some of it, this was definitely not a math video.

"Kaz, you have one minute to tell me or play that video. I want to know what you're up to."

"Mom, seriously, it's no big deal."

I held my breath, clicked the video forward a few minutes in hopes that I'd get out of his coming out story, and hit play. The very built trans man talked about dealing with his changing body and the new way people interacted with him. I paused it again. At least we were in a spot that made it sound like he was talking only about bodybuilding.

"See," I said. "It's bodybuilding tips. Nothing about sex."

Brock had come up the stairs just in time to hear me say the word, "sex." Or maybe "bodybuilding" was what paused him on the landing. Mom heard the wood creak and turned.

"Do you know FTM means?" she asked.

"Nope," he said, leaning far enough through the doorway to see me at my desk and the paused video. "Killer delts on that guy, though. You bulking up, Kaz?"

"Maybe?"

Milo appeared next to Brock. Her worn, practical gray cotton T-shirt made his skinny-strap tank top look about as delicate as Mom's ventilated sweatshirt.

"Family meeting?" Milo asked.

"Oh God no," I said.

"Kaz!" from Mom.

"Sorry." I looked up, "Sorry, God." Did it count as taking God's name in vain if it had been more of a prayer? *Also, if you're listening, God, please make this stop.* "I'm just watching videos and mom thinks it about sex and it's not."

"It's about time you have some questions about sex," Milo said.

"Whoa, I'm out," Brock announced and headed down the hall to the bathroom.

"I don't have questions about sex!" At least not any that they could answer. I had a lot of questions. I wasn't even sure how to categorize them.

"I see," Milo said. She came into the room and stood behind my chair, then turned to my mom. "Carrie, could I talk to my grandkid alone for a minute?"

"I'm her mother!"

"How much did you want to talk to me at fifteen?" Milo asked.

Mom looked away. "One of you has to tell me what this is about."

"Sure will, after we talk," Milo said. "Why don't you make us some tea and get the pie out, I'll be down shortly."

After Mom left, Milo shut my bedroom door.

"He is a handsome man," she said, pointing at my screen.

I shrugged.

"He looks happy. Is this one where they dramatize his transition or it's no big deal?"

"You...know what this is?"

"I'm a little ashamed that your mother doesn't." Milo sat on the edge of my bed. "Do you have a friend who's a trans man?"

"Yeah," I said, still blown away to hear "transition" and "trans man" come out of Milo's mouth. I mean, I should figure because she's cooler than cool, but...whaaaaat? "Uh, he goes to the high school. You'd like him."

Milo scooted back to sit against the wall, her short legs stretched out across my bedspread, gray work pants contrasting with my brighter brown and red bedspread colors. Wolvie had been sleeping by my desk but hearing Milo get on the bed, Wolvie hopped up and settled next to her with a put-upon dog sigh, like it was such a big deal to keep track of all these people. Milo scratched her back.

I said, "I met him in the queer and trans student group. There's an unofficial one. I go with Aisha."

"With or *with*?"

"Just with. She's dating Meta, I mean, this other girl, whose real name sounds like that."

"And you like this boy you met there?"

"Yeah. No. As friends. He's just a friend. He has a girlfriend. Milo…what if I'm like him?" I waved at the letters FTM on my computer screen.

She cocked her head to one side, frowned, nodded. "Then I think you'd make a fine man. Is that what you want?"

I grinned like mad because that was so much better than everything I'd heard from my mom about gender. "I don't know," I admitted. "I'm trying to figure it out. Aisha's not into guys, but now she's with Meta anyway. And…how did you get this cool? How do you know what all this stuff is?"

"Nessa's been talking to me," Milo said. Seeing my puzzled look, she added, "Vanessa Warren, Aisha's mom. Are you shocked that we talk about you?"

"Uh, yeah. Like, what?"

"Let's see, when I returned her copy of *Between the World and Me*, we talked about you and Aisha and if the two of you would end up dating. That was early December. Then Aisha started dating that other girl and you've been dressing more trans masculine—"

"Whoa," I said.

"Did I say that wrong?"

"Exactly right. Just, wow."

I lunged across the room and hugged her hard. Then I settled on the other side of her from Wolvie, her arm still around my shoulders, even though I had to hunch down for that to work.

"Has Aisha told you the story about her aunt coming out?" Milo asked.

"That it was really awful for her aunt back then, not details."

"She's Nessa's big sister and they grew up close, like you and Brock, but when she came out as lesbian, the family disowned her. Their parents forbid any of the kids to talk to her."

"Fu—shit, crap," I said and Milo chuckled.

"Once she got to college, out of her parents' house, Nessa got back in touch with her sister. You might not see it, but she's got a big rebellious streak. She even took a class in LGBTQ Lit, though she was the only straight person in there. And when Aisha came out to her, she told her parents, Aisha's grandparents, that the first time she heard a homophobic word out of their mouths, they'd be the ones cut off from their grandkid."

"She's a badass."

"She is. Makes me regret some things. Not spending more time with my uncle when he was alive." Milo loosened her arm so she could turn and meet my eyes. "My uncle, your great uncle Matty was...well, we thought gay but these days I think if trans had been an option Matty would've been a lot happier. And I haven't always been good about this. Lesbians maybe, I knew some in the seventies, but not gay men and definitely not trans anyone. I lost a lot of time I could've spent with Matty. We all have our blindspots but I wish mine had been smaller."

She sighed and leaned her head back against the wall. I rested my head on her arm.

"I don't want to regret anything about how I helped raise you," Milo said quietly. "I asked Nessa about Aisha, about how she felt, what she'd learned, what she regretted. Now we have a two-person book club. She doesn't know much about transgender people either, but there are some who come to her pharmacy, so she's been learning. We're reading *The Transgender Teen* together."

"I love you so much," I said. "Can it be a three-person book club?"

"Love you too, kid. Do you want to invite Aisha and make it a four-person club?"

"Yeah."

"Kaz, what should we tell your mom?"

"That I had awkward questions about boys?" I suggested. "And sex. But, like, super awkward."

"I got it," she said. "Do you want me to go with 'can I get pregnant from touching a doorknob?' or is that too sixties?"

"Yeah, like the 1760s. Better go with period stuff instead of sex. No one ever wants to talk about that."

Milo smiled and asked, "And you? You know I'll fight for you to have the life you want, best I can. What do you really need?"

"I don't know. There's so much I like about being a guy, but I don't know if I want to go through all the stuff to be one all the time. Like I'd be climbing out of one box and into another. I don't like the boxes."

"Good thing you're at that age where you're supposed to try some things and see what fits," she said.

"Everyone else has it figured out by now," I said.

"I will bet you twenty dollars and two rides to the destination of your choice that they don't. They only look more together because you're seeing what they want the world to see, not all their worries and fears and struggles."

"Telepathy isn't one of my superpowers," I admitted. "That's more Aisha's thing."

"Are you talking to her about this?"

"I..."

"You should. There, that's all the advice I've got right now. Can I watch that video with you?"

"Sure," I said and scooted back to my desk chair. I scrolled it back to the beginning and started it. We watched that one and another, then Milo went downstairs and I don't even want to know what she told my mom about my fictitious period questions, but I got a lot of "oh, honey" from my mom that week.

* * *

I practiced like Zack said, wearing the binder and standing with my shoulders back. I didn't have to practice sitting with my legs spread; that felt normal. The shoulders thing was hard; I'd gotten used to rolling them forward to hide my boobs.

But suddenly I was dreaming about having boobs—and about how it had felt for that one second when mine pressed against Aisha's, before I'd freaked out. How it could be the best thing ever. As if now that I didn't have to have boobs all the time, I did want them some of the time.

Random mornings I woke up with my boobs feeling interesting. Like touching them was a good idea rather than an annoying nuisance. And when I did, it seemed like some other things would also be a good idea: things that didn't involve a rolled up sock or having my business stick out from my body.

One afternoon in July I came in from yard work—I'd picked up a bunch of Brock's old jobs because he had a gig at a coffee shop now—all covered in sweat, flat-chested, in a sleeveless T. I stepped out of my shorts and pulled on the baggy guy jeans I'd found in a second-hand store. My hair was slicked back with sweat.

I watched myself in the mirror, struck my most guy pose and thought...no.

I can't do this all the time.

I'm not a guy.

Maybe I'm a guy sometimes and a girl sometimes?

Could I be genderfluid if I sucked at fashion and only owned one set of clothes and wanted those to be guy clothes?

The times I looked online at people who were genderfluid or nonbinary, they looked great. But the patterns hurt my brain. Like too often my brain translated the looks into boys-in-skirts and girls-in-vests. Like there were still only two options and you could only blend these two. Like blue and red and a lot of shades of purple, but I was green and gray and water and the whole night sky.

How did people ever grow up into these bodies?

* * *

Some days the binder felt just right and other days it was fine to wear a bra. What did that even mean? File that under the general heading of "puberty" and hope my body sorted itself out.

We only had a few weeks of school left. I didn't want to wear the binder during the school day and deal with questions. But I decided to wear it to one of the last GSA meetings before finals.

I'd already learned from wearing it all Sunday one weekend that more than seven hours made my back sore. Zack had warned me that wearing a binder all day wasn't a great idea, particularly if I was still growing. But at least this one was a little too big so I didn't figure it would smash all my ribs together.

I changed before last period, because we'd go right from there to the meeting and I didn't want to be ducking into the bathroom and making it all obvious while Aisha waited for me. Standing in the stall, unhooking my bra and balling it up in my bag, pulling the tank top on and then the binder, I felt like a superhero changing into my crime-fighting suit.

I didn't look that much different, but I did. Because boobs aren't like elbows. They're not some random part of your body. They're this whole identity thing. People see boobs and they assume everything. Like that you're going to be a person who wants to giggle and get pushed into gliding delicately down a slip-n-slide instead of a person who knows what all the trees in your neighborhood are.

I'd worn the military shirt to school, knowing I was going to put the binder on. I still had on girl jeans, but the tails of the shirt covered my hips, giving me a broad-shouldered, narrow-waisted look.

Aisha waited for me at the north doors of the school where we always met to go to GSA. Since Meta was in tenth grade, she drove over with kids from the high school.

"You look taller," Aisha said and studied my feet, like I'd changed shoes during the school day.

"Binder," I said. "No boobs."

"Oh! You look great,"

"Thanks, but I'm pretty far from Kate Bishop style cuteness."

"I'm not into her anymore," Aisha said.

"Who are you into?" I asked.

She shrugged. She didn't name Meta. We headed away from the school, down tree-lined streets, past houses.

"Hold up," she said and stopped to blow her nose. She was getting over a late spring cold, her eyes still red-rimmed, her cheeks carrying a hint of gray. She'd pulled her hair into a bun, which was her "screw it" hairstyle, but curls must've started escaping earlier in the day because she'd tucked a few behind her ear.

I'd seen Milo and Pops nurse each other through colds every year. Pops got sick more often and Milo always made a huge pot of soup, bringing him bowls as often as he'd eat them. He made soup for her if she got sick first or instead of him. I wanted to bring Aisha a whole lifetime of bowls of soup. If I got sick, there's no one I'd rather have sitting next to me in bed listening to me whine.

She tucked her tissue back into a pocket. Before she could start walking again, I asked, louder, "Who do you like?"

"You know who," she said and slipped her hand into mine.

We walked toward Main St. I figured she'd drop my hand well before we got to Five Star Chinese. We didn't need another fight from Meta, like the one they'd had that day with the slip-n-slide. Aisha held my hand until we reached the end of residential streets, about to turn onto Main, and then her fingers loosened, paused, squeezed mine, let go.

Too late. Coming out of the gas station on the corner, Meta saw us. She whispered intently to the girl next to her, the pretty one who kept the meetings going, and the two of them beelined for the restaurant.

"Cat's in the bag now," I muttered. To Aisha's quizzical look, I said, "It's something Wolvie says. Maybe it won't be that bad. Friends hold hands."

"No, I'm screwed. Let's do this."

Bright side: with finals coming, the meeting was at half attendance. Jon and Zack were there, plus the rest of the trans crew from the high school. Meta sat with the pretty girl, whose name I could never remember, and the sporty lesbians.

As soon as we'd crossed the threshold, Meta stood up. "You want to tell me what I just saw?"

"Not really," Aisha said. Her fingers found the back of the chair in front of her, but she didn't pull it out and sit.

"Then let me tell you. I see how you are with Kaz. You keep saying it's nothing but I see your eyes light up. I think we're good, but when I see the two of you, you're full-on sparkles. I get half that, I get leftovers. Are you honestly going to keep telling me you're not in love with Kaz?"

Aisha took the world's longest breath in. Everyone else in the room held theirs. When she let it out, her shoulders didn't drop from their scared, defensive height.

"No. You're right," she said. "I made a mistake."

Meta shouted, loud enough to be heard at the front cash register, "Are you calling me *a mistake*?"

"Don't you dare put words in my mouth," Aisha's voice rose almost to Meta's volume.

Around the room bodies stayed statue-still.

"What did you mean then?" Meta asked. "Because you sure as hell did not mean that I've spent five months on a mistake, did you?"

"Meta, I like you. A lot. But we both knew this wasn't going to last forever."

From the way Meta flinched on that last word, she hadn't known that. Her eyes squeezed shut on the pain and opened with hard fury. Leaning forward, palms on the table top, she said, "Last? When did it even *start*? You used me to get Kaz to say yes to you."

"Kaz hasn't said yes," Aisha replied.

"But she would. Ask her. You'll see."

"Um hey," I said, wincing as all the eyes turned to me. "Awkward timing, but I've been meaning to ask everyone if you'd use they/them pronouns for me. Except not if my mom's around."

Meta glared at me and back at Aisha. "Fucking ask them. Get it over with already."

"No. I am not going to pressure my best friend. Nobody has to date or define themselves or anything before they're ready."

"Fine," Meta said. "Ask whoever you want whatever whenever because we are done. We are over."

Aisha said, "Sorry" and fished in the pocket of her jacket, coming out with the tissue. She turned and sneezed into it. Only I could tell she'd faked the sneeze, that she held the tissue to her nose to cover the tears gathering in her eyes.

I wrapped my fingers around Aisha's elbow and drew her back out of the room, saying, "Bathroom" loud enough for everyone to understand that we'd be back.

Five Star Chinese had single-occupant restrooms and I locked us both in the women's room. I put an arm around Aisha and she curled toward my chest. Stepping back, I leaned against the door, both arms around her, pulling her closer. She pressed her face into my shoulder, crying.

I tried not to think about the sweet almond and coconut smell of her hair or how extremely happy I felt about the end of her and Meta. Tried to get all the ways this could hurt: that she genuinely cared about Meta, hated hurting her, felt embarrassed about all that happening in front of many of our favorite people. I ended up balanced between one-third hurt empathy and two-thirds wishing I could scoop her up in my arms and fly us to the treehouse and kiss her.

Probably not the right time for that.

Aisha pulled away to blow her nose and wash her face.

"Do you want to talk about stuff?" I asked.

"About Meta? No. About you and me, maybe soon. I don't want to put that off forever again."

"Yeah. For the record, I'd say yes. If you asked. But would you even want to with me like this?" I asked, brushing a hand down the flat front of my chest. "Even if I'm not a girl or only sometimes a girl or don't know what 'girl' is? Even if I don't know what I am?"

Aisha held out her hand and when I put mine in hers, she tugged me toward her. I dropped her hand to put both arms around her. She rested her cheek on my collarbone and sighed, our bodies fitting together perfectly.

"Especially because," she said. "Because you're Kaz and I want to be around you all the time."

I pressed my lips to her forehead. "Same. But I can wait. I made you wait. It's only fair."

"It's not. But after everything Meta said. Ugh." Aisha pulled away and blew her nose again, so I wasn't sure if that last "ugh" was about Meta or mucous.

Aisha was flying out to California in ten days to spend almost two months with her aunts, so I said, "I could ask you after you get back from Cali, as long as you promise not to say yes to going out with anyone else before you get back."

"You jerk, like I would," she said, but a huge grin crinkled her nose and made her eyes smile.

"Great, now I've got two more months to figure out how to ask you out." I tried to sound cheerful, but I hated that she was leaving for that long.

She opened her mouth, taking a breath in like she was going to say something and then closed it and beamed at me.

More even than asking her out right then, I wanted to beg her to stay. But I couldn't. I knew how much she loved it there with her aunts. She'd asked me to visit and I really wanted to but I had a bunch of dog walking jobs, and time at the lake, not to mention there wasn't money for a plane ticket, but I didn't want to tell her that. At least we'd get to hold hands and sit close every day until she had to go.

When we walked back into the GSA meeting, Meta had gone, along with the pretty girl and two of the sporty lesbians. Everyone else crowded around us, half comforting Aisha and the other half clapping me on the back and congratulating me about my pronouns.

CHAPTER TWELVE

Summer 2017

The first afternoon Aisha got to Cali, right after the plane touched down, she sent a pic of her in the sun, sunglasses on, deep smile, everything about her shining in that bright light.

I sent her a pic of me doing yard work in a sleeveless shirt with the binder on. Sweaty as anything, but better than doing it in a bra.

She sent me a pic of her at dinner with her aunts and cousins and their families: a long table with seven fabulous women and a few guys looking way out of their depth.

I texted back: *Say hi from me!* and sent her a two-second video of me waving and Wolvie wagging her tail.

She sent me a pic of herself and her cousin with blue and purple hair grinning into the camera.

I sent her a pic of the new comics pile, then sat in the treehouse and tried not to cry about how much I missed her.

I did not spend two whole months in the treehouse. For the three-sometimes-four-person book club with Aisha and Milo and Mrs. Warren, we finished reading *The Transgender Teen* and started reading *Mindful of Race*. Mr. Warren joined us for that second one because he understood the meditation parts more than the rest of us. He tried to teach us to meditate, but I kept laughing and then Mrs. Warren joined in, at which point Milo did too. Mr. Warren decided laughter meditation was the way to go.

I wanted Brock to read the book too, but no way that would happen. Apocalypse's mind control of him had been getting more complete; Brock thought our country was headed in a good direction. And he seemed to only want to listen to people who thought the way he did, probably one of Apocalypse's strategies. That voice in Brock's head seemed more real when the people he talked to said the same things.

Maybe Mom would read it if she wasn't too busy at work. Or I could ask Sofia. She'd been part of our lunchtime group in ninth grade and would be in tenth with us. With Aisha in California and Jon at gay summer camp, we'd been hanging out more. But I didn't know if as a white person it was okay to ask my Asian American friend to read a book about race that mostly focused on black lives. How could I even start *that* conversation? Way easier to stick to music and TV and safe topics.

* * *

I was in the treehouse when Aisha got back two days early and surprised me. I didn't even turn when I heard the door open. I figured it was Mom coming to get me for dinner, since Milo would've yelled from the deck.

Instead, Aisha said, "Hey" and I leapt up, almost smacking my head on the ceiling. Wolvie got to her first. Aisha let herself be knocked over by dog love and then I jumped in, so we ended up in a human/dog/human pile on the soft, sanded planks of the wood floor.

I'd been trying to think of the most awesome way to ask her out, searching through our comics to find the perfect panel that I could copy and put new text on. I wanted to use *Black Panther* but couldn't figure out if as a white person I should be using images with two black women, so I fell on the careful side of "probably not."

And now Aisha was here and I didn't have anything. I hadn't completely worked out how I fit into all this, so what came out of my mouth was, "What if I'm just a person?"

"Um, hi? I'm glad to see you too," Aisha said.

She rubbed Wolvie's belly vigorously, which got Wolvie to lie on her back between us, putting us face to face. Her glorious grin greeted my dorky one. I didn't know how to kiss her grinning.

"Do you date people?" I asked.

"If they're you, I do."

"For real?"

"Why not?"

"Because…boobs," I said and flushed hot and hugged Wolvie in an attempt to hide that.

"Cart super ahead of the horse there," she said. "You don't have to be a girl for me."

"Are you sure?"

"I know you. You're Kaz. Someone who names a big dog 'Wolverine' and is going to chase a girl with a little dog down the street just to make sure we're okay. Can we for real talk about all this now? I've been waiting."

"You have?"

"K, in my old school, I was already in the GSA by sixth grade—it was still called 'gay-straight alliance' back then and you know I was not the S. I told my parents I like girls when I was eleven. And you know I don't just like girls. And I *know* that you sometimes light up when I treat you like a guy, but not all the time. So, you want to tell me what you're thinking about for yourself?"

"I don't know how to be what I am."

In the semidarkness from the roof and leaves outside the window, Aisha's eyes were deep, wide. "I'd be scared if I didn't know," she said.

"Yeah, I am. So sometimes I try to be other things. Like a girl or a boy."

Her hand slid from Wolvie's belly to find my hand. I wrapped my fingers tightly around hers and put our joined hands back on Wolvie so she wouldn't kick us in a bid for attention.

Aisha said, "You know when someone gets their superhero powers for the first time and it completely freaks them out because they don't know how to control it and they don't know what all the powers are? Maybe this is like that."

"I wish," I told her.

"Why not?"

I turned my head, indicating the comic books all around us. "Nobody looks like me."

"Anyone come close?"

"Maybe, but you'll think I'm a freak."

"I promise I won't," Aisha said.

She sat up, untangling from Wolvie's legs and my fingers, and searched the stacks of comics until she had *Black Panther* #1. She turned the pages to show me Ayo and Aneka kissing.

We'd gotten this issue a few weeks before Aisha's birthday, spring of eighth grade. After school, we ran over to her house and sat on the bed, leaning into each other. I sat on her right so she could turn the pages as we finished reading them. When she got to the one where Ayo and Aneka touched palms and kissed, she didn't turn the page.

She sat and sat, her eyes wet and glistening, shining from inside, like she couldn't see this enough. I wondered if this was the first time she'd seen a comic book image of two black women kissing. Or maybe it was that they were heroes. Or that they loved each other so much. Now I thought it was all of that: they're powerful and loving and kissing each other. And now I also knew it was about how dark they were; that they looked more like Aisha.

Back then, I'd lifted her fingers off the edge of the page so she wouldn't think she had to turn it for me. She'd curled her hand around mine and I held onto her. When she did turn the page, she used her other hand. We read every page of that issue, even the bios at the end, and then we read it again. Aisha wore her hair in short twists like Aneka for the rest of that year.

Now I closed *Black Panther,* gathered up the others I'd been reading and put all the comics in the big storage box.

"The ones I want to show you are in my room," I said. "Come on."

We climbed down and went into my room. I got another, smaller box from the back of my closet, an old comic book box fraying at the edges. Wolvie hopped on the bed and took over the entire foot of it, so me and Aisha sat outside my open closet door with the box in front of us. I lifted out a few comics in plastic bags.

"These were my dad's," I told her.

Best thing my dad had ever done for me was leave his comic book collection. I had a hazy memory of him sitting on the couch with me and Brock, reading us these comics, but I think he spent more time with Brock than me. And no matter how cool he might've been, Milo and Pops were better. He'd left when I was six, so I barely remembered him as a parent, just remembered how upset Mom had been.

I put the stack of comics in Aisha'a lap and told her, "These are how I know I like Beast. And I remembered them a while ago and read these again. They're really goofy but, okay, read these parts."

Aisha read what I showed her. She had a few very on-point questions, like: "Did this character just turn into a guy because she's crushing on this woman and doesn't know lesbians exist?"

"Basically. Keep going."

When she got to the end, she turned back the pages and re-read the ending. "Whoa, cool, so Cloud has both a boy body and a girl body and can switch back and forth between them?"

"Yeah. When Cloud got to Earth, they were trying to communicate with humans, so they copied the bodies of the first two they met: a girl and a boy."

Aisha turned back a page and forward again, touched her finger to a panel, "So Cloud is a being who can be a girl or a boy or both at the same time in two side-by-side bodies?"

"Yep."

"And Cloud is also a nebula, so they're really big. They're this vast place where stars are born but they have a girl body and a boy body too? Is that you?"

We sat so close, her shoulder leaning against mine, the usual way we read a comic book together, but with electrified, shimmering sparks and icy jabs of nervousness under my skin. I leaned more into her, needing reassurance.

I told her, "It's super close. Not boy and girl and nebula side-by-side, but all in the same place. Not half and half, I'm all. I'm a whole girl and a whole boy in the same place with something else, that's what the nebula stands for. How my body feels changes within that range, like sometimes the girl is more in front, or the boy, or the nebula. And there's definitely a point where I'm too girl or too boy."

I stared at the drawings in the comic, the outline of two bodies on the backdrop of a field of starts.

Aisha's lips pressed my cheek.

"Okay," she said without moving away. I felt her breath and shivered.

I reached for her hand and her fingers caught mine.

Now that I could talk, I kept going. "I don't understand why boy-girl are the only choices. People are so many things, why do we have to get stuck with those two?"

"Because you're also a nebula?" she asked.

"Yeah. Or trees, that works too. Sometimes in the treehouse it's just me and our tree and I understand that a lot better than I understand how people do 'girl' all the time."

"We're not *doing* 'girl' Kaz. Some of us *are* girls."

"Are you sure?"

"Yeah, bae, I'm a girl all the time. It's not something I have to do or put on, it's me."

"I'm not like that," I said quietly.

"I know."

"But I could be for a while. I can do girl."

"You don't have to," she said.

"But you like girls."

"You don't have to be a girl for me. I don't *only* like girls. If you were going to be a guy all the time, maybe then it would be different... but *you*... I like how you are."

The whole time, talking, our bodies got closer and closer together, further entwined, her fingers around my fingers and she threw one leg over my leg. I'd been leaning back on my other arm and I moved it forward until it stretched across her back, she scooted closer.

I'd missed her so much and all that missing reinforced how I felt, but missing her didn't help me know what to do now that she was here. I knew that I wanted to go on with her sitting inside the curve of my arm. But I didn't understand what she was saying. I wasn't a guy all the time. But how did we fit together?

Her free hand rested on the comic spread open on our legs, one finger on the drawing of Cloud. She set it to the side, put those fingers on my arm, rubbed her thumb on my wrist.

"You're wonderful," she said, watching her thumb move on my wrist. "How you are is amazing. I'm sorry about this winter, about not talking to you about everything first."

All my breath caught in my throat while the words slipped away, so I took my hand off the floor and wrapped my arm around her. She rested into me, her whole body sighing. My hand curled around her lower ribs, small and delicate for holding all the intensity of her lungs and her heart and all those other parts she'd know as a doctor-in-training.

Her head rested on my shoulder, tucked into the curve of my neck, her forehead on my cheek. I tipped my face down, pressing my cheek to her skin, to the soft density of her hair, trying to see how much of a smile she had going. Thoughtful smile, from the curves at the corner of her mouth, happy, from her dimple, maybe nervous too. I sure was.

"I was trying to figure out how I am, so I'd know if we'd work together," I told her.

"I got that, eventually. After I thought a whole bunch of other stupid stuff."

Then she got quiet again. I needed her to keep talking because she was better at it than me, so I asked, "Wonderful-amazing for real?"

"Literally," she said, the corner of her mouth quirking in as her smile deepened. "Full of wonder. The most…"

"But that's you!" I said.

She grabbed the hand I'd rested on my knee—and tugged, as if I could get closer. I turned toward her as her face tipped up, eyes shining. Her lips pressed mine—and I was so scared that I was going to panic again, or that I wasn't going to pay attention, remember this, that I almost didn't feel the kiss—warm, dry, too brief. She rested her cheek on mine and whispered, "Is that okay?"

I nodded, got my free hand to the side of her face. With my thumb on her cheek, fingers trailing down the side of her neck, I couldn't turn her back to me. She pressed into my hand, brought her lips back to mine. I kissed her lips and then her cheek so I could kiss her mouth newly and then her other cheek and her nose, which made her laugh and sit back.

Her cheeks had gone the dark berry red they got in winter when she froze and then warmed up. I put my thumb there, grinning that I got to be the one who warmed her up now, and this winter, and…I wanted it to be forever.

"All those pictures you sent. I looked at them for so long," she said. "You look great in every one. I want to kiss every one of you."

Leaning forward, I missed her lips and kissed the corner of her mouth. She grinned and kissed me, longer.

And with all of that, I forgot to ask her out.

CHAPTER THIRTEEN

Early September 2017

All I remember of the week before starting tenth grade, official high school, was kissing Aisha. As soon as we were alone, one of us would reach over and touch the other, lightly, anywhere, to bring us together, I'd play with her hand, she'd touch my shoulder or my collarbone. We'd kiss at first on the lips and, as the days went on, soft kisses on each other's faces, necks, she kissed my hands and wrists, I kissed from the hollow of her throat up to her ear until she laughed and pushed me away saying it tickled. I kissed her eyelids, she kissed the tip of my nose.

It was like a musical score in which the notes were kisses, layers of melody built over days, soaring arias of touch over the bass beat of our hearts.

She always sat next to me or sideways across my lap so when we kissed, we didn't press chest to chest, and I was so grateful. She'd already been the best person in the world, so this made her double-best.

"You want to be my girlfr—, uh, my person?" she asked two days before school started.

I'd thought that was implied in all the kissing. And worried that I should've asked. I had my arm around her shoulders, both of us sitting against a pile of pillows in her bed, books fallen to the sides, her legs draped over mine.

"Yes," I said, fast. "Do you want to be...er, will you be my girlfriend?"

"Kind of hoping I already am," she said with a grin.

"Oh my God, you walked me into a formal girlfriend question and you're not even going to say yes, you're such a punk."

She kissed me hard, but I could feel her suppressed laughter through her lips, then sat back and said, "Yes! Absolutely."

"Good 'cause you kind of have been for a while."

"I beat out all those trees?"

"Oh shut up."

Aisha grinned and reached behind her shoulder to get the parasaurolophus and the hummingbird who was really a phoenix. Snuggling them together, she draped the phoenix's wing over the parasaurolophus, the phoenix full of colors and the dinosaur speckled white and brown, slightly dapper with its head crest.

I plucked the phoenix out of her hand and kissed its beak. She pulled it away and gave me her lips to kiss instead.

When we stopped, we had to fish around in the pillows to find the little phoenix. She put it on the shelf, cuddling the parasaurolophus, to the right of the middle where she'd see it as she fell asleep each night.

She said, "You know, I think Day and Riq have been placing bets on us."

"Are you going to tell them?"

"Soon. Not yet, if that's okay," she said. "I want them to know, and my folks and, pretty much, everybody in the whole world, but maybe not right away. I don't want to know what they all think about this and you know they're going to tell me."

"Yeah, and then you're going to tell me what they say, right?"

"Pffh, they'll tell you too," she said. "Is your family going to be okay with this?"

I shrugged. "Depends who. Milo will be great and she'll make sure Pops is. Brock, you know a year ago I'd have said he'll think it's cool, but now, who the hell knows. But Milo will handle him if he gets shitty. Mom, I don't know."

She sighed and asked, "They know I'm black, right?" The words sounded like a joke, but there wasn't any laughter in her.

"Nah, I never told them." I said and kissed her cheek. She cuddled against me and traced a circle on my knee of my jeans.

I watched her finger moving on the light blue denim. I saw the colors of our skin differently when we were alone. Not some foolish "we're all human" ideal that erased her experiences. When we were alone, her skin held so much information: temperature, softness, variations in texture and color, how she moved, her expressions, how my skin felt touching hers.

As soon as we went someplace with strangers, all that information collapsed down to one color and one idea. I watched how people looked at her. I worried about if she was safe or not. Weird because she was the one of us who really liked people and I was the one who wanted to stay home with Wolvie.

Wolvie had taught me a lot about how to handle people by the way dogs moved around each other at the dog park, deciding who should interact, who was okay. That helped me see when someone started moving toward Aisha in a way I didn't like. Mostly that happened in stores. A clerk would start to follow her and then I'd move in, like Wolvie policing a badly-behaved dog, and put my body between that clerk and Aisha.

She'd see that, of course. Aisha was onto the store clerks before I was. But sometimes I could give her an extra few minutes to get what she needed, or she'd catch my eye and nod toward the door and we'd drop the stuff we were no way going to buy now and leave.

Since we were dating now, could she take my hand and pull me away? Or was that a terrible idea?

"How much of a thing is this going to be, me being white?" I asked.

"Way too much," she said.

"And that didn't happen with you and Meta, or did it?"

"Not the same. Her family...well, Indian American and black are pretty far apart sometimes. But out in public we were two brown girls together and that's great even when it's bad. Darius was trying to tell me because he dated a white girl for a while—not that I'm calling you a girl, but same dynamic—"

"Got it," I said. "And thank you."

She nodded and placed a tiny kiss on my jaw before saying, "Some people, here, maybe a lot of people, are not going to be okay with us. Badly not okay. And I don't know what that means because all this Minnesota nice..." She trailed off into heavy silence.

"Hey," I said. "Maybe I'll finally get my superpowers and then I can beat them up."

"Yeah," she said, but her voice stayed low.

"You're scared?"

Aisha pressed her cheek to my shoulder. She said, "Sometimes I think I know this place and I don't. Minnesota is different. Back home, I wouldn't care. If someone had a problem, they'd say it to my face. Here people don't say anything but you've seen it. Harder to deal with when I can't see it coming, when I can feel it but folks want to tell me I'm making it up."

"Yeah," I said and held onto her tighter. "You're not making it up. I see it. Hear it, too."

"I hate that. But thanks. At least it's not like it used to be." Her voice fell all the way to a whisper. "Mom's grandfather, my great-grandfather almost got killed for dating a white woman."

"Fuck."

"They got stopped by the police and it was just luck she was driving. She was a court stenographer but she played it like she was a lawyer. Police wanted him to get out of the car and you know they were going to beat him, not care if they killed him, probably try to. She told them she was taking him to the courthouse for a trial. She had to tell them if he showed up at the courthouse all beat up, the jury might feel sympathy. If she'd hadn't been smart like that..."

That wasn't so long ago. Milo's mom had been alive when I was born. I hadn't thought that when Milo and Pops' parents were young if they'd tried to date like this that it was life and death. That people killed people like us for a whole lot of reasons.

"I'm scared for you. Is that okay?" I asked.

"Heck yeah, I'm scared for you enough, might as well."

"Yeah, sometimes I'm scared for me too. So we agree to never leave our houses again."

"No. We're going to leave the house, Kaz. And we should tell people."

"Can I be the one to tell Riq?"

"Sure."

But we didn't tell him before school started. And once it did, we had a lot more to worry about.

* * *

Our junior high hadn't been that big. You could walk across it before you realized it: one main hall with classrooms off it and one hall along the back with our lockers. Each of the three grades held about two hundred kids. A bunch of them I'd gone to elementary with. I had my same group of friends all three years, mainly Jon and Sofia, with Aisha joining us in eighth grade. Aisha had that group plus some girls from the soccer team, plus some friends from her Spanish class. Each semester, she picked up more friends. She liked people; I did too, but at a distance.

This high school was three times bigger than the junior high, nearly two thousand students. Aisha and I didn't have as many classes together. Since we were Kaz Adams and Aisha Warren, the alphabet split us any time there were multiple sessions of a class.

At least we had World History and AP Chemistry together and lunch. The first few days the two of us ate lunch sitting at the end of a long table of studious kids who ignored us. Brock had a different lunch period. Not like we'd sit with him anyway.

He was popular and hung out with a bunch of other popular guys. Jon wasn't in our lunch period and we hadn't seen Sofia at lunch yet.

Those first few days of school, I spent too much time trying to figure out where I was supposed to be, what the class was doing, where my next class was, how these textbooks could be this many pages. Luckily we only had three days until the weekend.

On Saturday, I fell asleep leaned against the wall, sitting in Aisha's bed. I woke up tipped sideways with my head on a pillow on her leg. I still had a headache. Aisha had her other leg bent up, a textbook braced open on it.

"Is that Chem?" I asked groggily. "Read it to me?"

"You okay?"

"I've had a headache for two days," I admitted. "Two thousand students is so many. It doesn't bother you, does it?"

"I like all the rush and busy and noise. You could ask them to move your study hall so it's not last period, give you a break mid-day."

"You're a genius," I told her and closed my eyes.

She curled a lock of my hair around her finger and dramatically read me the intro to our Chemistry book.

I thought high school would be perfect if Aisha and I could navigate it from a two-person bubble, but that Monday, walking into the cafeteria, Sofia stood up from a table and waved at me while I was in line. I waved back. She texted: *Come sit with us.*

I couldn't see who "us" was over the crowd. The juniors and seniors were way taller than anyone in junior high had been. I got to the end of the line and waited for Aisha.

"Sofi said we should sit with her," I told her.

"She's in this lunch? Why hasn't she been sitting with us?"

I shrugged. "We're bottom of the pack again."

Aisha flashed me a smile and wrapped her finger in my sleeve, pulling it tight so it hugged my wrist. I grinned back and rubbed my shoulder against hers. If I hadn't been holding a tray, I'd have taken her hand, except we hadn't talked about touching at school and how out we wanted to be. I assumed pretty out because she'd been out with Meta last year, but then I was white and everything felt so new. Better to ask.

Sofia waved us to the empty spot on the bench next to her. The purple streak at the front of her black hair looked freshly dyed and she wore a burgundy sweater that managed not to clash with that vibrant purple. There wasn't quite enough space for two people, but we made it work. We were used to sitting close, especially in the treehouse when we had a ton of comics covering the floor.

Across from Sofia sat a tall girl, short bleached hair, tan white complexion, sports jersey, broad mouth that turned down at the corners even though she was smiling. Next to her sat a smugly pretty girl with creamy pale skin and eyes about the same color as her long, wavy brown hair. Her stylized athletic shirt was mostly frill.

"This is Kaz and Aisha," Sofia told them.

"I'm Trina," the brown-haired girl said, looking at me. "And Eve." Eve nodded as Trina said her name.

"Kaz is Brock's little sister," Sofia said.

"Oh? Is Brock still dating Jillian?" Trina asked.

"He broke up with her mid-summer. He's going out with Lisa from the cheer squad," I said, then shut my mouth, wondering why I was gossiping about my brother with this stranger.

"She's so pretty," Trina said. She turned and looked across the room like she was going to see Brock and Lisa. She elbowed Eve and said, "Look, you could go for him. He's almost tall enough for you."

Eve shook her head. "I don't know."

"I'll find out if he likes you," Trina said. "How about you, Kaz? Seen anyone cute yet or did you have a boyfriend last year?"

Blood rushed into my cheeks. My face felt heavy enough to fall off, slide right down into my mashed potatoes. My favorite person in the world was sitting next to me—and the only person I'd ever really kissed or wanted to. And she was being much too quiet.

"Oh there is someone? Who is it?" Trina asked.

Aisha put her foot over mine and pressed, I thought about what she'd said about her great-grandfather, took a big bite of my hamburger and shook my head.

Trina laughed. "You can't keep it a secret forever. Sofi, did you find out the name of that guy in your homeroom? Or a pic of him?"

"Not yet," Sofia said.

The table got quiet. Trina scrutinized the room while the rest of us ate.

"You came from the smallest junior high, didn't you?" Trina asked me. "What do you think of this place?"

I had my mouth full, and I didn't have a good answer anyway, so I shrugged and looked at Aisha.

"I like the academic standards," she said. "Junior high was too easy. At least I can get college credits here."

A flash of shock crossed Trina's face. Then her eyes narrowed, mouth tightening. What did she have to be angry about?

Trina corralled her face into a plastic smile. "You have to pass the exams to get college credit." Her tone suggested that would be way beyond Aisha.

Aisha's face was expressionless, which meant she was pissed. But she kept her voice even as she said, "I know. I'm going to."

Trina shrugged and gazed across the cafeteria. "I guess you like a challenge."

"I'll let you know the answer to that when I find something challenging here," Aisha said and turned her attention back to her lunch.

Next to me, Sofi wasn't breathing. I contemplated our hands on the table: Sofi next to me with naturally tan skin and Eve across from her with sun-tanned, almost as close in color, but worlds apart in meaning. Trina's pale white was one shade pinker than mine.

Eve had been eating her hamburger, but now pointed with the half-eaten hamburger, reaching across Trina. "There's Caden, who's he sitting with?"

"Oh those lacrosse guys. He could do better. He needs to try out for football. I'm going to tell him." Trina pushed up, holding her tray. She bussed the tray and went over to hang on the guy who had to be Caden. He had a very defined chin and beyond that I'd never be able to pick him out in a crowd of brown-haired white guys.

"They've been together all summer," Sofia said. Her gaze flicked to Aisha and her eyebrows went up like she was worried or sorry.

Aisha didn't see it. She stared steadily down at her tray, stabbing at the green beans.

"You play basketball?" Eve asked Aisha. She didn't look up at first so Eve repeated it, louder, "Hey, you play basketball?"

Aisha's face came up, jaw set. "Soccer," she said.

"Huh, really? How tall are you?"

"Five-four."

"Kind of short I guess. Still you could try out," Eve said.

"Um, thanks? I'll think about it." Aisha folded her napkin, put it on her tray under her fork. "I've got to stop by my locker. See you."

She walked away with her shoulders rounded in. I got up without saying anything and followed Aisha.

As I bussed my tray, standing a few people behind Aisha, giving her a minute, I played through the conversation. How quickly had Aisha seen this group wasn't safe for us? When Trina didn't say anything to her or even look at her as we sat down? Or before that, when Sofi only called me over, not Aisha? But that could've been because I spent more time with Sofi this summer.

Definitely by the time Trina demonstrated how shocked she was that Aisha was articulate. I'd seen that look way more times than I ever wanted to, since Aisha tended to speak up first and said things better than I did. Seen how a white person's eyes would widen and their head jerk back a fraction. Watched how fast they caught themselves. Mom did it plenty. Not sure if Milo ever had because two years ago I wouldn't have noticed. And for every time I noticed it, Aisha had to see it two or three times as often.

And Trina's anger? What was that about? Plus the way Eve asked her about basketball, the demanding sound of her "hey," like Aisha owed her an answer.

I caught up to Aisha in the hall. "You okay?"

"Yeah," she said, but low and quiet.

"I'm sorry. That was fucked up."

She peeked at me, corner of her mouth lifting. "Thanks. Was it all the way as messed up as I thought?"

"I'd give it a seven, maybe eight," I said. Aisha had introduced me to the zero-to-ten pain scale doctors used and we now used it for all kinds of painful situations.

"Sounds right," she said and uncurled her shoulders.

* * *

Our first class after lunch was World History. We got seats together near the middle, left side.

As the rest of the class crammed through the door in advance of the bell, I saw Eve's paintbrush-style blond hair beside Trina's messy brown updo. I hadn't realized they were in this class; they'd just been part of a mass of loudness before I'd met them today. They settled into the middle of the louder right side, behind two rows of boys.

Class started: details and lesson plans and a short lecture on ancient Greece. I scooted my foot across the floor until I touched the side of Aisha's foot. She tapped the edge of her shoe against mine, tap, tap, tap. When she stopped I tapped back. Maybe we should learn Morse code.

After the bell rang, I hung back and let Aisha go ahead of me, as if I could literally watch her back.

"Hey Kaz, wait a sec," Trina said and I stopped in the aisle by reflex. She fished in her purse and held out a pinkish bottle. "I got two of this nail polish in a bag of samples, do you want one?"

"I don't much wear it," I told her.

She got up and pressed the bottle into my hand. "So give it to your mom or see if Brock wants to pass it on to Lisa. It's not doing me any good, someone should have it. My mom gets tons of samples, what do you like?"

"I don't really…"

"What do you use for that blue in your hair?" she asked. "Is it Splat?"

"Yeah."

"Great, I'll score you some. More blue or another color?"

"Uh, blue. Thanks?"

With a grin and a nod, she followed Eve out the door. The bottle in my hand was a semi-translucent creamy pink color called "Naked."

It wasn't like Aisha and I never played with nail polish. She'd even gotten me a flat chrome color like Wolverine's claws that I loved. And it wasn't like she never wore light colors on her nails. This one would look good on her. But no way would I let anything from Trina touch her.

And "naked?" Way too close to peach crayons being called "flesh." Like there was only one color a person could be.

On the way out of the room, I dropped it into the trash.

* * *

We didn't talk on the bus home except when I asked, "Treehouse?" and Aisha said, "Sure." I missed when we could walk, but the high school was a half-mile farther from our houses than the junior high.

The bus dropped us at her house. We went through her yard, across the alley and into mine. I sped up the stairs to the treehouse, Aisha right behind me. For the first time, I wanted us to be younger than we were, just a few months, early summer.

When she got up the stairs and sat, I held out my hand. Aisha wrapped her fingers around mine and tugged. I crawled toward her, put my arms around her. She held onto me as I pressed my lips to the side of her face.

Milo must've seen us go up the treehouse stairs and let Wolvie out, because seventy pounds of dog love pelted up the stairs and body-checked both of us. We were a pile of human limbs and dog body for a while. Aisha got laughing from the way Wolvie kept head-butting her chest, trying to get even closer, and I realized I hadn't heard her laugh at all at school the four days we'd been in tenth grade.

"I want to tell people you're my girlfriend," I said. "Is that okay?"

"I don't know," she answered.

The way she said it sounded so low that my breath stuck in my chest. "But we are, right? We're going to stay together no matter what...right?"

She turned her face and kissed me. Pulled back only enough to press our foreheads together.

"We are," she said. "Of course we are."

"But it's not safe?" I asked. "And it's less safe for you than me?"

She shifted back to sitting next to me, Wolvie now wriggling into both our laps. I put an arm around Aisha and rubbed Wolvie's belly with my other hand.

"Yeah," she said.

"Do you think it would be different if I didn't look so much like a girl? More like a guy?"

A long quiet followed, only Wolvie panting and Aisha saying "Oof" when Wolvie kicked her in the boob.

She said, "If you looked one-hundred percent like a guy, maybe, except that you grew up here being seen as a girl and people don't forget that. You know, that whole history of white women and black men, I think that trumps me being a girl."

I shuddered. As a white guy with Aisha, people would think I was experimenting or...worse. But when I was read as a white girl...historically black boys and men got killed if white women even said the men, or boys, had been flirting with them. I felt dangerous, and sad, but that was for me to deal with later because I wasn't the one who'd get hurt. I was the safe one, the one with superpowers in this situation.

"You want to give it more time and see?" I asked.

I clicked my tongue at Wolvie and patted the space next to me so she'd stop squirming in our laps and settle at my side. Then I tugged on Aisha until she sat between my legs. I wrapped my arms around her and she leaned against me. She pulled a comic book over from our to-read pile and opened it on her knees so I could read over her shoulder.

"I don't care what people think," she said. "But I don't want to hear it and I don't want to have to deal with it until I know how bad that school's going to be."

I almost said, *Maybe it'll just turn out to be Trina and Eve,* but I didn't believe that.

CHAPTER FOURTEEN

Mid September 2017

I got up early and walked Wolvie and Pickles while Aisha was still groaning over a cup of coffee. I walked Wolvie most mornings before breakfast, at least a few blocks, and stopped by Aisha's back door to get Pickles if I saw the light on in her kitchen. Her mom worked a lot of evening shifts and Tariq had a wild schedule, so I didn't want to wake them up if the house was dark.

On this morning's walk, I told Wolvie and Pickles about lunch and Trina, about the nail polish and hair color. They paused to sniff a tree at the corner and Wolvie looked over her shoulder at me like: *That girl is trying to mark you as her territory.*

"Yeah but what do I do about it?"

Pickles glanced over at Wolvie, both their tails wagging thoughtfully, like neither one wanted to answer. Finally Pickles lifted a leg and peed on the tree roots.

"I'm not peeing on *anything*," I told them. "We have to come up with something else."

At home, I changed into good jeans and a heavy button-down flannel. Aisha had on a gray waffle-pattern sweater I hadn't known she owned and put her hair back in a tight bun. We'd both dressed for a fight.

Come lunch time, I hauled ass to the cafeteria and saved a spot in line for Aisha so we could have our pick of places to sit. No way did we get stuck with Trina and Eve again. When Aisha came into the cafeteria, I waved her over.

"Saved you a spot," I said.

The heavyset, paste-white guy with generic brown hair behind me in line told Aisha, "No cutting, go to the back of the line."

"Hey," I stepped between him and Aisha. "I *saved* her a spot."

I had to look up to meet his blue eyes. I crossed my arms.

He crossed his and said, "Then you can go to the back of the line with her. There's no cutting."

"It's not cutting when you save a spot. Have you never saved somebody a spot in line?"

He glanced away, so he definitely had, or had someone save him a spot. Brock did it for his buddies all the time.

Glaring over my shoulder, he said to Aisha, "Why don't you tell your friend how it is."

"Oh no," she said. "You don't get to do that."

We'd been moving in fractional steps until we reached the trays. I held my ground, making space in front of me. "Go ahead," I told Aisha.

He turned back to his group of friends as I picked up my tray. Whatever he said made them laugh. Didn't take much to imagine about what it was, even if I hadn't seen him point from me to Aisha and laugh harder.

I could roll the video in my mind and see what happened in different endings to this lunch line bullshit. If I'd been perceived as a white guy and it got physical with no-cutting guy, we'd both have been taken to the office, given a stern lecture and probably been let off with that. I'd bet money someone would say "Boys will be boys."

White girls vs white guy, he'd have gotten suspended, even if I hit him first. But if Aisha tried to step in and save me, no matter how it ended up, she'd get the worst punishment of any of us. She'd get hit more than me in the fight and then get punished worse than me from the principal's office. Even when people treated her worse than me, she couldn't afford to fight back.

Aisha and I got a spot at the end of a table. I studied the room as more students filtered in, got trays and food, found tables. This school was really white, more so than our junior high—and that had been pretty freakin' white. There were some brown faces, mostly sitting together, some with white friends like me and Aisha. All my teachers were white.

I shoved a pile of peas across my plate. "A, in first grade, did you have black teachers?"

She had her Spanish book out on the table but wasn't reading it. "No."

"When did you?" I asked.

"Fourth, we moved to a better neighborhood. I mean more diverse, not better like the folks around here mean when they say that."

"You had three years of school with no teachers who looked like you?"

"Yep," she said.

Those same years, I'd had all white teachers. I'd had one black teacher in fifth grade. If I calculated the total number of teachers I'd had first to sixth grade it would be about twenty, and nineteen of them had been white. Almost all of the people that my school system deemed fit to teach me were white like me.

"Shit," I said. "And you have all my same teachers this year?"

"Yep."

All our teachers were white. So was the principal.

I'd seen photos of Aisha in fourth through seventh grade, photos with classmates, friends, the soccer team, class photos. At a guess, about one in six kids in her school was white. Most of the kids were black or Latinx, and there were more Asian kids than white kids.

But that was only four grades out of ten. What did it feel like year after year, every day to have to go to a school where most people didn't look like you?

I had some sense of that from walking around in a world where every single person was clearly identifying themselves as a man or a woman. I'd grown up not seeing people who looked like my gender and that made it so hard to know how to be a person in the world.

What if I could've gone to school with some teachers who weren't exclusively men or women? What if I could learn from people who were people, where everything wasn't gendered and distracting? Because gender was a huge deal all the time. And so was race.

No wonder Aisha still missed California. When she complained about the cold in Minnesota, she didn't only mean the weather.

* * *

Wednesday I wore another heavy shirt and Aisha kept her hair in that tight bun. I waited for her by the cafeteria doors and we joined the back of the line together. We ended up sitting with Trina, Eve and Sofia again because Sofia had saved us seats. At least this time she saved two. Sometimes Trina went to eat with Caden and the boys or Caden came over to eat lunch with us. This became our lunch default for the rest of that week and the start of the next.

They talked about classes and TV, white celebrity gossip. I chimed in if they said something I cared about, which wasn't that often. Aisha stayed quiet. I could see why. The first time I brought up black celebrity gossip, Trina and Eve stared at me like I'd sprouted a second head and the table turned coldly quiet until Sofia changed the topic.

I hated how much of my time with Aisha every day got taken up by the two of us listening to other people talk about topics we didn't care about. I hated how Trina and Eve ignored her and made her invisible.

But also, I could see how when we were in a bigger group, with popular girls, the no-cutting-the-line guy stopped watching us. I knew how his bullshit would go with Trina there: she'd cut him down verbally so fast and deep he'd have to slink away for good. Not because she was doing Aisha any favors, but because she liked the power she had, wanted to use it, and wanted to gain more power from knowing Brock through me.

And if Aisha wasn't there, Trina would join no-cutting-the-line guy in his jokes.

* * *

In World History, in the third week of class, we got rolling on class projects. Our teacher, Konrad Fogg, was a tall, big-handed history buff—a complete geek for historical detail—who didn't let us call him "Foggy" in the classroom, but didn't seem to care when we did outside it. He had more brown hair in his beard than on top of his head, not because he'd started balding like Aisha's dad, but because he kept the sides shaved high and tight. He left a mop of brown bangs flopping over his forehead. His face was so long, you almost couldn't see his bangs and his beard at the same time. He liked patterned suit jackets over T-shirts. I hadn't decided if he was trying to be cool and not quite managing, or if he legit had a quirky sense of style.

The World History classroom featured one wall of old Greek and Roman dudes, one wall of white guys, and one wall that was a mishmash of people of color and women, but that was the short wall. The room carried the wood and graphite smell of pencil shavings along with a toasted ham-and-cheese sandwich odor. How he could be toasting them in the classroom, I had no idea.

When he told us to get into groups of four, Trina waved at me, saying, "Kaz, come on."

She had a gray beanie over her long brown hair and it mismatched her gray skinny jeans in just the right way to show off the verdant green of her sweater. Next to her, Eve wore a dark green sweatshirt and had combed back her bleached hair, which looked almost the same as when she brushed it up.

We ate lunch with her, Eve and Sofia every day now. I really wanted them to know I was dating Aisha. I got up and tugged on Aisha's sleeve. She followed me over to Trina and Eve.

"I'm sorry," Trina said, making an apologetic face that was heavy on the face and light on the apology. "Caden's in our group too. We don't have room for both of you."

"Oh," I said, cheeks burning. "We'll get another group."

While we'd had this brief, unproductive exchange—with me and Aisha the only students standing in the middle of the room—everyone else had clumped into groups of three or four, based on the people near them. I didn't see a group of two that we could join.

Mr. Fogg came over. "Problem?" he asked.

"It's groups of four, right?" Trina asked.

"Three or four," he said. He pointed across the room. "They need an extra student."

Aisha walked over and sat down in that group of three.

"But we study together," I told him.

"The whole class is covering the same material," he said. "This is only one project. You'll be fine."

We only had this class together and Chemistry, so even with lunch that meant more than half of each school day without Aisha. In junior high, we'd had most of every day together. I didn't want to give up more than I already had. Plus it might be one project, but it spanned the whole semester.

"No, you don't understand," I protested. "We belong in the same group. Take someone out of that group and I'll join them."

"It's only a project," Trina said. She stood up and put her fingers on my elbow. "One class. You'll be glad you're with us. We're very accurate. You should've seen what we did last year in US History."

"Can we have a group of five?" I asked Mr. Fogg.

"Unnecessary," he said and walked back to the front of the room.

Trina leaned in to me, "Are you worried she won't do as well without you? You can give her your notes after school." She was *not* whispering. Students near us could hear her. Aisha could hear her, even though she had her back to us and acted absorbed in her history book.

I stared at Trina and said, louder than her, "Aisha's smarter than me."

"Don't sell yourself short," Trina replied.

"I'm not," I insisted.

"Take your seats," Mr. Fogg boomed from the front of the room.

Trina tugged on my elbow and drew me into a seat. I sank down, glad of the chair even as I hated where it was.

I scooted the chair back and sideways, further from Trina and Eve, but facing them more fully. "Aisha is really smart. If you knew how smart, you'd want her in this group instead of me."

"Sure," Trina said. "She'll be okay without you."

"I'm not worried about *her*," I insisted. At least not the way Trina meant. Is that what they thought about me always being around her—that she succeeded because of me and not the other way round?

Of course it was. Shit.

CHAPTER FIFTEEN

Mid September 2017

World History turned out not to be our worst class together. The winner for shittiest tenth grade class experience fell to Chemistry.

We had AP Chem fourth period, right before lunch, so Chem should've been the start of the good part of the morning. The first few weeks, it was. Our teacher Mrs. Alexander evoked an ad for hearty Midwestern living: big hands, wide hips, lots of long skirts in earthy, solid colors, chunky heels, brown hair that she always wore up.

I'd met her over the summer because she taught a science camp the school sponsored. I'd gone for two weeks while Aisha was in California. I liked her teaching style: she was big on questions and having us figure things out for ourselves, but she had a good sense about when to step in if we got stuck. Plus she collected practical household chemistry facts about baking and cooking. She made chemistry feel useful and her classroom smelled like someone had cleaned out a dozen apple pie tins with bleach. Plus it was in the quiet part of the school and weirdly dark because it only had windows on its narrow side.

Three weeks into the semester, Aisha came in late to class. She and Chloe, this white girl in her Algebra 2 class, both walked in more than five minutes after the bell. Mrs. Alexander had been giving out assignments for a class-wide project about testing household chemicals.

Chloe walked in first and said brightly, "Sorry I'm late, Mrs. Alexander. Aisha's with me too, she got stopped by the hall monitor, but she'll be right here."

Of course she did. This would be the second time she'd gotten stopped in three weeks. How many times had I been stopped? None. Not even when I was fifteen minutes late because I'd forgotten my book in the cafeteria, then stopped to pee, then stopped to look out the window at a massive, fuzzy Newfoundland being walked next to the school.

"Oh," Mrs. Alexander said to Chloe. "I've given all the assignments out. What's your lab partner doing?"

Chloe popped into her spot and scanned the page her lab partner held out. "Checking the manufacturer's websites."

"You two can split that one."

Aisha came in, face scrunched with annoyance, and sat on the stool next to me. I put the tips of my fingers on the side of her thigh.

"I'm sorry for being late," she said, sitting up straight, addressing Mrs. Alexander.

"I told them," Chloe said.

"We're doing a project," I told Aisha. "You can do my part with me."

Mrs. Alexander came down the aisle between the desks, pausing in the middle of the room and asked me, "Which part are you doing?"

"Posting our results online."

"We already have enough people for that. Aisha, you keep track of the amounts of household items and chemicals."

"Sure, Mrs. Alexander."

Over the next few days, we all brought in cleaners and other chemicals from our houses. I don't think Aisha had imagined—I sure hadn't—that Mrs. Alexander honestly meant for her to pour out all the contents of these and record how many milliliters of each we had. Every day. Because the amounts decreased as we tested them. Not only was this boring as fuck, but it left Aisha with a bunch of glassware to wash at the end of class. This class backed into our lunch period, which was only thirty minutes.

I stayed back with Aisha to wash glassware. At least we didn't have to listen to as much of Trina, Eve and Sofia's boring lunchtime chatter, but we missed the best food. After two days, Aisha packed us lunches.

She handed me one as we sat at the cafeteria table that Eve, Trina and Sofia had vacated. We had six minutes to eat. I unpacked my bag and stared down at the roast beef sandwich, apple, chips. The sandwich had fresh butter lettuce and the right kind of horseradish: the kind that was strong enough you could see the texture of the grated root.

"You wanted something else?" Aisha asked.

"No, just, I love you."

"Because I brought you lunch?" she asked, grin going huge across her face and I realized what I'd said.

"Oh shit, I totally meant to say that way more romantically. I almost had a plan but the treehouse is getting cold and if we lit candles at your house we'd probably set off the smoke alarm so I was thinking maybe Christmas lights—"

She reached across the table and wrapped her fingers around mine. "I love you too. And let's say it again when we're home so I can kiss you."

"Yeah. A bunch. You always make things better. Even with the chemistry crap and everything. Sometimes I want to curl up in my room and never come out again, except to go over to your room."

"I've got more people than you," she said. "And I curl up in my room plenty. You've seen that."

"You're always cuter than me about it," I insisted.

"Matter of perspective. You're cuter."

"No way." I grinned and rubbed my thumb over her fingers. "This whole chemistry thing is a pile of steaming shit. Mrs. Alexander should know you couldn't help being late."

"You think she's going to admit to herself that the hall monitor stops the black kids way more often than anyone else?" Aisha asked. "If she could be bothered to notice. And you know I'm only *acting* calm about this shit."

"Yeah, still I couldn't."

"You could. If you didn't have a choice. You know what happens if I get mad about this, I'm just another angry black woman, and I mean 'woman' not 'girl.' You know why the hall monitor stopped me this time? He didn't think I go here. He thought I was twenty. And then he had to look at my ID for forever because my hair's different in that photo."

This wasn't the first time white people around us thought Aisha was four or five years older than me, rather than four months younger, despite her being shorter and smaller. More of Apocalypse's mind control: change the way groups of people are perceived so it seemed natural to treat them differently. Of course I wanted to find that hall monitor and yell at him, or growl and bare my teeth Wolvie-style.

I put my hands under the table, clenched my fists and pressed them hard against my thighs.

"Okay." My voice came out rough, so I cleared my throat and started over. "Okay, you don't have a choice, then I don't have a choice. I'll bring lunch tomorrow. PBJ or PBB?" The second "b" was for banana.

"PBB," she said. "And Saturday, we both curl up in my room, right?"

"All day," I agreed. "With kissing. And I tell you again that I love you."

* * *

We only spent half of Saturday in her room because we decided it was time to start telling our families we were dating. We figured we'd tell Tariq first because he'd be cool and excited for us—and he was the least likely to give advice. Then we'd tell Darius and Aisha's folks, followed by my house, starting with Milo or maybe everyone at once over dinner.

That Saturday when Aisha's folks had gone to run errands, Tariq was planted in front of the Xbox with a pop and a giant bag of Cheetos. How he kept the orange cheese powder off the controller, I couldn't figure.

Aisha plopped onto the couch next to him and patted the spot on her other side so I squeezed in. He paused the game and looked over. I usually sat in the armchair because that fit me and Pickles—and because then I wasn't tempted by being next to Aisha—so both of us being on the couch was weird.

Tariq paused the game, eyebrows high. "You're ganging up on me," he said.

"We're going out," I told him.

"Where to?"

I froze and turned to Aisha.

She grabbed my hand and said, "We're dating, numbskull."

"Oh shit!" he yelped, and looked around to make sure their parents were gone. He dropped the controller on the coffee table and stood up, paced a bit away and turned back to us, stared at our joined hands. "Fucking epic. Day was right."

"You guys really had a bet going?" I asked.

"Informally," he said, like that made it better. "No actual money. Just bragging rights."

"Hold up, you thought we *wouldn't* get together?" Aisha asked.

"You had that other girl. Don't look at me like that. I don't know how you all do things, crazy kids. So, who asked who?"

"She did," I said. "Except I pre-asked her not to say yes to anyone else, I don't know if that counts."

"Yeah, yeah, I get it. You're the complicated one, not like you don't have game. Mysterious and kissable counts as game. Never got it to work for me, but congrats. Damn you two are cute. Who's telling Day?"

"Skype him," Aisha said.

"You Skype him."

Aisha sighed and ran upstairs to get her laptop.

"You're grinning like she's the only girl in the world," Tariq said to me.

"Isn't she?"

Aisha put her laptop on the table and called Darius. It was two hours earlier in Cali, but it looked like he'd been up and to the gym, sweat darkening his tan T-shirt around the collar.

"Why are you all calling me? Folks okay?"

"They're great," Aisha said. Then she put her hand on my chin, turned my face, and kissed me.

"WHOA! YEAH!" Darius hollered, bounced back from the screen, and we heard him yelling, "My lil' sis is finally going out with her longtime crush!"

Two people off camera cheered and one of them snarked, "Riq owes you money, man."

Darius came back to his chair. A pretty black girl with a lot of curly dark hair leaned over his shoulder and peered at the screen. "Aww, babies," she said.

"Wow, nobody ever got this excited about anybody I've gone out with," Tariq grumbled.

"There's a real reason for that," Darius told him.

"Yeah, but that one girl."

"Nah, you never had that one girl. I'll tell you when you meet that one girl. Or that one guy."

"Or person," Aisha said.

Tariq sighed. "I'm done with every single one of you. Except Kaz."

"You want to go live at my house for a while? I'll trade you," I offered.

"Yeah? I might. How big's your room?"

"Same as yours, but it's got a better closet."

"When I hit my dapper phase, we'll talk," he said.

"Can I have my dapper phase at the same time?" I asked.

"Oh hell yes, my sib from another crib."

We told Darius the story of me not asking Aisha out, her dating Meta, us finally getting ourselves together, and her asking me out even though I'd already sort of asked her.

After he got done making cute, appreciative sounds at us, his mouth turned grim. "Aisha, you got to call me later."

"We're talking now," she said.

"I've got something to tell you."

"There's nothing you can't say in front of Kaz."

"Thought I should tell you first, then you can decide," he said.

She picked up her laptop and walked up the stairs. I heard her bedroom door close. Tariq handed me the other Xbox controller and switched it to *Rocket League.*

We'd only made it through one game, a few minutes, when Aisha came back down the stairs, tears gathered in her eyes, one streaking down her cheek.

"Tell Kaz," she said in a strangled voice as she put the laptop on the coffee table facing me. "I'll be back."

"What happened?" I asked, moving the screen to face me as Aisha went back upstairs. Panicking that someone had been shot, maybe killed—no, not someone, Aisha's trans cousin in LA. She was the most vulnerable of all of us. "Is everyone okay?"

"Yeah." Darius sighed and sat back in his chair. "I'm going down to LA next weekend to see family. And Mom asked me to bring a bunch of stuff, like always, but also…she wants me to drive around, check out some houses on the market."

"Yeah," Tariq said, like no-big-deal, then looked at me and added, slowly, "Shit."

"No," I said. "Just, no."

Darius said, "I think Dad's searching for a job out here. Mom doesn't like how much Aisha struggled in math last year. It's not like her. And there's something about a chemistry teacher?"

"She gave Aisha a bunch of crap work to do," I said around the tightness in my throat.

"Mom emailed the teacher about it and called, didn't get an answer."

Tariq groaned. "She hates that. So rude."

Darius nodded. "And the next two years of high school are important for Aisha getting into a great college. Next year especially."

I looked from Darius's face on the screen to Tariq and back. "You can't move."

"Maybe it's her backup plan," Darius said. "But I thought you should know."

I ran up the stairs and into Aisha's room. She lay face down on her bed crying into her pillow. I knelt next to the bed and put my arms around her. She turned and grabbed me and pulled until I was in the bed and we could hold onto each other.

She said, "I love you. I shouldn't have to choose between you and a school that doesn't suck for me."

I couldn't talk. I nodded a lot, small motions of my face against her hair. I was probably holding her too hard, but she didn't protest.

CHAPTER SIXTEEN

Early October 2017

"We have to tell my parents," Aisha said the next day. "At dinner. And then you go walk the dogs and I'll field all my dad's weird questions."

I kissed her ear because that's what I could reach. If her mom knew we were dating, she'd stop the whole house search, moving-back-to-California thing, right?

So we told Aisha's parents at the family dinner that Monday. I'd had an open invitation to their family dinners for about a year and usually joined them on Mondays, which set up the whole week. Mrs. Warren would ask Tariq and Aisha and me about our schedules and write down anything important that wasn't already on their calendar. I loved that she included me.

She'd ask Tariq about his job and the two of us about schoolwork, what assignments were due, if we needed help on anything. I didn't use to say yes, but now sometimes I did because Mrs. Warren dug into our chemistry homework like she actually enjoyed it.

After we'd shared our schedules and schoolwork, Mr. Warren would ask for highlights of the previous week. He was big on accomplishments. And lately he'd added some other categories, so it became three As: accomplishments, acknowledgements, awesomeness. One thing you'd done well, one thing someone else did well, and one reason to be grateful.

This week, when dinner got to the three As, Aisha said, "I'll go first. My three A's are all the same thing: I'm super grateful for the fact that when I asked Kaz—whose pronouns are still they/them, Dad—to go out with me, they said yes. As in 'we're dating,' I'm Kaz's girlfriend."

I said, "That's mine too because yeah, of course."

"I'm glad to see you both this happy," Mr. Warren said, sitting back and resting his hands on his thighs. He couldn't resist asking, "What goes with girlfriend? Personfriend?"

"Works for me," I told him.

Mrs. Warren said, "Congratulations, you two. Aisha, you're leaving your bedroom door open from now on." She had the biggest smile I'd ever seen on her, so her serious tone didn't land very hard.

"Mom!"

"Same rules as anyone else, you know that. You didn't argue when you were dating Dani Mehta."

"But Kaz is also my best friend. We have secrets and stuff."

"You can whisper. You leave your door open."

Aisha pursed her lips like they were holding back some choice words. I didn't like this any better, but I appreciated it. And anyway, we had the treehouse.

"Thank you," I told Mrs. Warren. She gave me a forehead-wrinkling look, so I added, "For not treating me different."

"You're making me look bad," Aisha grumbled. I caught her hand under the table and squeezed it.

No weird questions came up *at* dinner, but Mr. Warren was terrible at having private conversations. His voice carried. Like he didn't realize that his voice being on the high side made him easier to hear, so he'd talk louder. Also I'm guessing he'd lived in houses with a less open floor plan. Aisha and I were pretty used to making a quick exit from the living room when he and Mrs. Warren were having a conversation we did not want to overhear—or getting quiet if we did.

Things we did *not* want to hear: romance, gross attempts at sexy talk, money.

Things we did: anything about us.

So after dinner when Tariq went out and we sat in the living room with our homework, we didn't run upstairs when we heard Mr. Warren ask, "Does this change anything?"

"The two of them dating?" Mrs. Warren asked. Her voice was muffled. I caught, "…worried if they break up…best friends…"

Aisha looked over at me like: *Do you want to run for it now?* And I shook my head: *No.*

Mr. Warren said, "Aisha has so many friends. It would be harder on Kaz. Do you think she's told her family?"

"*They've* told *their* family." That was clear enough because Mrs. Warren said it loudly and firmly, followed with, "I don't know if they've told their family. We could ask them."

"'Them'—both of them or just Kaz?"

"Jack."

"Are you going to talk to Aisha about sex?" he asked.

"Mmhm, I'll talk to her about why she's still too young to be having sex and the emotional implications of being sexual with her best friend. But in terms of emotions, I'm guessing the horse is pretty far from the barn at this point."

"And all the other stuff?"

"Sweetie, she's known the other stuff for years. Including why I want her to wait until she's at least sixteen, preferably seventeen, consent, safer sex, having good experiences, and not being the victim of any fool's black girl stereotypes. Am I missing anything?"

"I love you so much," he said. "Can I hear that talk about good experiences?"

"Not in the kitchen you can't. You know those kids are listening to us from the living room. I haven't heard a peep or a page turn since you said 'sex.'"

Mr. Warren leaned his head around the dividing wall and saw us both staring. We didn't even try to pretend we hadn't been.

"I'm telling my family soon," I said.

"And you have to get better with pronouns, Dad," Aisha told him. "It's disrespectful."

He ducked back around the wall and muttered, "I'm not ready for these kids."

I couldn't make out Mrs. Warren's reply, only her laughing, soothing tone.

* * *

That was not the end of awkward conversations about me at the Warren family household. A few days later, hanging out in the living room, we'd been playing on the Xbox. When we got bored, Aisha opened her laptop, playing Angel Haze videos, looking at a million photos of Angel.

"You could rock that hat," Aisha told me.

"I don't know how to wear a hat. Aren't I supposed to take it off inside? And then I'm hat hair all day."

"That shirt?"

"Yeah, that shirt."

"Jacket?"

It looked great on Angel, but it wasn't me. "What if I'm not that...masculine?"

She kissed my cheek, her fingers finding mine, and we should've run up to her room because we were about to get all kinds of cuddly. But the garage door went up and she pulled away.

Tariq and Mr. Warren came in wearing workout clothes: a navy T-shirt and cut-off gray sweatpant-shorts for Tariq and a much sweatier light blue T-shirt for Mr. Warren, along with full gray sweatpants that gathered at the ankles and looked highly dorky. Not to mention the actual, for real, light blue headband around his forehead.

"You go to yoga?" Aisha said laughing. "All downward dogging up in there?"

"Running and weights," Tariq sneered. "That's tight, who's she?"

"They," Aisha said. "Angel Haze, agender amazingness."

"Damn, perfect," Tariq said. "Aww, my babies have role models. You two should YouTube cover song them a love letter or something." He'd have been obnoxious except that he meant it and it was a pretty good idea.

Mr. Warren had stopped rubbing his neck with a paper towel and came over to stare at the screen. "Pretty girl," he said.

"Angel's not a girl, Dad, Angel's a pansexual agender person."

"She looks like a girl."

Aisha clicked onto another photo.

He said, "Okay...androgynous?"

"Agender, Dad."

"Right," he said, very doubtful and headed back into the kitchen.

Bullet dodged.

But not.

After dinner we'd retreated to Aisha's room and even did a little homework. I was sneaking to the bathroom—sneaking so Mrs. Warren wouldn't offer to help with our homework because we very much had *not only* been doing homework—when I heard her and Mr. Warren talking in the kitchen again.

"Honey, this word 'agender' have you heard it? What's it about?" he asked.

"People who don't have a felt-sense of being a man or a woman or some combination of those," she said. "Who used it?"

"Aisha, about some rap artist."

"Oh Angel Haze, right? Long hair, great hats?"

"How do you *know* this?"

"Some of the songs Aisha bought are explicit and she wanted me to know they're anti-suicide, so I wouldn't 'freak.' I looked Angel up online and I like Aisha listening to their music."

"Their? That's not even gram—"

"Sweetie, it is."

I missed the next bit because Aisha peeked out her bedroom door and saw me sitting at the top of the stairs. I put my finger to my lips. She silently slid the door wide and came to sit next to me.

Mrs. Warren was saying, "If the style guides say that they/them can be used as a singular pronoun, I'm not inclined to argue that one. We had a whole workshop at work about this."

"Workshop, for what, pronouns?"

"Jack, I dispense a lot of hormones to a lot of different people, I need to know how to make my customers feel comfortable so they can ask their questions without being afraid."

"You have customers who are…agender? And take hormones?"

Mrs. Warren made the "hrum" sound she did when she was thinking, then said, "I don't think I have any who identify as agender, though I do have one whose kid is. But I have a few who are nonbinary. And you know I can't tell you what I give them."

"Doesn't feel right to me," he grumbled. "Masculine and feminine are core archetypes of humanity. Every person is supposed to blend them in different amounts, but this is monkeying around with nature."

"You never say that about electricity." Mrs. Warren's voice came out light. I cheered silently at her point. Aisha put her hand on mine, weaving our fingers together.

"That's harnessing the power of nature. This is strange. People changing their bodies. What went wrong with them? Do people research that? When I was a kid, it was just men and women."

"No it wasn't. It simply wasn't safe for people to show themselves. Like Aisha and Kaz, my heart's still up in my throat seeing them go out together. The way they hold hands, like it's the most natural thing in the world, because it is, but it's not how things used to be. Don't you think it can be that way about gender too?"

"But that's exactly my point," he said. "It's better than it used to be. So this means people need to keep making it better for men and women, so they can be how they want to without thinking they have to change their bodies. Boys these days, they've got to know how to be a man, that they can be gentle, have feelings. They don't have to become women to have that."

"That's not what's happening. There are people who don't feel like boys or girls. I don't know what that's like, but I've read some of the studies."

"They need to do more tests. That's not normal."

I flinched when he said that and Aisha saw me. She leaned in and asked, "Trust me?"

I nodded. She slipped down the stairs and into the kitchen. I scooted down far enough to watch her.

"Hey Dad, Mom," she said, moving next to her mom. She put her hand up and whispered something to her mom, whose eyes went wide and flicked to the stairs. I ducked back behind the wall.

"Jack, would you chop the carrots? I'll be back."

"What? Why?"

"Carrots," Mrs. Warren said and pointed at the cutting board.

Only silence and then his sigh and the sound of a stool's feet scraping on the linoleum.

Mrs. Warren came to the foot of the stairs and looked up at me. "May I join you?"

"Yeah," I said, so she sat on a middle step below me. I asked, "Aisha told you?"

She nodded and said, softly, in a pretty fair imitation of Aisha, "'Please make Dad stop; Kaz is nonbinary.'" She paused and added, "I'm sorry. Grownups have things they need to work out too. He's not talking about you. He's talking about himself."

"Sounds like me," I muttered.

"Do you have people to talk to?"

"Milo knows," I said. "My mom..." I paused and waved a hand in the direction of the kitchen.

"Like Jack?"

I shrugged.

"Worse?"

Nodded.

"Can I show you something?" she asked, standing up and beckoning.

I followed her down the hall. She slipped into her bedroom and came out with her tablet, holding it so I could see a page from a book with a lot of lines connecting words about the development of human sex and gender.

Mrs. Warren said, "This is something I've been reading after that workshop we had, so I'd understand this better. It's by one of the top researchers about sex and gender development. See this diagram, it's a simplified illustration of how sex and gender are formed."

I considered that glowing page and all the lines. There were words linking to other words, spidering down the page, more intricate as it went. If this was the simplified version, how many pages did the complicated one cover?

"What's 'morphological?'" I asked.

"How your body is shaped. See up at the top here it says 'indifferent fetal sex' because for the first six or seven weeks, everyone's body is the same. People have different genes and environments, and that is what determines how the fetus develops. We act like there are only two paths a person can take, but human development is more like a sound mixing board, a series of sliding switches that can go all the way to the right or left or somewhere in the middle. So what gives you your biological sex and your gender is how all of these come together—and there's no wrong way for them to go together."

"Are you sure?"

"People are supposed to be different," she said. "Otherwise God would've made everyone five-foot-seven."

Aisha came up the stairs with a bowl of carrot sticks. We showed her the sex and gender development diagram. After her mom explained it again, Aisha said, "Well yeah, genes aren't light switches, I mean, epigenetic effects and all that."

Mrs. Warren put an arm around Aisha's shoulders and beamed.

CHAPTER SEVENTEEN

Early October 2017

I had a whole plan for telling Milo about me and Aisha. No part of that plan happened. On Wednesday in History class, Trina informed me that our group would start meeting twice a week, not just on Sundays, and the first Wednesday meeting was that night.

"This project can't take that much work," I protested.

"We do our other homework too," she told me.

"I do that with Aisha. And I can't make it tonight. I have a job walking dogs."

She sighed and put a hand on my elbow. "Kaz, this is important. Can I count on you to show up starting next week? And I'll see you on Sunday."

She didn't wait for an answer because it hadn't been a question.

Which is why Milo found me sitting on the back steps crying while Wolvie tore the bark off a fallen branch. I was crying about Trina and the study group, but more about Aisha's mom looking at houses in L.A. and the idea that I could get stuck here for two more years with Trina and Eve and without Aisha.

"Kiddo?" she asked.

"School."

She leaned against the porch railing. "Bullies?"

I couldn't talk about the idea of Aisha moving yet, not without losing it and bawling like a five-year-old, so I said, "I'm in this study group and I'm supposed to go over tonight but I want to study with Aisha, I always study with Aisha. And Trina keeps acting like Aisha's stupid and doesn't even know that she's my girlfriend."

Milo's deep-lined frown flipped into a smile, then settled into a tight-lipped, more serious smile.

"She's been holding your hand a lot lately, I was hoping," Milo said. "I know her dating that girl last spring made you miserable."

"You seriously have superpowers of observation," I told her.

"It's called aging," she said. "If you do it right. How'd you get into a group without Aisha?"

I told her the entire stupid story.

"Can you give it a week or two?" Milo asked. "You have a whole semester. See what your options are?"

"I guess. And I want to tell them she's my girlfriend. I guess I should tell Mom too, huh?"

"Family dinner night's tomorrow. Do you want to me to tell Pops tonight?"

"Yeah, thanks."

We didn't have any formal thing at our family dinners, not like the three A's. People just talked, often over each other or in two separate conversations, which usually fell out as Mom and Brock, then me, Milo and Pops—or me and Milo, with Mom joining in with Pops and Brock.

We went on like that for most of dinner. Toward the end, I got worried that Brock was going to leave before I did my announcement.

"Hey," I said. And again louder until Mom and Brock stopped talking about his sports. "Hey!"

They all looked at me and I wanted Aisha there. Her dad's weird questions were one thing, but I worried more about what Mom or Brock might say, so I'd asked her to let me do this by myself. Now I wrapped my hand over my thigh and gripped, like I could be holding her hand.

"I have news," I said. "I'm dating Aisha now. Um, and it's great and I'm super happy and her parents know and they're cool with it, of course, so, that's it."

A smile passed between Milo and Pops. Mom caught it and tried to smile; the muscles tensed around her lips but didn't move them.

"Very good," Pops said.

Brock got a look on his face like he had to poop and couldn't. Or like he was working out a complicated puzzle using his butt cheeks.

"What?" I asked him.

"I don't care who you date," he shot back in a tone that meant the opposite. "Just don't get all sappy at school."

Brock had a bunch of convoluted ways he could act okay with Aisha and Tariq but not with "immigrants" and other code words for people of color—like that wasn't the same. A year ago, I couldn't understand what had happened to him. Now I saw this as the evil of Apocalypse, the whole system of racism, changing the words and ideas it used so it could hide better.

I hoped that if Brock knew how much these ideas hurt people just like Aisha and Tariq, he'd stop thinking that way. But I still hadn't found a way to talk to him. And he kept pissing me off, so I wanted to yell more than talk.

"Why shouldn't I hold Aisha's hand at school?" I shot back at him. "I see a lot of kids snuggling, even making out in the halls." I glanced at Milo and added, "Not that we would ever do that."

Brock said, "People know you're my sister... er, sib, whatever, and you're already weird enough."

"Fu—" I caught myself. "Fart off, dillweed."

"Fart yourself," he said and almost chuckled because we hadn't said that to each other since we'd been way younger. My heart squeezed, hard and painful, remembering when I was ten and he was twelve, all the stupid games we played that we thought were awesome.

I'd wanted him to be happy about me and Aisha. And I'd known he wouldn't be, but having that proved to my face sucked. Before I could tell him to shove his farts back up his butt, he'd picked up his plate and taken it into the kitchen.

Milo reached for the salad bowl, lifting it in a half-toast to me. "I'm glad for you two. She's a very sweet girl."

Mom asked, "What did her parents say when you told them?"

I had to say enough to be real, even if I didn't tell her everything, so I went with, "Stuff about emotions, like it's going to get weird because we're also best friends. Or more like we should be careful because of that."

I didn't want to say the bedroom door thing, both because I didn't want Mom to think about that, but also because—this fear surfaced like a leviathan under ice in my brain—Mom would think it was because of Aisha, not because of me. Like Aisha was loose, even though all we did was make out. That is, Milo would say "loose" and be all polite, but Mom would be thinking "slutty." Because of—as Mrs. Warren had said—"any fool's black girl stereotypes." Mom didn't get to think that about my girlfriend.

Mom nodded, saying, "Well I agree with them."

Pops reached across the table for another dinner roll, saw Milo's frown, tore the roll in half and put half back in the basket with a sigh.

"Who asked whom?" he asked. "I don't know how kids date anymore."

I told the grandparents-appropriate parts of the story. We discussed current dating trends, and dissed Brock's last girlfriend, because that was a family favorite pastime.

After dinner, of course, Mom got weird anyway, by which I mean: racist.

Pops was doing the dishes, Milo had taken Wolvie out back, and I'd been sitting in my seat texting Aisha that it went okay. Mom came in from the kitchen with a cup of tea and sat in the chair beside me. She said, "There are a lot of girls you could date. Maybe it's not such a good idea to date your best friend."

"Um?"

"That girl Eve, she's athletic. Do you only like girls?"

I shrugged and said, "Kind of soon to tell."

"I always thought you'd go out with Jon. You two would be so cute together."

"He's gay."

He might date me as a guy, but I didn't want to be a guy all the time and anyway that would fry Mom's circuits.

"Oh, all right," Mom said with a sigh. "There's the girl down the street who always comes out with the lemonade when you're mowing."

"I'm not into her," I said. "I've known Aisha for years and she's great and I love her and you just named three white people."

"I don't mean it that way. It's going to be hard for you two. You're already dating a girl, do you really want it to be that complicated?"

"Honestly, no," I said. "I want to be growing up in a country that has handled its racist past—and present—but apparently I don't get to do that, so I'm not going to stop loving Aisha because it makes other people uncomfortable."

"It's not always about racism," she said. "I'm not racist. I don't know how you could even suggest that. I've never been anything but nice to the Warrens. You need to think about what you're saying before you go around calling people names like that."

I double-taked at her. Names? Like it was a personal insult? But I hadn't called her anything, I'd been talking about the system we were in. Oh but this was one of those Apocalypse strategies—one of the ways he defended his presence in her brain—making it into a huge deal about her, not about actual big deals like, I don't know, racism itself.

I wanted her to see what was going on in her brain, so I asked, "Why would you be cool with me dating Eve?"

"Eve's from Minnesota. You have a shared background. You haven't even met the rest of Aisha's family, you don't know what they might be like."

"What 'shared background?' Eve's family has always had money, she's never read a comic book in her life, she's a jock, and they're Catholic. The *only* thing we have in common is that we're white. I have way more in common with Aisha and Tariq."

"Where you grow up makes a difference," she said, quietly, turning red.

"It sure fucking does," I said, getting up so fast the chair hit the wall.

"Don't you swear at me!" She was on her feet too and very red.

"Why should it matter what Aisha's family is like? What did Dad's parents say to you after he left? Aisha's family would never have thrown us away like that."

"Go to your room. You are grounded."

I stomped up the stairs, called Wolvie into my room, and slammed the door. Then I had to sit on the floor and let Wolvie wriggle into my lap because she didn't like loud noises inside the house. And I needed to have my hands in her fur.

I was pissed. And scared because I hadn't won that fight in any way. I didn't know how to do that fight.

Apocalypse and his mind-control powers had gone deep into Mom's brain and I didn't know how to get her free from that. Same with Brock, and Trina and Eve at school. Milo told me how to get that conditioning out of my own brain, but not what to do with friends and family under mind control.

How do you tell people that a vast, disastrous, malevolent force they can't even see has gotten into their brains and hidden itself there? If I told them to fight Apocalypse, they'd see me as a comic-book-reading nerd gone too far. But that's exactly what I wanted to do: run to Mom, run through school yelling, "You have to fight him! He's not on your side! He's using you for his power, his survival, not yours!"

CHAPTER EIGHTEEN

Early October 2017

The first Saturday of October I'd walked my dogs, done chores, and sat on my bed with Wolvie, reading, waiting for Aisha to text and say I should come over. Saturdays we still got to spend most of the day together.

Wolvie furrowed her furry, black forehead, scrutinizing me from the foot of the bed. I had my Chemistry book in my lap and I could tell she was saying, *We need to have a talk about your lap and how often I'm not in it these days.*

I slid the book to the side and patted my thighs. She wriggled her way up the bed, pushing her head and shoulders across my thighs. I rubbed her neck fur, turned sideways to see the book.

"Sorry fuzz," I told her. "Aisha gets priority in my lap these days."

She blew out a heavy sigh, half-groan at my ignorance: *Bring Aisha over here and put me across two laps, that counts double.*

Laughing, I snagged my phone from my bedside table and texted Aisha to see if she wanted to come over.

Can you come over here instead? she texted back. *I've got a surprise.*

I wrote, *Sure! Can I bring Wolvie? She's being needy.*
Of course! Poor baby.

I hollered down the stairs that I was going to Aisha's, got Wolvie's leash and went over. Her mom opened the door and stepped to the side with a wave toward the stairs.

"Thanks, Mrs. Warren," I said and pelted up the stairs to Aisha's room. Pickles followed Wolvie, both dogs sniffing intently once I got into Aisha's room.

I put the baby gate across her door, to keep Wolvie from running around the house and knocking things over. Mrs. Warren had said I could bring Wolvie occasionally to hang out in Aisha's room, but no way was she reorganizing her house to deal with a big dog.

Aisha rose from her desk chair and stepped into the space behind her door, where her mom couldn't see from the hall. I caught her waist and pulled her close, kissed her. She sighed and put her arms around me.

She had her hair up. I touched the loose bits at the back of her neck, fingers playing with one tiny rebellious curl. My other hand was at the small of her back, thumb lipping over the top of her jeans, warm skin, so soft. I rubbed my cheek on hers and on the side of her neck. She laughed—parts of her neck got ticklish—and pushed at me.

"What?" I asked.

"I have something planned. If you want."

"Maybe?"

She went back to her desk chair. She'd brought in a folding chair so there were two chairs at her desk.

"Last summer, after you'd asked me to not say yes to dating anyone else..." Her eyes gleamed with the memory. "I wanted to know more about nonbinary people so I went to some meetings and met folks and they want to meet you. I can go do something downstairs if you want. Like if you have questions you wouldn't ask in front of me."

"I don't," I said. "And I don't want to meet new people without you."

"Okay cool." She patted the seat next to her. "I didn't know if you'd want this. I mean, sometimes when people are like 'hey meet my other black friend' it's just the weirdest thing in the world, especially if it's a party or something and we're the only two black people there and it turns out we don't have anything in common. But a few times it's been great, like Zack and Curt. That wasn't weird at all. Of course Zack's woke enough not to be like 'meet Curt, he's black.' Anyway, is it okay if I'm doing the whole meet-these-people thing?"

"Can I answer that after I meet them?" I asked with a half grin. I'd been petting Wolvie since I sat down, but I told her to go lie down. She immediately stole Pickles' dog bed next to Aisha's desk, even though only her back half fit in it. Pickles snorted in disgust, hopped on the bed and made a nest in Aisha's pillows.

She laughed. "That's fair. You'll like them. I'm calling Cori first, then Royce."

She hit the video chat buttons on her laptop and I scooted close enough to be in the frame with her.

The person who answered, Cori, had a heavy, grinning face, light-brown skin, orange hair piled up but also shaved on the sides. I guessed about five years older than me and Aisha, twentyish.

"What is up, folks?" Cori asked, grin widening. "This your friend?"

"Kaz meet Cori," Aisha said.

"Um, hi."

"Aisha would not stop talking about you," Cori told me. "Do you know how many times I had to walk her through the whole 'should I ask them out or wait for them to ask me' process?"

I was smiling so hard I felt like a massive dork. Cori had called me "them" for real. And it sounded so good. Aisha and Zack used it fluently, but everyone else in my life stumbled over my pronouns. And here a person I'd just met used "them" effortlessly for me. As if somewhere a whole world of strangers existed who'd say "they" and "them" like no big thing.

It felt like being invited in to a place full of warmth and safety. It felt like joy. Like how the world felt when it was only me and Aisha, when her fingers laced with mine and she smiled and put her head on my shoulder.

"Thanks," I said, trying to keep my shit together. "I mean, assuming you gave good advice."

"Oh you know I did. Aisha, call Royce, they shouldn't be missing this cuteness."

"Hang on," Aisha said and clicked to add another person to the call.

A second window opened on an angular face, blinking as if into bright light, a shock of short, straight, tousled black hair over brown skin. "Sec," Royce said and went offscreen to the sound of much thumping and fumbling. "You know what time it is?"

"It's ten," Cori said. "You've been up for hours."

"I was napping," Royce replied. "Hey is that your person-friend? Scoot over so I can see."

Aisha scooted sideways and I moved more into the center of the frame, saying, "Hi, I'm Kaz."

"Yeah," Royce said, long and slow. "I get it. Way to go, Minnesota."

I wasn't sure if Royce was addressing the whole state or if that was going to be my nickname in this group.

"Story time, please," Cori said. "We heard everything about how cute you are but Aisha didn't know when you realized you were into her, so I'm missing a significant plot thread in this whole fairytale."

"It's not a fairytale," Aisha grumbled.

"Yeah," I said. "It's a comic book series."

She grabbed my hand and held it really tight and I wondered what she was scared about. These weren't close friends of hers because she'd just met the two of them this summer. So if we didn't all gel with each other, was that such a big deal?

And then I got it: it wasn't that she was afraid we wouldn't gel—she was afraid we would. She was afraid I'd like Cori and Royce better than her. That I'd find people like me and I wouldn't want to be with her.

I squeezed her hand and snuck my other hand over so I could hold onto her with both. Just no way she wasn't in the center of my life.

"When did I know I was into A?" I asked, buying time because all I could think was: *for forever.*

"You call her A? Where's that from?"

Aisha said, "When Kaz and I started eighth, on the home rooms list everyone's name was initial and last name: we were K. Adams and A. Warren and it seemed really funny at the time."

I picked up the story. "We were in super different homerooms because of the Adams/Warren thing. And you said something about how it was too bad they didn't go by first name."

"And you said 'A and K,' maybe that's our superteam name."

I rubbed her shoulder with mine—remembering how amazing I'd found her two years ago and even more so now—and went on with our tale. "You made a joke about how of course A and K was our team name, but then in Minnesota everyone would say Ay-isha instead of Eye-isha."

Aisha's fingers tightened around mine, laughter in her voice as she said, "You made up a whole subplot about my character just trying to get people to say her name right and it cracked me up so much that I wanted you to call me 'A.'"

"Cori, you feel like you ate a pound of sugar that was so sweet?" Royce asked.

"Sure do. Now, romance story, give."

"Don't pressure them," Royce said. "You know how it is when you're young. Kaz might not have all their stuff sorted yet. Hard enough to figure out how to date, but if you've got to work out your whole gender on top of that."

"Do you two want to tell Kaz about yourselves?" Aisha suggested.

Cori raised their eyebrows at the camera. Royce shrugged and said, "Sure, my turn, huh? I'm not the easy one."

"Oh, *I'm* easy?" Cori asked.

Royce ignored that and went on talking. "I'm intersectional," Royce said, drawing the word out so it had a lot of ironic syllables in the middle. "I'm adopted and before my parents got me it was not a good time. I did a lot of therapeutic stuff when I was way little. That was so good. I met all kinds of people with different brain types and thinking styles and I figured out that gender comes across to me like a pile of bullshit. I don't get it. So I don't do it."

"Seriously," Cori said. "You take your eyes off Royce for a second and they'll start using they/them pronouns for everyone."

"I have a chart," Royce grumbled. "I know what's important to other people. Don't know why everyone wants to waste their time on all this."

"Because it's fun," Cori protested. "I don't want everyone to be the same. I don't want just people. I want all the wildness, the diversity, the variations. I met this demiguy I'm crushing on, he's so fine, prettiest hands I've ever seen. Why would I want a world without that?"

Royce grinned into the camera and gave us an epic eyeroll.

"Shut up," Cori said. "You like some people more than others."

"Yeah, I like smart, creative, funny. I just don't get all wound up about that other stuff. Who's this guy?" Royce asked.

"You haven't met him yet. Because you skipped out on the last meeting to play games."

"No regrets there. Tell Kaz your story before they realize how lame we are."

Every time one of them said "they" or "them" for me, a shiver went through me. Like Wolvie when she's getting petted—that pure physical joy. I pressed my shoulder against Aisha's.

Cori said, "I was assigned girl but I don't feel it. But I love femme stuff, so I kept trying to be a girl and it felt all wrong. You think it's all the same thing, but it's so not: being a girl or woman in our culture and being feminine. There's so many cool ways to be feminine. But I'm big to start so my boobs were freakin' huge. Hated that. It's been so much better since the top surgery. I can wear dresses now."

"What?" I asked. "I mean, sorry to be kind of stupid about this but you like being feminine but hated your boobs but now you wear dresses?"

Cori stood up, walked back from the camera and twirled, showing off their long, peach and purple dress. And they looked amazing. Their flat chest showed off their shoulders in the dress, the length of their body, their long legs, strong thighs, weighty hips and belly.

I liked how the shape of Cori's body made it so you couldn't settle on a biology for them. I saw tall and shoulders, which could read "guy," but also hips and big and soft, which could read "girl," and in the end my brain couldn't decide.

"Oh," I said. "People have to *see* you."

"They have to interact with me as a human. Plus my boobs never felt like part of my body."

"I have that sometimes," I admitted. "Like they're not even there and if something touches them it feels like static, like a signal's getting disrupted in my head."

"That's a cool way to describe it," Cori said. "For me, I literally kept forgetting I had them. I'd run into stuff with them, drop everything on them, and be surprised every time. Like: what on earth are these? I never wanted anyone to touch them. And now my chest is my chest. It's not a trans guy chest, it's a femme person chest."

I brushed my hand across my chest, looking down at it. I don't know if I'd want it to be flat always.

"Binder?" Cori asked.

"Yeah. But I wear bras too. Some days I can't stand the feeling of a bra, but other days they're like nothing, and sometimes they feel good. Like it changes, my boobs come and go. Is that weird?"

"Oh no, sugar, it's normal. Everybody's feelings about their body and their presentation changes, just some people more than others. You should see me on my non-femme days. Hang on, I've got a pic." Cori grabbed their mouse, peering at the screen and clicking. An image flashed up: a tall, light brown person with the same lopsided grin, hair back in a ponytail with a gray hat over it, soft sweater and baggy jeans. I'd definitely have read that person as a guy if I passed them on the street.

"How do you describe yourself?" I asked.

"Genderflux femme," Cori said.

"What's genderflux?" I asked.

"Genderflux femme means I'm more and less femme. I'm fluxing on the femme spectrum, more and less intense. But even when I go out looking like a guy, I'm not really a guy. I dress that way sometimes because it's convenient, like if I'm running out to the store. Genderfluid is when you're actually moving among different genders."

"Oh, that sounds pretty accurate," I said. "My friend Zack said I'm probably genderfluid, but I keep thinking that means both at the same time. And for real I sometimes wake up as a boy and sometimes a girl and sometimes both."

"You're the one who gets to say that. Sounds good to me, though. Royce, how are you identifying these days?"

"Agender or nonbinary, depending on who's asking," Royce said. "More questions! What's next?"

I asked, "When I talk to the trans guys, they're all super grossed out about getting a period, but I don't really care. Does that mean I'm not trans enough?"

Cori shrugged and said, "Definitely does *not* mean you're not trans enough. People get periods all kinds of ways. I always thought of mine as kind of a tough werewolf thing."

"Oh my God, I have a shapeshifter thing too," I said. "But getting my period makes me feel like an alien."

"How so?"

"Like this is a thing my body does every month because my alien body isn't completely adapted to Earth's atmosphere. There's a pressure differential and bleeding evens it out so I can live comfortably on Earth for another month."

"Oh," Cori said, looked at Aisha, added, "Oh honey, you've got to keep this one."

"That is really cool," Aisha said. "Can I have that too, even if I'm a girl?

"Yeah, sure."

"Was it always that way, from the start?" Cori asked, adding, "And there's no right answer to that."

"I think so. Mine was no big deal," I said. "I mean, I knew what periods were because Mom keeps her tampons out in the bathroom when she needs them and I'd asked some questions. But she's way over the top about girl stuff, so when I saw the blood, I went to Milo—she's my grandmom—and told her. She bought a few different kinds of pads and tampons so I could figure out what I liked and that was it. I guess she told Mom not to get weird about it. I already felt like an alien a lot, so the period thing really worked into it. How'd you come into being a werewolf?"

"The whole period thing was super embarrassing, partly because I'd been so into it before I got it. Most of my friends got it sooner than me, so I really wanted one. And then I got it and it was messy and not fun, and my mom told *everyone*. She told her hairdresser. I'm not even kidding. I think she told her mechanic. And maybe more than the period itself it was this whole 'my daughter's a woman' thing. But, you know, we're a family of awesome feminists so I tried to make it work. That's when I read stuff about werewolf legends and some cool novels and I got the idea that the whole point of having a period was so I could turn into a wolf—be badass and angry if I want to be."

Having finished their story, Cory asked, "What about you Aisha? You want to tell a period story?"

After a pause, Aisha said, "So...my dad."

"Oh no," I blurted.

"Ah yes. Mom was out of town. And he said 'yoni' and I simply could not."

"Baby," Cori said with sympathy.

"He wanted to do some kind of sweat lodge or other culturally appropriating badness, but I told him my cramps were terrible. As soon as Mom got home, I hid behind her. She had him back off and made sure I understood the mechanics. I'll take talking to Mom about my endometrium any day over taking to Dad about...any of that yoni business."

"Endo-what? What even is that?" Cori asked.

"Uterine lining," Aisha said plainly. "Oh yeah, Mom went into this whole follicular, ovulation, luteal phase thing. She dispenses a lot of hormones. I know so much about periods it's weird. I am definitely *not* going to be an OB-GYN."

"What's the werewolf phase?" Cori asked, grinning.

"Luteal," Aisha said. "Or maybe Lunar."

"What haven't we answered for you?" Cori asked me.

"What to wear," I said. "I mean, you look great in a dress or in pants, like just, in everything and I don't know that I could do that, so how do I even go around in the world without everyone automatically treating me like a girl? There isn't a set of clothes for nonbinary."

"Not one set," Royce said. "Because you get to be you. But I understand what you're asking. It can be hard. You should've seen Cori figuring it out. And, okay, I don't usually tell people this, and Cori don't be laughing, but I'm super into makeup and I haven't figured out how to wear it out of the house yet."

"Oh yeah, you should follow their Instagram," Aisha told me. "Beautiful."

"But that's all I do. I just make myself up and take pics because when I wear it out, unless it's to a trans event, it doesn't work. My parents get all: okay, we get it, you're a girl. Which I'm not. Or: okay, you're gay. Which I'm not. Right now I prefer women. Might not always be that way. And oh do not get me started about all the sex-related assumptions. Aisha, just, do not make assumptions about Kaz's body parts, 'k?"

"Hey, awkward," Aisha said. "Y'all are older."

"Well when you get to third base don't be all: I'ma slide across this plate without checking to make sure you're really playing baseball," Cori said.

"Truth," Royce agreed. "My last girlfriend was convinced I'm swinging a bat when I'm not even playing a sport. I'm a totally a co-operative person, but some girls don't get it when I'm like: can't we be painting a mural together?"

Aisha looked at me, eyes super wide like: "Oh my God" and "I'm sorry" and "I don't even know."

But honestly I appreciated it and I knew what they were talking about. "It's the same thing, clothes and bodies, the way people look at us and think they know what they're seeing, but they don't. They think boobs can only mean one thing."

"And there are three culturally sanctioned things you can do with them, or your business in general," Royce said, waving in a downward direction.

"Oh," Aisha said. "Oh. Wait, hold up, are you saying it's like when folks around here see I'm black and assume I'm going to be a line cook when I grow up instead of a surgeon?"

"Line cook, for real?" I asked.

"Yeah that totally happened to me in bio last year due to my skills with the scalpel. The teacher was all: you're great with that, you have a real future in the hospitality industry."

"Shit," Cori said and Royce looked like they were about to spit.

"Uh-huh, so I gave him Mom's ice-stare and said 'I'm going to be a pediatric heart surgeon.' I don't know what kind of doctor I want to be yet, but I hear that's a hard one so it made my point. Not that he got it."

"I want to go beat him up," I said.

"Yeah, that's how I feel when I see how people are with you about gender," she said.

I threw my arms around her and heard Cori say, "Awwww, babies." And then, "Hey, you two live in St. Paul, right?"

"Close to it," I answered.

"There's somebody there you've got to meet. Aisha, I'll send you her info."

I was up for meeting anyone these two recommended. They had to sign off and get about their days. I'd have stayed on Skype with them the whole afternoon.

CHAPTER NINETEEN

Mid October 2017

As Milo suggested, I went to the Trina & Co study group. We'd met for two Sundays before Trina dropped the bomb about adding Wednesday nights. Aisha got her World History group to move from Tuesdays to Wednesdays, so at least we didn't have more blocks of time apart.

My World History group met at Trina's house because it was big and central to all of us—close enough that I could ride my bike when the weather was decent. Mom freaked out with joy that I'd gotten in a study group with a junior in it. I wanted to tell her it wasn't a good sign that Caden had to take World History his junior year, but I was on thin ice with her.

Our assignment was to take a feature of an ancient culture that had parallels in modern American culture, to compare and contrast each. Our first meeting we'd brainstormed a list—and that was it. Trina turned the TV on and flipped around until Caden settled next to her with his arm around her. Eve pulled off her sneakers and started painting her toenails dusty purple.

"Aren't we supposed to have picked a topic by Tuesday?" I asked.

"That's days away," Trina said. "You know, Brock and Lisa could come over some time if they wanted."

"I don't think Brock has retained anything from sophomore World History," I said.

"Yeah but he knows a bomb about football," Caden said.

"And I need to know where Lisa gets her hair done," Trina added.

"Uh, yeah, okay, I'll let Brock know."

"Hey, I could really use some ice cream," Trina announced.

"Me too," Caden agreed. "Let's roll."

After they'd left, Eve went upstairs and came back with a whole bunch more pedicure stuff. "Come on," she said, "They're going to be gone a while."

"What?"

"They're going to make out in Caden's car and forget what they went out for and come back with some sad-flavored chips, like cheese and onion. And anyway, there's ice cream in the fridge if you want some."

"Cool. You want any?"

"Sure."

I brought back two bowls of mint chocolate chip, and sat on the far side of the couch, propping my feet on the coffee table like Eve. She'd brought down a whole box of nail polish colors, so I found a metallic silver for my toes. When in Rome, right? Which is where we should've been, picking a World History topic.

I texted Aisha: *Has your WH group picked a topic yet?*

Military, she wrote back. *Ancient wars compared to World Wars. That sounds boring af.*

So. Boring. Should I do the Harlem Hellfighters of WW1 or black nurses in WW2?

I texted back: *Nurses! I'll help.*

To Eve, I said, "Aisha's group is doing the military. What do you think we should do?"

"Caden's going to wish we'd picked that. I don't know, sports?"

I did not want to get stuck researching ancient or modern sports.

"We could do medicine," I suggested.

"Too gross. Anyway, if we pick something where Caden can do a model or replica, he'll do most of the work."

"Why do we have all these study sessions then?"

"To hang out," Eve said like that was super obvious. "Sofi usually comes over and sometimes Trina invites more people. You can bring someone if you want, or if you're into someone, ask Trina to invite them."

"Sure," I said, but when Trina and Caden got back, I didn't bring up Aisha.

And I didn't argue when Caden said he wanted to compare Roman religion with Christianity in America so he could build a Roman temple. In addition to the group presentation, we each got to do an individual paper, so maybe I could do gender and religion.

That had been two and a half weeks ago. With Aisha's homework and my dog walking—plus Trina adding Wednesday night meetings—Aisha and I didn't see each other most weekday evenings. But now that we'd told Aisha's family we were dating, and my family—tonight was the first Wednesday night session I'd attended—I wanted Aisha with me. Especially since nobody was working on the project.

On top of that, it was literally National Coming Out Day, October 11. Not a day I'd thought that much about in the past, except to enjoy folks posting on social about all their identities. I'd figured coming out wasn't a once a year thing, you told people when it was important, but it was too hard to pass up the obvious opportunity.

As usual, Trina and Caden made an excuse to run out for chips. How many of these study sessions were cover for them to make out in his car? Like, all of them?

I texted Aisha: *Can I for real tell Eve and everyone you're my girlfriend, tonight?*

After a bit she replied: *I don't think that's going to change anything. Least not in a good direction. But sure.*

Eve and I had the TV on quietly, an old season of *Pretty Little Liars*, and were painting our toenails again because this is what you do when half your study group ditches you. Milo was so going to roll her eyes at me when she saw this. Aisha might think it was cute, though.

"About inviting people over, and the dating thing, the boyfriend stuff," I said to Eve. Over the last three weeks, Trina had asked repeatedly who I thought was cute.

"Yeah, you like someone?" Eve asked. She had the biggest feet I'd seen on anyone and was doing a basketball stencil on her big toe.

"I like girls," I said.

She dabbed more orange on her toe and shrugged. "Okay, tell Trina. She'll be cool with it. Unless you want me to tell her."

"Nah, I can."

"You know, if you see a girl you like, Trina'd probably set you up."

I took a deep breath and said, "I'm not single."

"Really?" Eve paused in her toe-painting and cocked her head, scrutinizing my face. "I never see you with anyone except Aisha."

Eyes even with hers, I said, "Because she's my girlfriend."

Eve's eyebrows shot up and she stared at me for an awkwardly long time. Long enough that I could pick out the silver flecks in her blue eyes.

"What's *that* like?" she asked.

Most of my possible answers involved swearing ("what the fuck are you asking?" and "none of your fucking business"). I could tell from the angle of Eve's body, shoulder turned half away from me, how badly that would go over.

"Would've been great to be in the same study group," I told her.

"You should've just told us."

"In the middle of History class? Standing in the middle of the classroom?"

"Okay, point."

"And even if I had, last Sunday Trina had all these other people over—people that nobody is dating—but didn't even ask if I wanted to invite Aisha. Or invite Aisha herself. Aisha's with us at lunch every day but Trina acts like Aisha doesn't exist."

"Aisha's really quiet, hard to talk to. Trina probably forgot."

Forgot what? We'd been in tenth grade together for five weeks and at the same lunch table for four weeks. Trina saw Aisha almost every day.

"You all never ask her anything," I said.

"I asked her to try out for basketball and she blew me off. And I asked her about that one song."

"She doesn't play basketball," I pointed out. "And she doesn't listen to a lot of rap, so that's not going to be a very long conversation. Not to mention that's super stereotypey."

"I play basketball, what was I going to invite her to? Golf? Don't get all emo about it. Invite her to the next party."

"Can I do that?"

Eve switched to her other foot and dabbed with the tiny nail polish brush. "Sure. Why not? Trina's having a big thing on Sunday with her mom, everyone's invited, they got all the new winter colors in."

That solved the issue for about ten minutes, until I went to the bathroom. Trina's mom was a realtor but she sold cosmetics on the side. Their bathroom was full of skin creams, soaps, shampoos. The nearby hall closet was packed with samples. Trina had brought me up here a few times, to pick an eye shadow that went with the blue in my hair, to look at nail polish, to show off.

I opened the hall closet carefully, silently. I had an image of myself as the superhero Beast—covered in blue fur, with animal ears and claws—having climbed up the wall and crept in through the window, like this was a secret lab and I was checking for weapons.

I found the box of foundations and read the labels: Organza, Velour, Taffeta. A stack of cards listed all the foundation colors; it included brown tones like Chenille, Cypress, Suede. I lifted the top card, rubbed the colors with my thumb. My skin was Organza "light skin with pink undertones" and Aisha would be Chenille "dark skin with warm undertones."

This reminded me of the wood colors chart from Milo's workshop. The card had three colors for light skin, one light-medium, just like the four colors of white in my mind. And it had eight colors for medium to deep skin tones. I tucked the card into my pocket. Maybe I'd show it to Aisha as evidence for how accurate our thirteen-year-old perceptions about skin color had been.

But I'd rather be called Autumn Oak than Organza. Pretty sure Aisha would say the same about Walnut compared to Chenille. Trees had way more dignity than fabrics.

Next I checked the box of samples. Organza was there; Chenille was not. Did Trina's mom never use the dark skin foundation colors at her parties? Did she not invite anyone who wore those colors? Did she even know anyone who did?

I went into the bathroom to pee and stared at the bottles by the tub: four shampoos and three conditioners. I didn't have to look at the labels. I wouldn't use any of them. Neither would Aisha. They were for fine, straight hair. I'd started using Aisha's brand of shampoo a year ago because it didn't make my thick hair turn into a mass of frizz.

Aisha's mom got their shampoo and conditioner online and always ordered extra for me. Our local stores didn't carry the good products and if you wanted anything for "ethnic" hair, it was on a tiny endcap way in the back.

Would Trina's mom know the difference between a shampoo for straight hair and one for curly or kinky hair? Did she know other kinds existed or just think hair was all the same?

No way was I bringing Aisha to a party where none of the colors or products were right for her. Trina and her mom had a place for white skin colors, and maybe even blue superheroes like Beast, but not brown.

I said no to the party on Sunday and spent the day over at Aisha's. We were catching up on *Grey's Anatomy*. I counted white and brown faces, comparing it to *Pretty Little Liars*, which was always on in the background at Trina's. Yeah *PLL* had Emily, who was Filipino and queer and so cute, and her parents. But all the other main characters I could think of were white. *Scandal* and *Grey's Anatomy* were the only shows I saw regularly that had more than one black person in them. And I watched those mostly at Aisha's house—though I'd hooked Milo on a season of *Grey's Anatomy* before she declared the gross medical stuff too much for her.

So then I was mad. Being mad I did tons of World History research. Seeing all those pale-colored foundations in Trina's mom's closet reminded me of the cops coming into the drugstore and wanting to check only Aisha's purse and nobody else's. It made me think of all the ways she got singled out and then blamed for it. Not only the drugstore, but the hall monitor at school, our Chemistry class, our lunch table—and I'd bet her list of examples was many times longer than mine.

How could I show that to Trina and Eve, to Mom and Brock? How could I demonstrate it so completely they'd break free from the mind control and stop doing it?

There had to be a World History topic I could use. Areas in modern America where the racial disparities were obvious, like how healthy some people were compared to others, where they lived, what opportunities they had, how much money the people in their families had available to help each other out.

At our next study session, before Trina and Caden could disappear on some phantom errand, I said, "Hey, this religion topic isn't moving me. Other groups are dressing up for their presentations and I am not going to be a priest or a nun."

As usual, we'd sprawled around Trina's living room: her and Caden taking up the couch, Eve in an armchair with her big feet on an ottoman, me in the other armchair, legs tucked under me.

"My temple model is half done," Caden protested. "And it's epic!"

I untucked my legs so I could lean forward. "Guess what else Roman temples were used as?"

He shrugged. I looked at Trina and Eve to ensure they paid some attention to this. "Banks," I said. "We could compare how wealthy people lived."

"Oh!" Trina's eyes brightened. "Mom has a ton of fake gold coin jewelry from a Halloween party last year. This could work. I'll do a modern American. Eve, do you want to be a Roman lady?"

Eve shrugged. "Sure, why not."

To Caden, I said, "I guess we're the poor people."

"Cool. You have some sites I can look at for the temples that were banks? I've got miniatures for the people, I could paint up a banker or whatever. We don't have to wear togas, do we? I call dibs on the modern poor person."

I didn't argue. If I dressed as a Roman guy, I could get away with a tunic. At this point I didn't care what I had to wear as long as I got to say something worthwhile in the presentation.

Apocalypse, I'm coming for you.

CHAPTER TWENTY

Mid October 2017

Other than World History, I did all my homework with Aisha over at her house. Despite Mrs. Warren's open-bedroom-door policy, she or Aisha's dad tended to yell up the stairs if they wanted us to come do something. People didn't randomly walk into *her* bedroom. And by people, I mean my mom.

My mom had no qualms about walking into my bedroom, never knocked, even if the door was closed. It made me and Aisha a lot less likely to swap kisses while studying at my house, so Aisha's was our favorite place to be as the weather turned cold and the treehouse got uncomfortable.

Most of the time these days, Tariq fondly ignored us because of his intense EMT schedule and the centrality of his Xbox gameplay to his social life. He'd call, "What's up A and K?" as we went by him on the way upstairs and we'd say, "Same old," which always made him laugh.

Our current deal was that I got kisses for doing Algebra 2 and History, and she got kisses for Chemistry and English. We weren't sure who should be kissing whom for Spanish but it was usually me kissing her because she'd start talking in Spanish and I'd have to crawl across the room and press my lips to hers.

We'd gone about a half hour without any kissing, so I snagged her latest English paper to see what the teacher said could be improved. The front page had a "B" on it. I flipped through the next two pages. There were a few small corrections and on the last page the words, "good effort." What did that mean?

I dragged my backpack over and pulled out my paper. We had the same teacher, just different class times. I'd also gotten a B on the paper, but there was a note on the first page: "Interesting ideas. Develop more and cite more quotes in your next paper." On the second page a "nicely said" sat in the margins next to rather good sentence I'd written. One the third page, "Add a secondary source to strengthen the point you're making" and "Please include at least two sources per paper."

"Hey, A, can I see your papers before these?" I asked, staring at the two side by side.

"Yeah, why?"

"I'm breaking a code."

"K, you already broke that one," she said, but she pulled out her English notebook and got the papers out of the back. I didn't have mine with me. I'd tossed them into a box in my closet, but I remembered they had comments all through them too.

I skimmed through Aisha's top paper. She'd gotten an A and the last page only said, "Good!" The one before that was a B with the comment, "too short—assignment was 3 pages." She'd written two and a quarter. I'd done about the same. We'd been rushed that week.

Aisha scooted next to me and peered over my shoulder. "Anything new?"

"Mr. Bretherton writes way more stuff on my papers than yours. Like sentences on mine and words on yours. What's up with that?"

"You know," she said. "Same obvious reason he answers my questions last. Lets me stand around while he talks to everyone else. I'm sure he thinks he knows me, that I'm not going to be anything, so he doesn't 'waste' time on me."

"That's so not fair."

She shrugged one shoulder. "I'm doing good enough in English for pre-med."

"Next week, swap papers with me. We'll both write our papers like usual but we each hand in the other person's with our name on it. I want to see if he notices."

"I'm in."

"Oh hey." I turned to the last page of my recent paper and tapped the note about having more sources. "I think when he says our papers should be longer, this is what he's talking about. We have to quote somebody else, not just the author we're reading."

"Cool. Maybe I'll quote Malcolm."

"If we're switching papers, maybe *I* should."

Aisha half-grinned at me, not quite with enthusiasm, but at least fondly enough that I dropped our papers and kissed her. She pushed on my shoulder, signaling that we were too close to the open door. I scuttled back across the room into the space between her bed and her desk and she came with me. Here we could kiss for a few minutes before one of us got freaked out that her mom was going to come up the stairs—and if that happened, we had four seconds from the creaky step to the top of the stairs, plus an extra two since this was the least visible corner of the room.

I sat against the bookcase, arms open to her. Her grin got bigger, bunching up her cheeks. Kissing the side of my face and my neck, she ran her hand down from my shoulder and sat back with a startled, "Oh. You're not flat today. You're usually...I wasn't trying to..."

"It's okay. I was kind of in a boob mood."

She laughed. "Is that random or does something evoke the mood?"

"Um, maybe, you. I was getting dressed and thinking about us hanging out and it seemed like it would be fun. Is that okay?"

"Very."

"And is it okay if it's not always like this?" I asked.

"Because you have a girl body and boy body in the same space and sometimes you're more one or the other but you're also always both?"

"You're amazing," I told her.

"You realize you're saying that only because I'm smart enough to repeat you back to yourself," she said.

"And you're smart enough to know when to do it. And a million other things I really like."

It was hard to explain about boobs. Sometimes they were fine, but a lot of the time they weren't. Not okay for people to look at them, not okay for me to feel them. Those times, I wore the binder and feeling Aisha's hand slide across my flat chest was wonderful. When we sat together in the treehouse or in her bedroom and she curled into me with her cheek on my chest, I loved it.

But I also loved that she had boobs all the time and I felt like a hypocrite. She had to put up with people treating her like a stupid girl and other super creepy sexual variations. I felt like I was leaving her to deal with a heap of shit without me. I was a huge feminist, in part from hearing Milo's stories about when she was younger. So how unfair was it for me to wear the binder, to opt out of being a girl?

Except not that.

Because it wasn't easier to be a person who often looked like a girl and sometimes was a girl and sometimes wasn't. Not easy to feel my body changing based on who knows what. Maybe reacting to the people around me and internal measures I couldn't track. Hormones? Brain stuff? Some days I'd wake up and put on the bra—always the plainest white or a gray sports bra—and it was super wrong, like poison ivy wrong, slimy tentacles wrong, and other days it was fine, and sometimes it was even a good idea.

Aisha snuggled against me, her shoulders tucked under my arm, body diagonal to mine, cheek resting on my shoulder. Her fingers played with my earlobe while I nuzzled the parts of her face I could reach. I wanted to kiss her fine collarbones, where they peeked out from her sweater at the curve of her throat, but I couldn't bend that far without hopeless awkwardness.

"Does it bother you if my body changes?" I murmured. "If some days I'm more girl or more boy or more both?"

"Hmm, no. That's all you."

"Even if I can't be a girl all the time? If I always think of us as two girls, like Kate and America, I get worn out and kind of bleak."

"Depressed?" she suggested.

"Is that what that is?"

"Sounds like it. What helps?" she asked. "Do you know?"

I shrugged and brushed my fingertips over the curve between her collarbones. She put her hand over mine and pressed it flat to the middle of her chest. I felt the deep vibration of her heart.

"When was the last time you got exhausted?" she asked.

"Last week."

"And what happened before that?"

"We went to the movies and hung out with Jon and tried to get your mom to let me sleep over and…oh, I kept being a girl for all of that, like she's going to say yes if I'm a girl and we're going to make more sense to everyone if I'm a girl instead of a person."

"How do you know what you are?" Aisha asked.

"There's a way the inside of my body feels. But it's hard to feel that if there's a lot going on. So the shortcut is who I picture myself as. I could say that I feel tall and broad and like laughing and playing a lot—and the code for that, in my head, is that I'm Hulkling."

"And that's when you're more of a guy?"

"Yeah, but like more male without being a man, if that makes sense. I picked Hulkling because he's an alien shapeshifter. He's not an Earth guy."

She kissed my temple and nuzzled my cheek. "It doesn't have to make sense to me or anyone else, only to you. So, sometimes you wake up Hulkling and sometimes…?"

"If I wake up as Laura Kinney, new Wolverine, then I'm a girl. And sometimes, I wake up as Cloud, in nebula form. Or I wake up as a tree. And if I'm not a girl on the inside, it's really hard to keep being a girl on the outside."

"Do you want to just tell me who you are every day?" she asked.

I kissed her.

"But America doesn't go with Hulkling," I said. "You're always a girl, but you're never a straight girl. I don't want to make you have to be one."

She sighed. "That's a lot of categories. You think about gender way more than I do. How about I be Moon Girl?"

Moon Girl and Devil Dinosaur was a series we'd both been loving, even though it was written for young kids. Moon Girl was a mega-genius black girl in New York City whose best friend was a super-powered T-Rex.

"Am I supposed to be the dinosaur?" I asked.

"You're whoever you want to be. Moon Girl is, like, nine or ten in the comics, so we don't know what she'll be like at fifteen, but let's say she's all kinds of bi and pan—and you can be everyone you are, some days you can be the dinosaur—and we'll fit together all the time."

"So I'm a nebula and a boy and a girl and the dinosaur and you're the girl genius?" I asked.

"Sounds like us."

"How can I be sure this wasn't an elaborate joke to get me to agree to being a dinosaur?"

"You can't, 'cause I'm the genius," she said and pulled me around and down to where she could kiss me harder.

We ended up lying on the floor and scooted ourselves back up to where we'd look proper enough for parents.

She said, "I'm sorry that I don't understand all this."

"You do," I said. "You understand enough. You don't have to be the same as me. I mean, you put up with me being white."

"Yeah because you…oh, okay. You do the work. You make sure you understand things. I don't have to get what it's like being nonbinary to know how to make a space for you. And the more I read, the more it makes sense to me."

"How?"

"Different cultures do gender differently," she said. "Some maybe didn't do it at all like what we're used to."

"Like what cultures?"

"K, do you never Google this?"

"Some. I read the Native American Two-Spirit stories but I don't want to be appropriating. And when I'm looking it up, there's other articles that aren't good. They get stuck in my head. I can't look at things for very long sometimes."

"I get that. Sorry. How much do you want to know? Cori and Royce gave me a site to read and there's a local professor they want us to meet."

"You're the best girlfriend," I said.

"You've read more about race than I have about gender," she pointed out.

"Yeah, but I had a head start and…" I was about to say that gender wasn't as big a deal, but it was, only in a completely different way.

CHAPTER TWENTY-ONE

Mid October 2017

Another week passed of me having to go to World History study sessions without Aisha, of both of us washing glassware in Chemistry class and being late to lunch. I counted the days to Thanksgiving break.

By the end of the week, all the way home on the bus, Aisha's jaw was clenched. She stared out the window while I glared around the bus, though this probably wasn't the location of whatever had upset her. Even if no-cutting cafeteria guy had been on our bus, he wasn't nearly as bad as staying behind, day after day, in Chem class to measure liquids and wash glassware.

We walked to Aisha's house. She dropped her bag heavily by the side of the kitchen island and opened the fridge.

"Want to split one of Dad's ridiculous smoothies?" she asked, voice flat. She didn't even make a joke about how much better the store-bought ones were to those her dad tried to make.

"Sure. You okay?"

She poured the thick orange goop into two glasses. Best case: mango. Worst case: persimmon kale.

"I went to talk to Mr. Bretherton because I have questions about our next paper and I had to wait ages, like usual, and then he asked me to give some extra credit assignment to Hannah Porter."

"Who's Hannah Porter?"

"Exactly!" Aisha said.

Raising the oddly heavy glass, I took a sip of the alleged smoothie. It tasted like lawn clippings in orange juice. "You don't know her?" I asked.

"No, but I'll give you one guess what race she is?"

"Wait, what?"

"You know how it is, all the black kids must know each other, right? I looked her up." Aisha pulled out her phone and held it up for me to see a black girl smirking at the screen, no dimples, her skin a few shades lighter than Aisha's, her hair in box braids.

"I don't have any classes with her," I said. "Is she a sophomore?"

"Junior. Figured I'd better send her this so she doesn't get in trouble."

"That's super weird, him giving you her assignment. Should we tell someone at the school?"

Aisha took a sip of her smoothie and winced. "No. It'll make him mad and I don't want to deal with that."

"Can I tell Milo?" I asked.

"K, leave it alone."

The icy air of the kitchen clued me in that I was doing this wrong. Plus Aisha's body was turned away from me, shoulders curled in, tired, hurt and protecting against more hurt.

I hopped off my stool and moved closer. "Hug?"

She shrugged. That wasn't a no. It wasn't really a yes, so I put an arm loosely around her waist. She set her smoothie glass on the island and rested her cheek on my shoulder. I pulled her close.

"Aisha Warren, you have the most beautiful smile in this whole state, probably the country," I whispered. "And you're my favorite person in the whole world. You want to play some *Lego: Star Wars* and break stuff?"

Her sigh ended in a chuckle. "Yeah."

When we got into the living room, she put the big couch pillow on the floor. I sat on the back half of it, leaning against the couch, and she settled between my legs, leaning back into me. It wasn't easy to play with my arms around her, the controller in front of her stomach, me looking over her shoulder, but I didn't care.

When Hannah texted back, I played solo while Aisha got deep into that conversation, summarizing for me.

"She's doing a paper about this British poet who reworked *The Canterbury Tales*, and she's all into spoken word and she's out as bi!" Aisha said. "I mean the poet, Patience Agbabi, not Hannah, as far as I know."

"Oh, I thought Hannah *was* into spoken word," I said and Aisha laughed.

"She says it's funny to watch Mr. Bretherton try to be cool when he's freaking out about this black woman redoing Chaucer. Any time Hannah reads this poetry in class, everyone else likes it better than the original."

"Is Hannah going to tell Mr. B not to give you her assignments?" I asked.

Aisha shrugged. "Don't know. But I am definitely reading *The Wife of Bafa* to quote and mess with him if it happens again."

She read the poem and then read it out loud to me.

"Whoa wait," I said about some lines near the end. "Show me that."

She held her phone up and I scrolled the screen until I got to the lines I wanted to see:

Some say I'm a witchcraft
'cause I did not bear them children.
They do not understand your Western medicine.

"That part could be me," I said.

Aisha leaned back against me, resting her head on my shoulder. "Sometimes I think we're lost in the same place. I mean, the place where you and I are, where we lost ourselves to, is the same. I want us to go find where we belong together."

"Where?"

"I don't know yet. I'm looking."

I ambled through the Legos level, not really playing, more bumping into things as I paid more attention to Aisha sitting between my legs, leaning into me, her hands on the outsides of my knees, my arms around her, holding the controller in front of her stomach.

"Wherever it is," I said. "I belong with you."

* * *

That next week, we got our English papers back. We'd read *The Great Gatsby* and in the spring we were scheduled to read *Narrative of the Life of Frederick Douglass*, so Aisha wrote up a paper contrasting the autobiographical elements of *Gatsby* with *Frederick Douglass*. I put my name on that paper and turned it in.

She put her name on a paper I'd worked my ass off to write, comparing the women in *Gatsby* to Scout in *To Kill a Mockingbird*, which I'd read last year. I even quoted experts on both books and made sure my citations were done right.

October hadn't turned super cold yet and we could catch a ride home with Jon, so as soon as we got the papers, we ignored our bus and stayed in the school foyer to compare. The paper with my name got a half page of commentary from Mr. Bretherton, including "extraordinary research" and the recommendation of a book I could read for further study. I got an A+.

Aisha also got an A+, and thank goodness because I'd never worked that hard on any school paper in my life. It had more citations than the one with my name on it, but the comments to her only said, "Very good work!"

That is, my paper said, "Very good work!"

I showed her the "extraordinary research" quote and all his comments throughout my paper.

"What do we do?" I asked.

"Keep using secondary sources."

"This," I poked the paper with my finger, "it's so unfair."

She'd been checking something on her phone and glanced up long enough to shake her head at me. "First, we'd have to tell them we switched papers."

"Okay that could suck."

"Bae, it's a bad idea. Mr. Bretherton would fight it. And I don't know what anyone could do about it. I asked Darius why a teacher would write a bunch of stuff on your papers and not mine. He said it's that same effect that screws me up in math: stereotype threat. I get so afraid I'm going to be a bad stereotype, it's hard to think. Only now that's working on Mr. Bretheron. He's so afraid he's going to say something racist, he says as little as possible. Even though he's screwing with my academic future by not telling me how to do better. Like his fear of being racist is actually causing him to be more racist."

"I get that."

Aisha stared up from her phone at me. "You do?"

"The fear part. I'd never screw with your academic future." We grinned at each other. "But I used to feel that a lot and not bring up topics 'cause I didn't know how to talk about them with you, like I was going to screw it up and be really racist and you'd hate me."

"Seriously?"

"Very."

"But you don't feel that now, right?"

"No, 'cause I screwed up a bunch of things and we laughed about it and I got that I can manage myself not to say anything obviously awful and if I say something stupid, you'll tell me and I'll apologize."

"Like when you first started using 'they/them' and I messed up your pronouns," she said. "Or kept calling you 'girl' and was apologizing all the time."

"Yeah, I knew it was just habit and you'd get it. Like me not knowing what cornrows were or anything about the history of white people appropriating black hairstyles. Or me not knowing a ton of history, in general, that happened in my own country. Or the first time you said 'Malcolm' and I was like, 'Who?'"

"But I didn't know the names of any major trans people," she said.

"All my TV shows had majority white casts."

"My comic books had all cisgender characters," she pointed out.

"Or so you thought," I said. We'd decided a bunch of the characters were trans whether they said so in the comic books or not. "I like how we are now. I don't want to live in any world that's all one way. But shouldn't we give Mr. B the chance to get this too?"

"Let me think about it. We'd get in trouble for having switched papers."

"We don't have to say that part."

"I have a better idea," Aisha said, returning to her phone. Whoever she'd been messaging, the longer they talked, the deeper her smile got.

"Something good?"

"Yeah. I think I found the right place for us."

"Where?"

"The future," she said and typed a bunch more. "I want to go right now. Is that foolish?"

"No. I'll come with you. Where are we going?"

"College," she declared.

She zipped her jacket and I followed her out of the building. She turned left out of the school and left again, so we came to the bus stop on the big road heading to St. Paul.

"The Cities?" I asked.

"Dad will pick us up on his way home."

Buses came by often, since our town felt farther away from Saint Paul than it was, and a lot of people commuted. Aisha and I had taken this bus twice last summer to go to the gaming and comic book store.

We rode to the edge of Saint Paul and then had to change to another bus. The wind picked up and blew into the bus shelter. I tried to stand between it and Aisha so she'd freeze less.

"Where are we going?" I asked.

"Shh, wait, I want to see if this is going to be what I think," she said.

The second bus let us off at the edge of a college campus. Aisha stopped at a map, glanced at her phone, grabbed my hand and pulled me across a broad, grassy lawn. We passed red brick buildings and modern glass and metal ones. She drew me into one of the brick buildings, up two flights of stairs, slowly down a hall as she read the numbers next to the doors.

She stopped in front of #260 where a plaque said: Dr. Amanda Wade.

We stood there for about a minute while she stared at the door and shifted from foot to foot. Then she knocked.

"Come in!" From the sound of her voice, Dr. Wade was cheerful and big, either physically or personality-wise, or both.

Aisha froze, so I turned the knob and pushed the door open, but didn't go in. This was her thing. Or mostly hers, because when I saw Dr. Wade, I really wanted to go in. She'd stood up from her desk and she was tall and big-shouldered, broad and thick, heavy-jawed, soft eyed, kinky black hair down to her chin, warm brown skin.

Aisha went in, me right on her heels.

Shelves lined one wall of the office, filled with books, magazines, journals, stacks of papers. A window and file cabinets took up the short wall behind Dr. Wade's desk. The other long wall held framed posters from museums and one big painting, that was half collage, of six black people sitting and standing around a table, talking intensely.

"Aisha?" Dr. Wade asked.

"Hi, yes, this is Kaz, we're totally pleased to meet you," she said and stuck out her hand. Dr. Wade shook hers and mine. I felt the strong gentleness of her hand and wanted to stay here for a super long time.

She was probably trans. I really hoped. She could be a trans woman or maybe a cis woman with big shoulders, athletic, but I so wanted her to be trans. She had a kind smile but very no-bullshit dark eyes behind her glasses.

"I read your bio but Kaz didn't," Aisha said. "I wanted to be sure of you, like that you existed."

Dr. Wade laughed and said, "I get that a lot. I'm a trans woman butch lesbian sociology professor. Please, have a seat."

Aisha sat in one of the two chairs in front of her desk.

I said, "I'm some kind of nonbinary, probably genderfluid or something you can't say in English but I don't have another language for it." Then managed to get myself calm enough to sit down in the other chair.

"I can help you with that," Dr. Wade told me. "And Aisha, I want to hear more about your school program and what's going on."

Aisha told her everything about our Chemistry class and Mr. Bretherton. Dr. Wade took notes and asked, "Have you told your parents?"

"I don't want to. Mom's already looking at houses in California. I don't want to..." she repeated, trailed off and gestured at me.

"There are more than two options," Dr. Wade told her.

"You mean it's not a binary?" I blurted out.

Aisha flashed me a grin. "That should be one of your superpowers, not getting people stuck in either/or situations."

"Except I get stuck in them all the time," I admitted.

"Would you tell me about that?" Dr. Wade asked. "The research is very preliminary, but what I've read suggests that nonbinary people see themselves quite differently from men and women."

"Yes!" I about hopped out of my chair. "The thing is, I read some of that, and I talked to Aisha's friends, which was great, but almost everybody is like: I am *THIS*. Like they've got one or two or three names for what they are and it's all handled."

"Is it possible that because you're looking from the outside, they seem to have themselves more together than they do?" she asked.

"Maybe yeah but a lot of people are like: oh I'm androgynous or nonbinary. They don't talk about feeling different on different days. And yeah, they say flux or fluid, but I can't *see* that."

"Sight may be a significant part of the problem. We live in an incredibly visible time and culture. For tens of thousands of years, people did not rely solely on sight as much as we do now. There are cultures where a multi-sensory landscape was the primary way of getting around in the world. Hearing and touch were very important. At least one of these cultures didn't seem to have gender at all. Can I give you some articles to read?"

"Please! But how can a culture not have gender?"

"It's possible that gender is not a human universal. This is an imperfect analogy, but we might consider that humans have a universal drive to create and use language—and there are many different ways to do that: spoken, signed, written, typed, images, emoji, and so on. I suspect that humans have a universal drive to create social roles, but there are many different ways to do that: gender, age, seniority, geography, caste and class systems. We happen to live in a culture where gender is one of the strongest systems of social roles and it's anchored primarily in how people look."

"So some people are fluent in English and some are fluent in Spanish, but I'm fluent in both, but you can't see that only by looking at me?"

"Or more than two," Aisha said. "About four, from what you tell me."

"But then is gender even real?"

"Of course it is," Dr. Wade said. "English is real. Money is real, as is the U.S. Constitution, even though cultures created those. Some social constructions like gender, language, money, have more impact on us than the natural world, even to the point of changing our bodies. For example, our brains are now wired to speak English and it might be impossible for us to stop thinking in English if that's our only language. My brain is wired for me to be a woman as, I'm assuming, is Aisha's. Our brains evolved to shape and be shaped by our cultures."

"But then shouldn't I be a woman too?" I asked with a shudder.

"Cultures can come up with systems that are more restrictive than human beings are capable of. No one would say the creation of racism should've caused brains to adapt for it."

"Hell no," Aisha muttered.

Dr. Wade looked at me. "Your brain doesn't fit itself into a model that is too restrictive for you. That doesn't have to be a problem, it can be a strength. You can see where the social construction of gender needs to change. Can I give you homework?"

"Like the only homework I will completely look forward to in ever? Yes!" I said.

"You too?" she asked Aisha, who grinned and nodded. Dr. Wade said, "I don't like what that school environment is teaching you and your parents need to know about it too. All of it."

Aisha sighed and said, "Yes, ma'am," but she hadn't stopped smiling.

Dr. Wade took us over to the school union for dinner and Aisha's dad met us there. The seating area was smaller than our school's cafeteria, with wood and blue fabric partitions that kept the noise level low. And it didn't smell like week-old tater tots in a stale oil bath. I could definitely like college.

Mr. Warren and Dr. Wade had one of those boring adult conversations about their work histories and current projects, while Aisha and I jostled each other under the table with excitement.

CHAPTER TWENTY-TWO

Late October 2017

Aisha told her parents about Chemistry class when I wasn't around. She texted me that the conversation had happened, but didn't give details until a few days later. That Friday, Aisha's parents were having a dinner party and we'd been invited but it sounded dreadful. We opted to eat at my house and hang out there so we wouldn't get called down from Aisha's room to awkwardly meet a bunch of people from Mr. Warren's office.

Brock and Mom were out. We'd eaten with Milo and Pops, then done the dishes while they played *Bananagrams*. They'd said good night at nine and we hoped to have the living room to ourselves for an hour. We settled on the couch, my arm over Aisha's shoulders, her leaning back against my side, our history textbook open in her lap. I had a smaller book open on my leg. She underlined and took notes. I just had to read this for English. Since we had books out, no one was going to protest us being cuddled up together.

"What did your parents say about Chem?" I asked.

"Lots of stuff."

That meant she didn't want to talk about it. But I couldn't keep from asking, "Did your mom say anything about moving?"

"Dad likes his job here, but she's using this to get him to look for similar jobs near L.A. Now I think he has to because if he doesn't it looks like he's putting himself ahead of me, even though I told them I want to stay."

"Do you?"

She sighed and lapsed into a long silence before saying, "I don't know. There's a lot I hate about being here, a lot that I miss about Cali, but there's also so much I'd miss if I weren't here. Even if you could come with me, I'd miss Milo and Pops, and the marsh, the seasons that aren't winter. And if Dad couldn't have his job, that would suck. I'm only in high school for two more years and he's got to have a job for, like, ever. Plus being an EMT out in the sticks here is good for Riq. Closer to L.A., I'd worry about him."

She sounded so much older than me and I felt sad for all the ways she'd had to grow up.

"I wish we could make our school more like your old one," I said.

"Hah, me too, but we'd need at least a thousand kids of color, plus teachers."

Brock banged in through the back door and stomped down the stairs to his room. Not that he was mad or anything; he always stomped. Mom followed, nuking herself some dinner in the kitchen.

We returned to reading. I snuck peeks at the curve of Aisha's neck, brushed my thumb up the back of it and felt her press closer to me. I caught one of her curls and pressed it between my fingers, tugged it. She laughed and shook her head so her curls tickled my cheek. I kissed her shoulder.

She said, "K?"

"Huh?"

"You know I like what you're doing, right? But would you not play with my hair when our friends are around."

"When did I...oh."

I'd finally taken Aisha over to Trina's last Sunday for a fall-themed party. It did have great food. We'd spent most of our time in the living room watching TV, or pretending to, because that was less boring than the conversations going on around us. I remembered sitting next to her on the couch, my fingers tugging on her curls while I tried to figure out if it would be cool to have my arm around her. I'd decided "not cool" because all the other couples there were white.

Playing with each other's hair had started last spring as a friends-to-flirting move. Aisha tugged on her curls when she was concentrating. I'd leaned over during a study session and teasingly asked if it would help her to play with *my* hair or did it only work with curls. She'd spent the rest of that study session wrapping a lock of my hair around her finger, curling it, letting it go—which had been just the excuse I'd needed to lie with my head in her lap.

Days later, she'd taken my fingers and placed them on a curl at the back of her head. I'd tugged it out and let it spring back, like she did. Now sometimes she'd wrap my hair around her fingers when she was thinking and I'd play with her curls when I wanted to feel closer.

So I'd done that at Trina's last week. Now I remembered the expression she had when she'd come back from Trina's kitchen later: hard, closed, angry but not able to show it. Something had happened to her and I'd missed it.

"I'm sorry." I said. "I should've thought about where we were. I'll pay better attention. You want to tell me what happened?"

I pushed the book off my knee and wrapped both arms around her. Her back and shoulders stayed tight.

"Eve patted me." Her clenched jaw flattened the words.

"Fuck."

"Came up behind me when I was pouring pop and ran her hand down my curls, pulled at them. I spilled pop everywhere."

"Can I talk to her or did you? Or both?"

"I asked her to please not do that, but what are you going to say?"

I took a very slow, deep breath because I was furious. I considered a whole bunch of things I was not going to say, like: *Please don't pat my girlfriend like she's a dog.* And the fact that on the street people asked before they touched Wolvie and what the fuck that Aisha didn't get that courtesy.

"I'm going to say: 'You saw me playing with Aisha's curls because she's my girlfriend and that's a girlfriend thing to do, it's not okay to go up to someone you don't know that well and touch their hair, especially if they're black.' And then Eve is going to say some colorblind bullshit and I'm going to deliver a concise lecture on the history of the exoticization of black hair."

"The one my mom does?" Aisha asked.

"Yep."

"Okay. Cool."

I held her tighter. "A, I am sorry. I won't do it again."

"Except in private," she said quietly. "'Cause I like that."

I nodded and pressed my lips to her cheek. She sighed and relaxed into me. I kept both arms around her as she went back to reading, kept them there until she shifted and wriggled and pushed my hand back toward my book.

* * *

Later in the kitchen, after Aisha had gone home, Brock asked, "Why were you apologizing to her so much?"

He'd come up to nuke some mac-n-cheese, wearing gray sweatpants and a sleeveless black T-shirt—with giant, drooping armholes—that made him look like a skinny tool with goosebumps because the kitchen was chilly and he was too much of a dork to put on a sweatshirt.

"Wow, nothing good on YouTube tonight, huh?" I said.

"You were loud enough. All, 'I'm sorry, I'm sorry,' what'd you do?"

"You wouldn't understand," I told him.

"Is it some mysterious black thing? You don't have to be always apologizing to her for shit that happened hundreds of years ago."

Okay that was it. Brock was getting the whole lecture on the history of black hair in America, not even the concise version. And not even only about hair. Like how some white people said slavery was so long ago but didn't think how there'd been two-hundred and forty-six years of slavery on this continent followed by eighty-nine years of segregation. That was three-hundred and thirty-five years of being dehumanized and brutalized. And segregation had only ended sixty-three years ago. It was legal when Milo and Pops were kids. How long was it *supposed* to take people to get over all that? Especially in a country shaped by and carrying on its effects?

I wanted to yell at Brock. Beat on his chest until he heard me. But he wouldn't.

Aisha had to do this all the time, every day.

And if she didn't get to be angry, then I had to do better too. I ground my teeth, clenched my hands so they hurt, and said as calmly as I could, "I don't understand why you think I *shouldn't* apologize if I did something that made life harder for her?"

He took the mac-n-cheese tray out of the microwave and dropped it on the counter because he hadn't used an oven mitt. At least it landed dish-side down. He leaned against the counter and folded his arms.

"What'd you do?" he asked.

"I let some of my friends think it was okay for them to touch her hair without asking. That's a thing white people do a lot to black people, just touch their hair. Does anyone ever touch yours without asking?"

"No," he scoffed, like anyone would dare.

"And what would you do if someone came up and started playing with mine—a person I don't know well and maybe don't even like?" I asked.

"Probably hit 'em. Does that really happen?"

"Eve trying to play with Aisha's hair will be the third time it's happened to her this year. That I know about. Different people each time."

He shrugged. "Yeah but it's only hair."

"But you'd hit someone who touched mine."

"Her hair *is* different from ours," he said. "People are curious."

"It's not different from one-fifth of the people in the world. It's only that TV and movies didn't show black hair until the last few years so we didn't grow up understanding that it's only hair—" I stopped mid-thought because another idea rammed through my head.

Dr. Wade had said our visual culture made binary gender *seem* universal when it wasn't. I'd only seen white people's hair on TV and I'd only seen men and women, but a lot more existed in the world than that. Not only did I see TV characters who were exclusively men or women for most of my life, but I only saw certain kinds of men and women: they had to be slender or skinny or fit, men had to have muscles, women had to emphasize boobs and their waist.

Walking around my school I could see students and teachers who didn't fit those idealized gender images. And beyond that, if there was a kind of hair that didn't get on TV, there were also kinds of genders that didn't get on TV. And they were as real as the genders that did.

"There are plenty of black people on TV," Brock said.

"When have you ever seen a black woman on TV who didn't have her hair straightened or was wearing a wig?"

"What?"

The clueless expression on his face...had I looked like that two years ago? Yeah, probably.

"The last few years maybe Michonne on *Walking Dead* and the mom and older sister on *Black Lightning*. But we didn't grow up with that. We grew up being taught that black hair is weird and exotic."

And I thought: *Just like I grew up being taught that any gender that isn't "straight man" or "straight woman" was freakish or impossible.*

"Who cares?" Brock asked.

"I don't want people to see Aisha that way. I want them to see her like I do: this intricate, sweet, vast person who's into all kinds of cool stuff. So, yeah, I am sorry that I did something that made it easier for our white friends to reduce her to her hair and skin color. I *am* responsible for understanding how my whiteness interacts with Aisha's world. Sometimes I cause problems for her or hurt her in ways I don't mean, and when you hurt someone, you apologize."

"Seems to me you understand black people better than white people," he said. "What about us?"

"What about you?"

"Don't you care that we're being replaced in our own country?" he asked.

"Whoa, you do know we were very much *not* here first."

"That was hundreds of years ago. We're here now and we've done great things," he said. He jerked a drawer open, pulled out a fork and jammed it into his steaming mac-n-cheese. "White people made this the best country in the world."

"Yeah, by using slaves and then using racism to justify inequality that profits white people," I said.

"Why are you so fucking anti-white?" he snarled.

"I'm not."

"Yeah, you are. You'd throw me under the fucking bus in a heartbeat to help Aisha."

"It's not an either/or."

"What if it is? If there was a train speeding at me or Aisha, who would you pick?"

"I'd use my superpowers and save both of you," I said. "That train scenario is made up bullshit so I get to solve it with superpowers."

"You know what's not made up? Immigrants and people on welfare taking tax money from folks who earned it."

I wanted to yell, *Bullshit!* But even more than that, I wanted Brock to hear me. One of my superpowers was supposed to be not getting stuck in binary situations, so how did I get out of this one?

"Why are you so worried about that?" I asked, managing not to sound entirely pissed off.

"It's not fair. People who work hard should get rewarded."

"I agree. And that should be regardless of their race or gender."

"Yeah," he said. We shared a moment of shock that we weren't disagreeing.

"So how do we make that happen?" I asked.

"Make sure we don't let so many people into the country that they take all the jobs," he said.

I didn't argue even though I felt pretty sure that wasn't a big danger. "And then?"

He lifted a forkful of mac-n-cheese and let it drop back into the black plastic dish. Shrugged.

"I don't want to spend my whole life working in a shitty coffee shop," he said. "When we were little, Dad had money, a bunch of it. Where did it go? Where did *he* go? What if he's laid up somewhere, sick or hurt, and can't get the help he needs because so many other people are getting taken care of first? Would you pick Aisha's dad over ours?"

"Mr. Warren is a senior engineer at 3M, he's got everything covered."

"Why? Why is he here and our dad isn't? Why does he have a great job and a big house and Tariq has everything?"

"Tariq works his ass off."

"So do I! So do a lot of white people who just get shit for it and it is not fair! Why can't you see that!"

I stood there way too long with my mouth open. How did he not see that this argument applied many times over to people of color in this country? He must've not known that Aisha's family was the exception, not the usual experience for black families in our country. But how could he miss that the unfairness applied to our generation had been applied to ten generations of Aisha's family?

He grabbed his congealing mac-n-cheese and stomped down the stairs.

I stared after him, my sock-covered feet getting cold on the kitchen tile. Wolvie butted the side of my knee with her forehead because she wanted to go out.

"Do you think if I google 'privilege' I'll see a video of Brock just now?" I asked her.

She sat and peered up at me as if to say: *Remember that one time when you switched me to the better dog food and then tried to switch me back to that other stuff? I was mad too. You can't take good things away without offering something else good. At least not if you want me to eat my dinner instead of throwing pieces of it around the living room.*

I held the back door open for her, hearing the loud, angry rock belting up the stairs from Brock's room. Was Wolvie right? Did I have anything good to offer him?

CHAPTER TWENTY-THREE

Late October 2017

The next morning, Brock hauled ass out of the kitchen as soon as I came in from walking Wolvie. I wanted to be gone when he came home, so when Aisha invited me to run errands with her and Tariq, I about teleported over to her house.

Aisha talked Riq into driving us to Target. She had photos to pick up and I looked at dog toys. Then we walked down the street to the Applebee's for lunch. The temperature had dropped from mid-fifties two days ago into the thirties, but Tariq still wore light blue knee-length shorts above his white sneakers.

"You're turning into a Minnesotan," I told him.

He snorted. "Haven't done my laundry."

"Mom stopped doing it for him," Aisha said. "It's a crisis."

He ignored her and walked ahead of us into the Applebee's. When we were seated, Aisha pulled out the photo envelope and started spreading photos across the table. She got out her big school notebook and arranged a few on the front cover inside the plastic coating.

"Can I look?" I pointed at the photo envelope.

"Sure."

They were mostly black women, some historical, a few in sepia. We'd both been reading books and articles that Dr. Wade recommended about gender and race and the intersection of the two. I'd been amazed at the parallels. Like so many white scientists and leaders, decades and centuries ago, tried to prove that black people were profoundly different from white people, to justify racism. They'd failed, even if everyone hadn't gotten that info yet. And men scientists and leaders tried to prove—to make us believe—that only two sexes and genders existed, were natural, were mutually exclusive, and men were better. Now they were failing too.

I held one photo up toward Aisha. "Who's this?"

"Dr. Jane Wright, surgeon and cancer researcher. And this is Dr. Alexa Canady, pediatric neurosurgeon."

"Wow, badass." I saw a corner of a comic book illustration and pulled out a drawing.

Aisha said, "Dr. Cecilia Reyes, showed up in the X-Men sometimes." She fished around in the pile and pulled out a photo of a smiling woman with short hair next to an anatomical image of a dog's skeletal system.

I touched the dog and raised my eyebrows.

"Dr. Erika Gibson, first black veterinary neurosurgeon."

I studied that photo while she arranged two more inside the front cover of her notebook.

"This is what Darius was talking about, yeah?" Tariq said. "Reminding yourself every day that there are a lot of brilliant black women doctors…and vets."

"Vets *are* doctors," I said.

"You know what I mean."

"Stereotype threat," Aisha told him. "Dr. Wade sent me a bunch more about it so I'll know what I'm dealing with. So I won't freeze up because I'm afraid the whole school's going to see me as some stupid black girl. And so I see how possible it is to be a great black woman doctor."

Aisha slid another photo into her notebook. I reached for the one below it, pulled it in front of me. The woman looked almost familiar with her strong nose, bold face, prim smile. "She wasn't a doctor," I said.

"Who is that?" Tariq asked.

"Lucy Hicks Anderson," Aisha said. "She was born in Kentucky in the late 1800s—and we'd say she was assigned male at birth—but she said she was a girl and a doctor told her mom she could raise her as a girl, so she did. I asked Cori and Royce who I should print out for you...is this okay?"

I lifted the photo off the table, grinning. "She's for me?"

"Yeah, I made a bunch for you. Here, this is Hatshepsut, a female pharaoh from Egypt who was depicted with a beard. And this is the goddess Inanna from Mesopotamia, the one you were telling me about with the trans priests. I know they didn't call them trans, but we would. Here are hijras from India and fa'afafine from Samoa. Parinya Charoenphol from Thailand; she's the kickboxer from that movie we watched. I didn't find a famous trans vet, but I did get a picture of Joan Roughgarden, American biologist who studies animals and evolution, and Jowelle de Souza from Trinidad, she's a huge animal rights activist."

As Aisha named people, she slid them along the table to me and I fanned them out on the dark wood surface. In the presence of these faces, I understood what I hadn't been seeing for most of my life: people of all races, all ethnicities, genders, sexualities, body sizes and ability.

One way to fight our very visual culture's shaping my ideas was to keep looking at all kinds of people—to keep them in front of me so I never forgot the full wonder of human beings.

Aisha reached to the bottom of the stack and pulled out an illustration, saying, "And this."

The artist had drawn a boy and girl on top of each other, semi-transparent, with a nebula in the background. They looked like Cloud from the comics and like me because the artist had done their hair more like mine.

I loved it so much. "You had someone draw this for me?"

"I paid an artist online," Aisha said. "Is it right?"

"It's perfect. What nebula is that?"

Aisha smirked. "The California Nebula. I couldn't help it."

I beamed back at her. "From the future, where we belong?"

She nodded and returned to putting photos in her notebook. I contemplated the beautiful faces in front of me.

Brock didn't have this. Maybe he didn't look at Milo and Pops like I did, wanting to grow up like them. He didn't have faces of white men who were powerfully anti-racist. The really visible faces were the ones spewing hate about "immigrants" and others. Maybe he'd gotten as trapped by what he saw everyday as I had and didn't know what he wasn't seeing.

Could I give him other options?

* * *

Having the photos in my notebook—trans people from history and the drawing of me as Cloud, nebula and all—made school easier. But it also made me want to fight.

I couldn't let things go in Chemistry because I knew something Aisha didn't. I'd spent those two weeks last summer with Mrs. Alexander at the science camp, run by the high school. Mrs. Alexander taught the chemistry portion that I'd signed up for, figuring I'd get ahead for tenth grade. Plus it'd come in handy if I had to fall back on that career in Materials Sciences and I'd started thinking that I might really enjoy mixing things and occasionally blowing them up.

Most of the kids in the class were some kind of geek, but one girl clearly got dropped off there because her parents didn't know what else to do with her. She knew nothing about biology or the scientific method.

Mrs. Alexander had come to me and asked me to mentor this girl because I was good at explaining the concepts. And she'd checked on us at the end of class at least every other day.

The girl texted during lectures and laughed at things she read on her phone. Sometimes she put in her ear buds and ignored the lecture. Most of the other students were over her by the end of week one. Two of them moved across the classroom to get away from her texting, laughing, gum-chewing disruption.

I'd asked Mrs. Alexander if someone else could be the mentor for week two.

"She doesn't care about this," I'd said. "She doesn't want to learn." I did not say, but thought: *Let someone else waste their energy on her.*

"She's having a tough time at home," Mrs. Alexander told me. "Have you thought about why her parents might drop her off at a camp she's not interested in? She needs a friend and I think she's starting to look up to you. I'll try to help you out more if you'll keep mentoring her."

I got the tough time at home thing, so I'd said yes. And Mrs. Alexander did come by and explain things that I hadn't. I started liking it because I got to hear some real-world applications I wouldn't have thought of. Mrs. Alexander made sure that by the end of that second week, that girl was for real getting curious about biology.

But that girl had been white.

So for a white girl, Mrs. Alexander would devote her time and attention *and* other people's resources.

I'd let two weeks pass after Aisha got assigned the bogus measuring task, in case Mrs. Alexander was going to swap tasks around. She didn't. I added one more week, benefit of the doubt. No change. Then we had a two-day week because of teacher conferences.

By the last week of October: no more waiting. That Tuesday, I got out of English a few minutes early, by asking nicely, and slipped through the Chemistry class door as students from the earlier class left. Mrs. Alexander sat at her desk sorting her notes back into order for our lecture.

When she looked up, I asked, "Mrs. Alexander, do we need to keep measuring everything? Can Aisha work on the online part of the project with me?"

She put her notes into a stack and tapped them. "We have enough people online."

That was true, we probably had one too many. "Well then swap me with her," I suggested. "I'll measure and she can do the online stuff."

"No."

"What?"

"No. Class is starting, take your seat."

I walked back to my seat numb and cold with shock. I'd figured Mrs. Alexander owed me a favor since I'd done that mentoring thing at summer camp. I knew she remembered me by how she'd greeted me the first week of school. And I'd thought she liked me, I was even good at Chemistry, so was there any reason not to say yes?

"What did you ask her?" Aisha asked me as I stumbled into my seat.

"To swap you and me on the tasks so you can do the online parts," I said.

"Huh. Thanks."

"She said no. I'm going to ask her again."

Back to trying to fight supervillain Apocalypse's control of other people's minds. How could I do that if they believed his thoughts were their own? Or if, like Brock, they thought it was the truth of the world? How could I tell Mrs. Alexander that she was being mind controlled? Not in *those* words, for sure.

I knew what had happened: Aisha had left her third period class with Chloe but got stopped in the hall by the monitor because the voice of Apocalypse inside his mind had said: "Dangerous."

And then Aisha came in late to Chemistry and Apocalypse told Mrs. Alexander, "That girl's lazy."

But the hall monitor and Mrs. Alexander couldn't hear those words—they just obeyed them. If Mrs. Alexander could hear it, she'd have stopped when I asked her to swap with Aisha or do our assignments together. If she got how she was being mind controlled, she could've resisted it.

* * *

I waited two days, until we had a lecture day, nothing to wash out, and told Aisha I'd meet her in the cafeteria. Then I went back to Mrs. Alexander at her desk.

"What if we both do both?" I asked. "I'll measure things with Aisha and she can help me with my part of the online project."

She stood up, a few inches taller than me in her thick heels, and said, "I told you, no."

"Why not?"

"Aisha needs to learn discipline and precision."

"So do I," I said. "Way more than she does."

"Her answers are sloppy. She needs to learn to persist until she improves."

"She's bored. If you had me do all that, I'd be way worse. This is an AP class and you're having her spend most of her time measuring volumes. That's not fair."

"If she wants harder tasks, she has to show me she can do the basic ones," Mrs. Alexander said.

I wanted to say: *A fifth grader could do the basic ones.*

Instead, I asked, "How long does she have to show you?"

"What?"

"One week? Two weeks? How long does she have to get it perfect before you let her do something interesting?"

"I don't appreciate your tone."

"I'm sorry," I said and drew in a very slow breath. "Please, Mrs. Alexander, how many days does Aisha have to give you perfect numbers before she can work online with me?"

"As many as I think she needs."

"By what measure?"

"Kaz, this conversation is over. One more minute and I'm handing out detentions."

I'd have kept going, not caring if I got detention, but the way she said it plural, I worried that she'd write one for Aisha too.

I went into the bathroom and stood in a stall, not sure if I was going to shake or cry or punch the wall.

So that white girl from summer camp was just having a tough time—even though she was disruptive and not that smart—but Aisha needed to learn discipline?

Hell no.

CHAPTER TWENTY-FOUR

November 2017

I thought: *I should go to Mrs. Warren.* She'd emailed and called Mrs. Alexander, probably a few times. But she already had so much to deal with. She never let Aisha or Tariq out of the house without making sure they were well-dressed. I used to think she was super strict. In a way she was, but I could see how a lot of it came from her fear for her kids.

Last spring, I'd heard her and Aisha fighting about it. One morning, not long before Dani Mehta broke up with Aisha, I'd gone over early and had breakfast at her house. I was in Aisha's room packing my backpack when she went down to get her biology book from the living room.

I heard her mom say, "You're not wearing that to school."

"Why?" Aisha had insisted. "Any of my friends can go to school with torn jeans."

"Do *not* let your white friends get you in trouble. Go put on your nice jeans and bring me those."

"Mom, these look better."

"Not to your teachers."

"It's not going to matter." Aisha's voice went rough with anger. "They aren't looking at my *jeans*."

"I know, honey, but if you're proper, then you know and they know it's their problem, not yours."

"They don't know that," Aisha said.

"You're not leaving the house in those," Mrs. Warren told her.

Aisha stomped up the stairs and shut the door. There was a strong no-slamming policy in her house. The jeans she loved were torn at the knee and I agreed they were her best pair. Not that I wanted her wearing them to school for Meta to see.

My jeans didn't have any big tears, but the bottom cuffs and the edges of the pockets were fraying because I'd had them for so long. I put my thumbs in my pockets so my fingers fell over the frayed parts.

Aisha got out another pair of jeans, turned away and put them on. I didn't watch, of course, but from her breathing I could tell she was crying.

Mrs. Warren and Aisha should not have to deal with this on their own, or at all if I could help it. I decided to ask Milo if she could help. Milo and Mrs. Warren had become a dynamic duo since the election. They were teaching me about social conditioning and racism and learning about trans issues. Maybe together they knew how to fight this.

But first, because I knew there was a ton I didn't know, I asked Aisha if she'd be okay with me talking to Milo about Chemistry. We'd been playing Xbox and stopped to maybe watch a movie. As she flipped through the channel listing, I slipped my fingers under her free hand.

"What are you going to ask Milo to do?" she asked, eyes narrowing though she faced the TV screen.

"Milo knows everybody. She'll talk to the principal or something."

"Who will talk to Mrs. Alexander," Aisha said. "Who will take it out on me."

"Yeah. That's why I'm asking."

Aisha sighed. "Mom's already going to talk to her. She sent a bunch of emails and left phone messages. Mrs. Alexander sent her some brush-off replies so you know there's going to be a meeting." She got up and went to the stairs, since her mom was upstairs reading, calling up, "Mom, Kaz wants to talk to Milo about Mrs. Alexander."

Mrs. Warren came to the bottom of the stairs, facing into the living room. "I'll talk to Milo. Kaz, do you want to come to this meeting too?"

"Yes, please."

"All right. I am done playing with that woman."

She returned to her room and Aisha came to sit with me again. She rested the remote on her knee and wove her fingers with mine, then kept moving them restlessly.

"Wow," I said. "That all happened fast."

"What did you expect?"

"That you'd tell me you don't need me to fight your fights and I'm being kind of stupid and you've got this."

"See, you already know that," she said. "Except the stupid part, what's that about?"

"Apocalypse," I said. "I can fight the mind control in my own brain—I'm good at it now—but I know I still don't see things that you see."

"Sometimes you see things I don't. Like Mrs. Alexander treating that white girl differently last summer. And so much about gender. Is Apocalypse also the one who tells you that you can't be nonbinary? That you can't be both and all and everything?"

"Oh. Yeah," I stared hard at the leg of the couch because my eyes had gotten really wet.

We'd talked about Apocalypse as a metaphor for the kinds of racism that were super hard for white people to see they were doing. That they needed to get responsible for and fight against. Like all Mrs. Alexander's assumptions and the teachers who didn't see how a mostly white curriculum hurt everybody.

I didn't want to take away from that, so I hadn't thought much about how Apocalypse also worked as the mind control that made people think everyone fit neatly into the categories of man and woman, even though they were forcing people into those categories.

Aisha laced her fingers with mine. "He doesn't want us to be powerful. Because he can't really control us. So he's got to keep knocking us down, trying to tear us up inside, turning us against our powerful selves. You know how you see me? I see you like that too."

"But I barely exist," I mumbled. "How can you see me?"

"You're combining things. Out there, there aren't a lot of examples of you, but there are some. But here, up close, you exist the same way I do—in a 'multiplicity of senses anchored by hearing.'" That last part was a quote from a book Dr. Wade had loaned me and Aisha.

We'd talked about how in the world around us, in Western culture, we each got reduced to visible surfaces. Aisha was "the black girl" to everyone white around here and I was "that weird girl" to most people. The further we were from each other, the more cultural weight fell on "black" and "girl." At school I could see how everyone saw Aisha first as black. Here at her house, that vanished. And alone together, her skin had a color and mine had a color, we both had hair, and we both really liked the interactions of our skin and hair and fingers and lips.

Some days I watched the cultural weight come down on us. I'd walk over to her house, bringing anything Milo had baked the night before, eat breakfast with her, laugh with her Dad about whatever. We'd walk to the bus stop and wait and when we got on the bus, the first layer of weight came down. At school a second, thicker layer fell, and we walked around under that all day.

Sometimes we couldn't get all that weight off until nearly bedtime—like the days she got Hannah Porter's assignment, the days she got stopped in the hall, the days nobody at our lunch table talked to her except one pitiful question from Sofia, the days I got called "she" and "her" by nearly everyone, even the friends I'd asked to use "they" and "them," the days I got glared at or laughed at in the women's restroom or the girls in there huddled up and whispered about me.

Sometimes I didn't see the light come back into Aisha's eyes until we were saying good night. And sometimes I couldn't see it in her eyes because I didn't have enough light in mine.

Aisha was trying to tell me the whole world, all of space and time, wasn't like our country now. Lots of places existed where people hadn't based everything on how someone looked. Lots of places existed where social roles and categories *helped* you be yourself in the community. I just wished we could make this place like that.

* * *

The meeting got scheduled for after school that Friday. Aisha and I met Mrs. Warren and Milo at the west doors to the school, away from the buses. For work, Mrs. Warren always wore a white blouse under a lab coat, but now she'd put on a silver-gray suit over the white blouse. Milo had forgone her usual flannel for a navy blue sweater and black pants.

Mrs. Warren took the lead, walking with all the determination, confidence and fury of every Shonda Rhimes badass heroine ever. In the few minutes' walk to the principal's office, the air charged with pre-thunderstorm energy. The admin jumped up from his desk and waved us into the inner office.

Our principal reminded me of Lynda Carter, especially when she showed up on *Supergirl* as the President and then... well, spoilers, but I wanted our principal to be all that too. She had the same long brown wavy hair and blue eyes so pale they looked colorless. Plus she always wore a suit jacket: navy today with a tan blouse under it. She sat behind her desk with Mrs. Alexander in front of it. Mrs. Alexander had her legs crossed, arms crossed, looking about as happy as a wet cat.

Mrs. Alexander had taken the chair closest to the door, so we all had to go around her. Me and Aisha sat in smaller chairs in the back. I wore my very best jeans and the military-style button down I loved. Despite the cold, Aisha wore a green and white dress with a cool geometric pattern. She had black leggings on under it and a white sweater, but she still looked cold.

Milo took the middle chair and Mrs. Warren picked the left chair. Before she sat down she turned the chair so she could see the principal and Mrs. Alexander at the same time.

After very stiff introductions, the principal said, "I'm sure we all know why we're here. Aisha, do you mind telling us, from your point of view, what's been happening?"

Aisha pressed her hands together in her lap, kept her eyes on the principal and said, "I came in late to class because the hall monitor had stopped me again. He didn't believe I was young enough to go to school here and spent a long time looking at my ID card or I wouldn't have been so late. Chloe got stopped too, but he didn't ask to look at her ID. When I arrived in class, Chloe had been assigned to share her lab partner's task and I was asked to measure liquids, which makes me late to lunch most days. Other kids have changed assignments but I haven't, even though Kaz asked to switch with me."

"If your assignment was such a *burden*, why didn't you come talk to me?" Mrs. Alexander asked.

"Because my mom emailed you and called you. And then Kaz asked and you said no."

"But if you were so troubled by it, you could speak up yourself. You could have shown some initiative."

Mrs. Warren's face transformed to living metal or something harder. "You won't take that tone with my daughter," she said. "She's not the locus of the trouble. And why should she have to ask you when I had been emailing and calling you?"

"And I told you that all of my students have assignments that involve a level of rote work and discipline," Mrs. Alexander said.

"Umm…" The sound slipped out of my mouth and everyone looked at me. I swallowed and said, "The rest of us don't have anything that boring. And we're not expected to do it week after week. We rotate every few weeks. And you let those two groups at the front switch just because Tommy is afraid of fire. I've asked three times to switch or share jobs with Aisha. She could be learning so much cool stuff."

Pretty sure Mrs. Alexander was thinking of ways to kill me about then. With her red-brown hair piled up on her head and her light tan skin going ruddy, plus the red sweater she wore over her tan dress, she resembled a cartoon smokestack about to blow.

"You could also be leaning 'cool stuff,'" the principal said to me.

"Yeah but I'm only going to be a vet and I already know about animals. Aisha's going to be a medical doctor."

The corner of the principal's mouth twitched in an almost-smile. "You have that worked out already at...?"

"We're both fifteen," Aisha said softly. "I've wanted to be a doctor since I was ten."

"And for me it was between vet or animal trainer. But Aisha's set on doctor and I thought it'd be cool if we both were. And she's the one who likes chemistry, not me. Or at least she did."

"Aisha's never going to be a doctor or even a nurse if she can't follow simple instructions for a few weeks," Mrs. Alexander said. She picked at the sleeve of her sweater, like pulling off lint.

"Coming from a teacher who can't perform the simple task of responding to my calls and emails in a timely manner," Mrs. Warren said.

"Aisha never complained," Mrs. Alexander insisted.

"You singled out my daughter for a task that sounds very much like a punishment, even though being late was not her fault. Did you do that on purpose or were you too ignorant to see what you were doing? I'm here to tell you right now, it's going to stop and stop immediately."

Mrs. Alexander turned to the principal, her upper lip curled. "I don't think parents or their children should be telling me how to run my class."

"Aisha, Kaz, would you wait for us in the outer office?" the principal asked.

Mrs. Warren nodded and we went into the room outside the door. It was late enough in the day that the admin had left, which meant we didn't have to sit in the chairs on the far side of the room. Instead, we could stand right outside the door and listen. Aisha took the spot by the door and I stood close enough that our arms pressed together. I took her hand, squeezing her fingers.

We had no trouble hearing Mrs. Warren as she said, "You should know that there's nothing more important to me than my child's education and I will not tolerate any interference with that. So either you fix this issue or I will see that the school board and the local news are aware of the selective rules and guidelines you have here at this school for people of color. If you think this is an idle threat please know that my husband and I have a standing yoga date with a late night news producer; try me if you want to."

The principal spoke for a minute or two, I couldn't get most of the words. I stayed quiet in case Aisha could hear better than me. She whispered, "Something about other complaints and a warning and training."

Mrs. Alexander sat near the door and had a loud voice, so I heard clearly when she said, "I live in a very diverse neighborhood and my sister-in-law is African American. I do not need training or consulting or oversight. I am simply trying to teach my students the best way I see fit and that girl needs to learn to follow instructions and do work even if it is boring."

"My daughter is not 'that girl,'" Mrs. Warren told her. "And you think because you're counting the black folks in your life, I'm supposed to find you less racist?"

In a low, carrying tone, Milo asked, "I'm sorry if I've got this wrong, but help me understand, aren't you teaching an advanced chemistry class that prepares students for college? How are you preparing Aisha for college-level science?"

Silence stretched out, wide and deep. I heard Mrs. Alexander's surprise in that silence; she hadn't thought about Aisha in college. Not for one minute.

And she had less than no clue how often Aisha had to face that burning shock from a white person when she showed her smarts or talked about college. No clue the weight and pain that put on Aisha.

"I prepare *all* my students for college," she insisted.

"What are you doing for Aisha?" Milo asked.

"I am not going to treat her special just because she comes from some poor, disadvantaged background. She can do the work like everyone else."

Mrs. Warren gave a humorless snort. "You don't know Aisha's background so let me tell you it's far from poor. Kaz told us that at summer camp you set up mentorship for kids falling behind. Why do that for a camp and not in class? If Kaz wants to work with Aisha on this project, why not? What made you willing to spend extra effort on that summer camp kid but not on my daughter?"

"I don't like what you're implying. You're blaming me for stories these kids have made up. I don't have to justify myself to you. And I do not appreciate being attacked in my own classroom."

"You're not being attacked," the principal said.

"Yes, she is," Milo said, evenly. "She's in the wrong. I'm sure you see it too. Let's not try to sugar-coat this. Let's get it handled."

Mrs. Alexander's voice rose in pitch. "How can you say that? It feels like every move I make is under scrutiny and I can't open my mouth at all without some kind of terrible accusation coming at me. I don't know what's happening to our school system in this country, I honestly don't. I'm not going to give any student special treatment—"

"Yes," the principal cut in. "So I'd like you to rotate the tasks the students are doing so no one student has the same task for more than two weeks, including the time they've already spent at that task."

"Fine. Will that be all?"

"For now."

Mrs. Alexander stormed out of the office, pausing to glare at me where I was leaning against the wall, having leapt back from the door. She wouldn't even look at Aisha.

Mrs. Alexander had left the door half open. Even though Milo spoke softly, I heard her say, "I don't know the first thing about running a school and I imagine it's very difficult, but if you'll pardon me saying, I think you've got a problem here."

Mrs. Warren backed her up with a heartfelt, "Mmhm."

"I'll keep an eye on that class," the principal said. "And I'll talk to Mrs. Alexander when she's cooled down. If she won't agree to attend diversity training, she won't continue teaching here."

"Good," Mrs. Warren said. "Thank you."

"Yes," Milo agreed. "Now, have you looked to see what percentage of examples used in math, science, history, English are white people? Because looking at my grandkid's homework, it's above ninety percent. You think you can get that down closer to sixty?"

"Our district *is* above ninety percent white," the principal said.

"Are you preparing students to live their whole lives in this school district?" Mrs. Warren asked, disbelief heavy in her tone.

"No. But we're not doing something wrong here. Aside from some individuals who need training, we're teaching the way we've taught for years and no one's complained."

"Because they moved away," Mrs. Warren said. "You're in a middle-class district. Families of color here have choices. We leave. I've been looking at houses in L.A. for two months now. When my husband gets transferred out there, do you think we're going to stick around for a ninety percent white curriculum? You think I'm not going to put Aisha in the absolute best school for her?"

"We're a very good school with high standards," the principal said.

Milo sighed, a long, slow, low sound. "Jenny, a lot of schools are. We're losing smart kids to other districts. When was the last time we won a regional Science Bowl? And you have an opportunity to make a difference, to do things better. If we bring you some information, will you read it and think about it, really think about it? Get someone in here to consult on this?"

"The budget..." Our principal—her first name was Jenny?—trailed off. "Is Aisha that good? Is it worth riling up everyone?"

"How often do you decide what kids are worth when they're in tenth grade?" Mrs. Warren asked. "Aisha's going to medical school whether you get your act together or not. But you're failing hundreds of kids."

"I didn't used to see it either," Milo admitted. "Think about it. If you came in here and all the teachers were Asian American, and so were most of the kids and most of the examples—and I'm saying Asian American because that environment makes white people feel stereotypically stupid—and everybody expected you to fail because that's how white kids are, no discipline, how well do you think you'd do on your schoolwork? Do you think you'd tell anyone about it? Or do you think you'd go head down and break yourself trying to be better? How many kids are you going to let that happen to before it's too many? Because the way I see it, one is too many."

"As a district, we don't have a lot of diversity, that's not our fault."

"No, it isn't," Milo said. "But now it's your responsibility."

That word hung in the air for a long time, until the principal said, "I'll think about it."

"Thank you."

Mrs. Warren and Milo came out of the office, saw us sitting in the chairs—because with the door open we could hear fine—and gave us a wave to follow them.

On our way across the parking lot, Aisha said, "Thanks, Mom. That was badass."

Mrs. Warren grumbled, "Lord help me, that woman. Milo, you know the principal, will she take action?"

"She'll watch that class like a hawk. Beyond that, my best guess it'll take a year or two to get some real training going, and the teachers who really need it won't get it. So I'd like to propose a two-part plan."

"Which is?" Mrs. Warren asked.

"First, pick up dinner, plus wine for you and beer for me. Then, we see how many friends I still have on the school board."

"Your kitchen or mine?"

"Yours, I'll bring the second half of that Bundt cake and that book you lent me last week. Kids, you're telling us if that teacher doesn't switch up the tasks by Monday."

* * *

Dinner blurred by, all of us over at the Warren household, Milo and Mrs. Warren retelling the story of the meeting to Pops,

Mr. Warren and Tariq. Congratulations turned into serious talk and strategizing. Under the table, Aisha rhythmically bumped her foot against mine.

Afterward, she said to everyone, "We're going to watch X-Men cartoons, holler if you're all watching something that isn't boring."

I followed her upstairs and sat on her bed, where I had hundreds of times, her beside me, her laptop in front of us. This was where I needed to keep sitting for the next two and a half years until we graduated high school.

She did turn on X-Men cartoons, fairly loud, and I tried to watch. My eyes burned no matter how much I blinked them.

Aisha said, "Hey," really softly, and rubbed her thumb across the wet streak on my face.

"Your mom said 'when,'" I whispered. "Not if. *When* your dad gets a job, you're not going to stay."

"I heard."

"I'd run away, hop a train, come to L.A., but I don't think I could bring Wolvie."

Aisha tugged my head and shoulders into her lap and curled over me. "Mom hasn't made an offer on anything, I asked. We have time."

"How much?" I asked. "Because it's not enough. If it's not forever, it's not enough."

Her cheek pressed to mine and her barely voiced words, "I know," breathed cold across my tears.

CHAPTER TWENTY-FIVE

Late November 2017

The next week, Mrs. Alexander did switch the classroom jobs around and (shocking!) eliminated the measuring and washing job. I guess she couldn't get her head around giving that to a white kid. I almost asked her about it, but I was afraid that would blow back on Aisha if I did.

Of course our going to the principal was going to blow back on Aisha anyway because Apocalypse does not rest. He was saying all kinds of evil into Mrs. Alexander's brain and she didn't know how to fight him because she was so wrapped up in defending her so-not-racist self.

We got emails that she'd be taking a leave of absence in the spring and there'd be a new AP Chem teacher. We also got our updated spring schedule and Aisha had been moved to another Chemistry class—*not* an AP class. Before leaving, Mrs. Alexander had tanked Aisha's grade enough to bump her out of the class. Mrs. Warren was back in the principal's office in a flash. But two white kids had also been reassigned to the easier course, so the school was delaying with some business about not wanting to treat Aisha differently than any other student.

Not being in AP Chem was a setback to getting into the International Baccalaureate program next year. Aisha hadn't been getting a great grade in Chemistry, but only because she was so pissed every time she had to go into that classroom. Now she'd have to sit in boring, regular chemistry thinking about how Mrs. Alexander had screwed her. How hard would it be to learn anything feeling that way?

I spent a week furious and trying not to vent around Aisha. She'd been a bundle of locked-jaw rage for days.

I skipped my Sunday World History session and asked Aisha to walk the dogs with me. She bundled up in full down coat, scarf, hat, mittens, even though it was still in the mid-forties and I hadn't switched from wearing my fall jacket.

I had three dogs in the neighborhood that I got paid to walk on weekends. We picked up the easy one first and then went to the house with two big rambunctious dogs. We brought them into the fenced yard and let all five run around sniffing and playing before we tried to walk them. The two big dogs romped while Wolvie got the two smaller dogs to chase her.

I kept stealing peeks at Aisha, trying to gauge how okay she was. I wanted to see her cheeks bright with cold, her eyes laughing. Instead she looked metallic, glints of steel in her eyes, like she wanted to have the bladed claws of the superhero Wolverine instead of the mental powers of Jean Grey.

I told her, "When you're a doctor, you're going to come back here someday, for a conference or whatever, and Mrs. Alexander's still going to be a high school Chemistry teacher. When you start winning awards, maybe I'll happen to forward some of those news stories to her."

She bumped her shoulder against mine. "And your awards. Send those too."

"Yeah, when I'm famous for figuring out how to train cats."

"Nope," she said. "For exposing how cats have been training people."

"No way! I've sworn never to tell. Don't even let the cats know you're in on it—you know how they get."

She almost laughed.

I said, "I think we need a plan."

Aisha watched the dogs running in circles. Pickles bossed the lot of them, herding them to one side of the yard and then the other. Wolvie helped without appearing to help, moving her body on the other side of the group from Pickles.

"We're the X-Men, right?" Aisha asked.

"Or X-People," I said with a humorless smirk

"But we're not, like, Iron Man or Dr. Strange. We don't fight solo. I think we need more X-Men. We've only got my parents and Milo, that's hardly a full team."

"And we need a lot of people to take on Apocalypse. He's really deep in some people's brains."

"Exactly," she said.

"There's Dr. Wade and Tariq. I can talk to Jon and his new boyfriend. We need more white people too. I'll make a list," I said. "White people need to be doing more in this fight."

She flashed me a grin. "I'll talk to Meta and Sofi."

"What do we do with our team?"

Aisha said, "I don't know about AP Chem. I can push it, with Mom, and get back in. But who knows what the teacher's going to be like. If I'm back in that class with some white teacher who thinks I got the other white teacher suspended, it's going to be a real crapfest."

"So what do you want to do?" I asked.

"Truth? Take Physics. It's way cooler than Chem, sorry."

"Can you get into second-semester AP Physics?"

"No. I've been looking at the textbook but I'm not there yet. I talked to Darius and he said maybe I could get an independent study. Meta did one last year because our school doesn't have Hindi."

"She knows Hindi?"

"She doesn't; that was kind of the point of studying it," Aisha said. She picked up a stick and tossed it to keep the big dogs running around. "She had a teacher track her progress and did it through an online course."

"You have a teacher in mind?"

"Mr. Saito, but I haven't asked him yet because…I had this other idea."

"I like your ideas," I said.

"I signed up for the Science Bowl."

Our school's Science Bowl was supposed to be an informal, fun competition where students could show off their science smarts. But in reality it was a cutthroat fight for bragging rights and resources. Each grade had its own competition level. At the tenth grade level, students weren't going on to regional competitions, but placing in any of the top three spots meant you'd have teachers' attention and they'd give you time and supplies and answers when you needed them.

"Oh hell yes," I said. "I'll help you study for it."

"That's what we need a team for. Not just studying, but being there. Can you be okay with me inviting Meta and her family?"

"Yeah. Of course. Who else?"

"Sofi and…" She trailed off.

"Are you going to invite Dr. Wade?"

"I thought about it. Do you think she'd come?"

I said, "I'd love to have her there, selfish reasons, of course. You want me to ask her?"

"No, I got it. Will you ask Jon?"

"Yep. Maybe this new guy he's with can bring some friends from Saint Paul." I hadn't seen much of him since he'd gotten a steady boyfriend, but I figured he'd still say yes. "What about Eve and Trina?"

"Might as well ask, they won't come anyway," Aisha said.

"I could tell them it's a makeup party."

I clicked my tongue and Wolvie came over to get attached to her leash, the other dogs following her example.

"I don't think they've got the right foundations for that party," Aisha quipped. I'd told her about the makeup closet at Trina's.

"Huh, well then, it's a World History study group."

"Pretty sure Trina and Caden shouldn't be making out during Science Bowl," Aisha said, almost smiling.

CHAPTER TWENTY-SIX

Early December 2017

The smart thing might've been to ask each person separately and deal with whatever they were going to say, but I didn't have the patience for that.

I texted Jon: *Can you come over to Trina's with me on Sunday and agree with everything I say?*

He wrote back: *Depends. Are you going to diss Sam Smith again?*

I didn't diss him the first time, but yeah, I'll leave him alone. I need people to be better backup for Aisha, that's what we're talking about.

He waited a few beats longer than I wanted to reply, but then he said: *I'm there.*

Trina had given up the pretense of World History project sessions now that Caden had the temple model finished. She invited a bunch of people to come hang out and told the rest of us to invite anyone we wanted. I'm pretty sure she didn't expect me to show up with Jon. She triple-taked and I gave her the head shake I hoped was the universal gesture for: *We're still super gay.*

Trina's living room was mainly filled with girls talking about TV shows and sports and eyeshadow, but Jon fit into that group easily. He wasn't a super girly gay guy, but he did love his eyeliner.

I nibbled Doritos and figured out how many people in the room I knew. In addition to the core group, there were four other girls from World History, two from the basketball team sitting with Eve, one guy that Caden had brought with him, plus the guy Sofi had been hanging out with the last month, though they weren't officially dating yet. Out of dozen people, I knew the names of about two-thirds. And everyone except Sofi was white, but this time that actually worked into my plan.

I stood up and said, "Hey" a few times to get people's attention.

"Speech?" Eve asked.

"Yeah," I said. "Look, I need your help. All of you. Students of color at our school have a shit time of it, everything from being stopped in the hall excessively by the hall monitors to being given grunt work in class to being expected to fail all the time. Plus what we're learning is super white and it's not preparing us to live in the diverse world we actually live in. Aisha and her mom and me and Milo already talked to the principal, but I need your help too. We can help change this."

"Why isn't Aisha here?" Eve asked.

"Because she shouldn't have to be. And she's studying for Science Bowl. You don't need 'the black girl' to show up and tell you it's wrong to have a school where whiteness is the norm and everything else is an exception. I'm telling you and if you keep watch for it, you'll see it too."

A confused look passed from Trina to Eve, a rustle in the room as people shifted and didn't talk. I raised my eyebrows at Jon.

"Kaz is right," he said. "Like, have you all seen those country flags in the hall?"

Lots of nodding happened, since those flags had been up since the start of the school year three months ago.

"And how there's Ireland, Germany, Japan, Mexico, and dozens of other countries. But there's only one flag from Africa and it's for Ethiopia," Jon said.

My chest ballooned hollow and big to fit all the pride I had for him. I'd complained about this to him a few weeks ago and he remembered.

"So?" Trina asked.

Jon looked to me, so I said, "Africa has fifty-four countries in it. As far as I know, no one in our school is from Ethiopia. Local African immigrants are mostly from Somalia and Kenya. Plus a lot of our African American students have families from West Africa."

The blank stares suggested that no one in this room knew the difference between East and West Africa, or why black kids whose family had been in the U.S. for generations would have West African genealogies.

I said, "Sure, we don't know where everyone's family is from, but they could put up the ten most likely flags along with the Pan-African flag and it would be great."

"Or just find out where everyone's family's from," Trina suggested.

I opened my mouth, but Jon got there first. "Um, Trina," he said. "Some people don't know where their families are from."

She cocked her head at him. "They could ask."

"There's nobody to ask," I said. "Nobody knows. Slave owners didn't keep records like that. People didn't even get to keep their own names, none of the white people in this country cared where they'd come from or who their families were."

The room got super quiet, the air dense as smoke.

Trina started crying and put her face in her hands. Eve was there in a flash, an arm around her, Sofi on the other side and some of the other girls I didn't know so well. I heard bits of what Trina was saying, "...so sad...I just feel so bad for these people... can't imagine what they went through...awful..."

I went into the kitchen to get another pop and get away from all that. Jon came with me.

"So," he said.

"It's going to be all about Trina for the rest of the day now."

"She seems really broken up about it."

"Yeah maybe, but my mom does that too. Like if I'm watching a show about black history, she'll sit and cry and talk about 'those poor people' and not change a thing about how she treats folks in her day to day. I used to think something was getting through to her, but it's like she thinks if she gets really upset about it now and then, she's off the hook. And she still says stupid shit about Aisha and doesn't realize it."

"She...what?" Jon's eyebrows went most of the way to his hairline. "You didn't tell me that?"

"You want to hear about every time my mom drops some casually racist bullshit?"

"Yes, I actually do."

"Thanks."

"You know, you could talk about this more because you're a badass about it," he said. "And I don't know one-fifth of what you do, so start with me. I'd watch some history and not cry. And I won't even make it about me even though, as a gay, you know that's one of my God-given skill sets."

I laughed and he ducked into the fridge for the orange juice. He handed me a Sprite.

Sofi came in and filled a bowl with chips and one with pretzels, but didn't carry them into the other room.

"You should go back and talk to Trina," she told me.

"Why? I'm not into The Trina Show."

"She asked questions. She took a risk. She's got to start somewhere."

I stared at Sofi, her black and light purple hair falling across the side of her face, her steady, dark eyes. I hadn't thought nearly enough about what life must be like for her as the one Asian American girl in our sophomore friend group. And I had never asked. I still had so much to learn.

"Oh," I said. "I didn't see that. Thank you."

I turned toward the living room, but Sofi's fingers on my arm paused me.

"I noticed that about the flags," she said. "Because they don't have Laos either or South Korea. I didn't know who to tell."

"Do you have Foggy for World History too? What period?" I asked.

"Yes, sixth."

"Want me to meet you after your class Monday and we can talk to him together?"

"That'd be great," she said. "What else can I do? Is there something specific?"

"Aisha's in the Science Bowl, so show up for her, cheer for her, support her," I said.

"I'll bet we can find someone with a great set of flashcards for that," Sofi said. "I'm on this."

I thanked her again, braced myself and went into the living room to tell Trina that she was brave and on the right path and then to gently deliver How To Be A Badass White Ally 101.

CHAPTER TWENTY-SEVEN

December 2017

Sofi brought us one set of flashcards and Zack came with extensive notes. I hadn't seen much of Zack since school started, with him being in eleventh grade, and was so glad to have another trans person in the friend group. Since the GSA had been founded from an International Baccalaureate prep class, it turned out to be a not-so-secret network of academic brilliance. Aisha's living room became a war camp for Science Bowl strategy.

I caught her mom watching us: me, Zack, Meta, Sofi, Jon and a few other kids. Most of the time the white kids were the minority and I prayed that her mom, seeing this, was deciding Aisha could stay here, that we'd take good enough care of her.

I'd only go home when there were too many people for me, too many voices talking at the same time, or when I had to show up for dinner so mom wouldn't get on me. Over at Aisha's, everyone used they/them pronouns for me, most of them doing it easily, except Mr. Warren, but he tried. At my house, I hadn't even asked. Though I noticed that Milo had stopped using pronouns for me at all and I was so grateful.

If Aisha could take on the whole school, I could at least talk to my family. At dinner, in a lull, I said, "Hey, so I'd like you all to use they/them pronouns for me."

Mom threw Milo a razor-sharp look and Milo caught it in her steady, clear eyes like she was daring Mom to come at her. Mom said, "You didn't tell me that was for Kaz."

"I wasn't telling you only for Kaz. I didn't know their pronouns. Just figured you should know that it's something the kids use these days."

Brock asked me, "You going to be a dude?"

"No, I'm nonbinary. I don't fit in those boxes."

Mom let out a big sigh and said, "I'm sorry, honey, would you explain that to me again. I'm used to men and women."

"Hang on." I ran up to my bedroom and got the notebook where I'd been putting info from Dr. Wade, photos from Aisha, images I'd found on my own.

Back at the table I offered it to Mom. She read the cover where I'd scrawled: *Kaz's Big Book of Gender* and took it. Paged through it with Brock leaning to where he could see over her shoulder.

They looked at the examples of cultures with three, four, five, even six genders, cultures where people easily switched genders or had multiple genders at the same time, cultures without gender. And facts about biology, like how all humans had all of what we called "sex hormones," most of us in really similar amounts; everybody needed all these hormones.

Plus statistics because I went all out! Over sixty percent of adult cisgender (not trans) men experienced some breast enlargement during their lives. About forty percent of cisgender women could grow facial hair and at least seven percent had amounts and patterns of body hair considered "male." If there were only two discrete biological sexes, how come so may men got boobs and so many women had mustaches and beards? Because we all started out the same and we all had the same hormones—and as we grew, there were so many different pathways we could take.

I said, "Humans are super adaptable, there isn't one right way to do things, there's a bunch of right ways and some work better than others. It's pretty recent that Western culture decided that if you have certain characteristics, like boobs and ovaries, then you have to do this social role called 'woman.' That's not what my body means. My body means I'm a person. My hormones and my parts don't define me and who I'm going to be. I get to be all the ways I'm capable of being."

"Yeah but what bathroom do you use?" Brock asked.

"Any of them. Toilets are toilets."

"Who's Dr. Wade?" Mom asked, because her name was in the notebook.

"A college professor who's helping me think about all this. She gave me some books and articles. I figured if I got it all organized for myself, then I could explain it to other people and maybe use it for papers the next few years."

"You're doing a project for a professor?" Mom asked. "Wow. I've never seen you this organized."

"That's 'cause you haven't seen my dog training stuff."

"Can I meet Dr. Wade?"

"Sure. Next time me and Aisha go to see her, you could come pick us up and hang out for a bit. Hey also, do you want to come to the Science Bowl? Aisha's on a team with Jon and they're going to slay. You too, Brock."

"Nah," he said. "That shit's boring."

"You're not there for the science, you'd be there to support Aisha."

He shrugged. "The tenth grade one doesn't matter anyway. And she's got lots of support."

I considered Brock's pink-white face. When had the strength of his jaw and the close set of his eyes gone from looking heroic to clueless?

"Hey." I took my notebook back from Mom and turned to the back so I could get the color printouts I'd done at school that week. I pushed them across the table to him. "I made these for you."

"Captain America? Why?"

"Chris Evans, the actor who plays him, he's a pretty great human being. And that's Matt McGorry, he's another actor, and Justin Baldoni, he acts, directs and makes movies."

"Yeah, who cares? I don't want to act or do any of that."

"Because we don't see enough good white guys on TV," I said.

He picked up the pictures, tapped them on the table to line up the edges, then tore them in half. Dropping them on his dinner plate, he got up and walked out.

"Asshole," I said. Nobody at the table got on me for language.

Milo lifted the pictures off Brock's plate, wiped the back and put them by hers.

* * *

I finished my World History paper—the part of the project I got to do on my own. We did a presentation in class too, for which we got all of fifteen minutes and I had to wear a tunic and sandals in December. But Caden's temple model was amazing and got displayed in the back of the room with my charts comparing wealth inequality in the Roman Empire to modern America.

Spoiler alert: in the U.S. today the top one percent of households owns forty percent of the country's wealth, while in Rome the top one-and-a-half percent owned twenty percent. So our country was doing a lot worse than ancient Rome, and we knew what happened to them.

More than our teacher reading the paper, I wanted Mom and Brock to read it. Considering how unlikely that was, I waited for our next family dinner. Brock hadn't shown up. We weren't talking since he'd ripped up the pictures I gave him.

"Do you all want to hear parts of my World History paper?" I asked Mom, Milo and Pops when we'd finished eating dinner.

"Isn't that a group project?" Mom asked.

"It's both. We did a group presentation plus individual papers. My group compared banking in ancient Rome and the U.S., and I did a paper about two families in Minnesota."

"We're all ears," Milo said, waving a hand to include Pops. She'd already read the paper in an early draft, but being the best grandmom in the world, was totally up for hearing it now.

We moved to the living room, with Milo, Pops and Mom on the couch. I ran up to my room for my paper and notecards, so Wolvie ran up and down with me, then turned around a bunch in her dog bed before settling.

I started out with the info about how wealth inequality in the U.S. is way worse than in ancient Rome and asked, "Why is this?"

Mom shrugged. Milo grinned at me and said, "I trust you're going to tell us."

"One of the main pillars of wealth inequality in our country is racism," I said, reading off my notecards too much. "And to show you how this works, I want to tell you a story about two families. Now I know in our family that when you got together…" I pointed at Milo and Pops. "Pops's dad helped you buy your first house. And I asked Aisha about her grandpop and grandmom. They didn't own a house when they got married or for a long time after. So let's start there, but let's look at the same family under two conditions, whether that family is white or black."

I'd been tempted to call the family the Wadamses after Warren + Adams, but that sounded too flippant for the topic, so I went middle of the alphabet and picked "Long" as the family name. I had printouts of a white couple in front of a house and a black couple in front of an apartment building and held these up while talking.

"In the 1940s, a white family was twice as likely to own their home as a black family, for lots of reasons including having higher income, banks being more likely to lend to them, housing discrimination, etcetera. So, if our average family, the Longs, are white, they've probably got great-grandparents who own a home while that same family, if black, doesn't. The grandparents of the white family are also much more likely to own a home and to get help from their parents to do so."

I'd been ignoring the thumping in the kitchen that meant Brock taking off boots but now he came around the corner, through the dining room, to the living room doorway. He leaned there and crossed his arms. I put my chin up, realized I couldn't see my notecards, looked down and went on with my report.

"Now let's look at the income of those white grandparents—and no snickering, Milo and Pops, I did averages and I don't have the math to adjust everything for inflation, but you'll get the idea. An average white man without a Bachelor's degree makes about a million dollars over the course of his working life—and because of racism, an average black man with the same degree would make $730,000. That's a lifetime tax of $270,000 just for being black. That hasn't changed between 1980 and 2015, and before 1980, it was less. Since women still make less than men, the grandmom in the white Long family would make about $820,000. But if she's in the black Long family, she'd make about $700,000."

"Kaz, I made more than that," Milo said.

"I know, but you have a degree, and I rounded it down to a million to make the math simple. See, with my average family, the white grandparents together make $1,820,000 but the black grandparents only make $1,430,000. And if the cost of living is $1.4 million, the white family ends up with $420,000 in the bank and the black family with $30,000."

"There's no way," Brock said from the doorway. "There's reasons for that."

"Yeah there are," I said, louder than him. "Study after study shows that black Americans are given fewer promotions even when equally qualified, are hired less—"

"I don't believe it," he said.

"I have some of them printed out in my room. I'll bring them down for you."

"The studies are biased."

"All of them? Let me finish this." I returned to my notecards, flipped over one I didn't need. "If you think my math is unrealistic to show that the black family has seven percent of the savings of the white family, national statistics show that black households actually have closer to five percent of the wealth of white households. Because they're also more likely to be targeted by predatory lenders and have to borrow money for emergencies at higher interest rates.

"And that's just savings based on earnings, that's not even looking at investing. Since the white grandparents have more money, let's say they've got enough to invest $1000 a year in the stock market. Over forty years the $40,000 they've invested would grow to over $200,000. Since the black family has five percent of that wealth, let's say they invest $50 a year—and let's go benefit of the doubt that they don't have to take that money back out for an emergency—at the end of the same forty years, they've managed to save about $11,000.

"My grandparents have been putting money away for me to go to college since I was born. I have $13,600 in the bank for me to go to college. Thanks, Milo and Pops! In the black family I've presented today, given the average wealth gap in our country, do you know how much would be in the bank for my future? Not because my family didn't work hard, but because of everything stacked against us. Can you guess how much? Six-hundred and eighty-five dollars."

"No! Way!" Brock about yelled from the doorway. "There are so many other reasons: drugs, single mothers, violence."

"Our country is *full* of systems that are biased against black people," I shouted back.

"You only give a shit because of Aisha!"

"I am lucky enough to know how ignorant I was because of Aisha. I would hope that I—and everyone in this family—would be a decent enough human being to recognize when something is grossly unfair and fix it."

Mom, Milo and Pops all turned sideways on the couch, so they could look from one of us to the other. Pops had his hand on the couch arm, ready to push up in a flash if our argument got too heated.

"Why fix that first when so much else is fucked up?" Brock asked.

"Like what?" Mom asked and it took me a second to register the question had come from her. The weight of her words said she knew the answer to what Brock wanted fixed, and then I did too, even before she said, "your father has a new family now. He doesn't want anything to do with us."

Brock stomped out through the kitchen, slamming the back door.

"I'll talk to him," Pops said and followed.

I knelt and put my arms around Wolvie, who'd pressed against my leg, shaking, as she felt the anger in the room. But I watched Mom's face and wondered how much I didn't know about our family.

If I asked, she'd tell me whatever she knew about our father. Probably that Brock had tried to get in touch with him again and been ignored. And I didn't want to know that yet. I'd heard how she'd found where my dad was living with a new wife and new kids, and gone to him for child support that he paid sometimes, and I ignored all that. So what if he had a new family? I had a new family too and mine was better. I had Milo and Pops and Aisha and all the Warrens.

And I didn't want this fight to be about Brock or about me. No matter how upset Brock got, that didn't make it okay to use terrible contentions about other people to get ahead.

"Can I show you the rest of the report?" I asked Mom.

She patted the couch cushion between her and Milo and I tried to sit there, but Wolvie beat me to it.

CHAPTER TWENTY-EIGHT

December 2017

Our school auditorium usually smelled like ass feet—like a pair of feet had grown out of unclean buttocks and walked the room for days. But for Science Bowl they managed to switch it over to an antiseptic smell with a note of inky intelligence. They hadn't swapped any of the sports team banners, but they'd set up the stage with long tables draped in deep blue cloth edged with gold. Those were our school colors and they made it pretty classy.

Aisha had been studying for weeks, with me and Jon, plus online, and with Darius, Sofi, Zack, Meta and anyone else who'd run through her flashcards. I'd given her a pep talk the night before that included more holding her close and giving her little kisses than talking.

Now Aisha sat in her spot, behind her nametag, wearing a peach sweater and dark pants, with her hands twisting together in her lap, keeping them from shaking. She was so scared. Not about the math or the kids up there with her, but this audience. So scared that she'd screw up and prove their stupid stereotypes right. Most of our teachers were here, including Mrs. Alexander in the second row on the other side since her "leave" didn't start until after break.

The competition went in two rounds. For the first, students competed in pairs. The top three pairs made it to round two and went against each other individually. Of the twelve students in the first round, nine were white and two Asian or Asian American. Aisha was the only black person and one of three girls. The auditorium had half filled, we still had fifteen minutes until the start time, but already it looked as white as our high school.

To be fair, I noted that Jon was the only out gay guy. He and Aisha had been joking that their team name should be "Team Queer." The formal contest didn't have team names, but the study group all called them that.

I walked to the side of the room, leaned against the wall, crossed my arms. Some people looked at me. What did they see? Some babydyke? Okay. A tomboy? Less okay. A boyish girl or girlish boy? They could look but they probably couldn't see me. It didn't matter right now, I only needed Aisha to see me.

I wore the binder and slim-skinny guy jeans that I loved— dark blue denim, no tears, no wearing—and my amazing light blue *Jay & Miles X-Plain the X-Men* T-shirt that combined the X-Men and trans symbols. Over that I wore a dark brown men's shirt, unbuttoned to show my T-shirt. But I also had my hair up in a topknot, and earrings, light makeup, so I didn't come across as just trying to look like a guy. From the double-takes, this combination confused plenty of people.

Aisha's head tipped up, gaze sweeping back and forth across the audience. Searching for me. I straightened up. She *saw* me.

I nodded once, slowly, grinning, acknowledgement and joke. Her lips quirked and she nodded back. She put her hands on top of the table and sat back in her chair.

She stared out over the audience. The front three rows were sparsely populated on this side. Mr. and Mrs. Warren came up and saved seats for me and Tariq, and a few more for Milo and Pops.

Meta came in with her mom and dad and her sister and three of her friends. I swallowed my pride and waved to her, calling, "Hey, Meta, we saved seats up here!"

Her family and friends slid into the row with Aisha's parents and got to catching up about parent stuff. Meta came over to me. "Why aren't you sitting?"

"So Aisha can see me better."

Meta opened and closed her mouth, turned and looked at Aisha. "Got it," she said and stayed facing the front, leaning against the wall.

"Thanks," I told her.

Sofi and Jon joined us.

Trina and Eve came in with some other girls and they were all wearing X-Men buttons. "Do they know what those mean?"

"Conceptually, sure," Jon said. "For real, no. I bought a bunch for them to wear. Figured it was the right way to support our team. They did say they'd come see *Black Panther* when it's out."

"Wow, let me know how that goes."

"You could come with us," he offered.

"Maybe. But I'm seeing it with Aisha first."

"Wish me luck," he said and went up to take his seat next to Aisha. I couldn't hear what he said to her, but from her eyeroll it was a failed attempt at a joke.

The competition started and Aisha stayed middle of the pack even though she knew all these answers. Heck, I knew most of the easy ones at this point, but she kept looking up at her parents and over at me and at her hands. Mostly at her hands.

Jon got one right and one wrong, putting them in fifth position.

The next question was: "One of the strongest materials manufactured by processes within mammalian bodies, this polypeptide's alpha helix forms a coiled coil. Its harder versions have up to 8% cysteine, while the more flexible versions go as low as 2.5%. What is this protein affected by heat, which can be curled, waved, or straightened when manifest as human hair?"

Aisha hit the buzzer and said, "Keratin." She got it right, but her forehead pinched, lines between her eyebrows. It took a second for me to get how she'd feel about being so quick to answer a question about hair. She was worried that people thought this was all she knew.

She sat through the next four without even trying for the buzzer. Jon got one right about laminar flow and turbulent flow, which was badass.

The questioner asked, "The first disease ever linked to a single gene, this condition's abnormal protein—especially prominent in black people—can protect its carriers against malaria if they carry it on only one chromosome; two copies of the mutated gene, however, can impede blood circulation and cause strokes and seizures. What is this condition named for its misshapen or unusually shaped red blood cells?"

Nobody moved.

Aisha hit her buzzer and, voice strangled, said, "Sickle Cell Anemia."

She looked madder than I'd ever seen her. Way to load on the stereotype threat. She didn't move through the next six questions

I wanted to tear down this fucking school.

I felt like we were in that scene at the end of the *X-Men: Apocalypse* movie when Apocalypse is beating the shit out of Professor X, has him pinned to the ground and is this huge, terrifying force in his mind. And Apocalypse has already beaten all the X-Men, immobilized or caged them. He's going to wreck them and then the world.

The same way this school was wrecking us. The way the force of Apocalypse, that hidden racism and sexism in the minds around us, beat down so many young heroes.

As the X-Men are all dying, Professor X calls to Jean Grey, "Unleash your power!...No fear!" She's afraid that her power is too destructive. Like Aisha being scared of being the angry black woman or falling into any of the stupid stereotypes she'd been offered.

In my mind I called to Aisha: *Unleash your power!*

But neither of us was that good at lip reading, so I squared my shoulders and the next time she looked my way I mouthed: *I love you.* And I hoped that my eyes showed how much that was true no matter what.

She and Jon were in fourth place with only a few questions to go.

"Archaeologists confirm that a largely alphabetical system of writing provided the foundation for extensive trade, philosophy, and poetry more than two thousand years ago in a system of city-states whose descendants survive in what modern nation?"

Aisha slammed her hand down on the buzzer.

"Greece," she said. "That's *your* answer. But it's equally true of Ethiopia."

She got the next one right too, edging her and Jon into the third spot and the second round, where they would each compete as individuals. Jon wasn't going to make it far into the second round; science wasn't his thing. But how far would Aisha make it when all the attention was on her alone and each question felt like a trap?

On the break I asked Sofi to save my spot and went to walk around the parking lot, pissed at so many people in that room and one who wasn't. Brock didn't even pretend he'd show up and at this point I didn't want him to. I'd tried to give him something good and he'd shredded it. He'd always be my brother and I'd have a place for him if he wanted to wake up and be a decent human being, but I wasn't wasting any more time on him, not when I had friends like Jon and Sofi who did want to create a better future together.

I stomped the length of the parking lot and back, still had a few minutes before the break ended, so I crossed it again, heavy steps, arms swinging, trying to burn out my rage.

On the strip of snow between parking lot and street, I stopped to watch a bunch of cars, driving by in a line, like for a funeral. The two bumpers I could see bore rainbow flag stickers. The next car had a trans sticker and a Black Lives Matter sticker.

My superhero reflexes kicked in faster than thought. "Hey!" I hollered, waving my arms. "Hey, over here!" I ran after them, waving and yelling, "Here! Here!"

The last car pulled over and a girl got out, college-aged, stout and dark-skinned, in a red hijab. "We're looking for the high school auditorium," she said. "Do you know where that is?"

"Right here!" I pointed behind me. "Those other cars are heading for the junior high."

"Oh!" she pulled a phone out of her purse and texted quickly. "Thank you."

"You're here for Aisha, aren't you? Please say you are. Please."

"Are you Kaz?" she asked and I nodded. "I'm Hani. Why are you out here? Did Dr. Wade tell you?"

"No, it's just luck or magic or telepathy or all three."

Hani grinned and ducked back into the car so they could pull into the parking lot and help wave down the other cars. There were seven cars and a lot of people. Hani explained that Dr. Wade had invited all the students from her sociology classes to this event, saying it was a study of implicit racism in suburban Minnesota.

From Dr. Wade's three classes, more than twenty students decided to road trip down to our little town. I saw light brown faces, medium brown, dark, red-brown, tan, more races and ethnicities than I could name. Dr. Wade got out of her car with a curvy black woman in an orange shirt under a gray suit that I'd have worn even if it was a women's suit.

Dr. Wade introduced her as her wife and was about to introduce the students, but I hopped in place and said, "We have to get back inside. The first round already happened. Come on!"

We got to the auditorium three minutes before the end of the break and filed up the wide aisle between the two sets of bleachers and chairs. Conversation stopped. The tension of all the other white people in the room pressed hard against my skin.

I turned toward our side of the room and yelled, "Milo, how many seats are still open up there?"

That hit pause on the rising tension but it did not dissipate.

Milo rose up from the row in front of Aisha. She beamed the way she did when we worked on a woodshop project together and it turned out just right.

Without seeming to yell, she raised her voice enough to carry through that vast room. "Dr. Amanda Wade, I've been reading your papers." With the entire audience silently watching, Milo crossed the front of the room, still talking, came down the wide aisle, hand extended. "I'm so pleased to meet you. How many seats do we need?"

"Twenty-four," Dr. Wade said. "And it's wonderful to meet the famous Milo."

Mrs. Warren was on her feet, calling to the back of the room, "Milo, Dr. Wade, we've got eight open here. More if we could add some chairs."

"Spare chairs are over there," Milo pointed. "The kids will get them for you."

Amid the resumed hubbub in the room, I scrambled with Sofi, Meta, Zack, and Tariq to get more chairs by the side of the front rows. We managed to fit in ten more chairs. Then Jon planted his feet, looked at Trina's group and said, "Would you all move back a few rows?"

Trina opened her mouth, but Sofi cleared her throat pointedly and said, "Caden and the guys will help make room, won't they?"

"Yes, they will," Trina said and got up.

Damn. Sofi must've had a talk with her. I wanted to know what she'd said.

Conversations started again as Dr. Wade's group came up to fill in all the empty chairs. Aisha blinked hard, trying not to cry as the front three rows on her side got filled in. I kept fiddling with the chairs, because I was also on the edge of tearing up too.

I was far up enough toward the front that I could see how it might look to Aisha: the only white faces in the front three rows now were Milo and Pops. Plus me standing on the side. Rows two and three were all brown, tan, cashmere, chenille, walnut, mission oak, mahogany faces—two-thirds of the wood chart from Milo's workshop, of the foundation colors on the card—most chatting with each other but also glancing up at Aisha and smiling, grinning, or giving a thumbs-up. All of us looked at her like she could say anything and it would be the best thing in the world.

The second round started.

Aisha was fire. Totally phoenix.

Exactly that moment in the movie where Jean Grey is so scared but she walks out of the building, walks straight out in the air because she's that powerful, frees all the other X-Men, including Beast. Together they disintegrate Apocalypse— literally turn him to dust and blow him away.

Aisha *was* Jean Grey. And Storm if she wanted, and Dr. Maggie Pierce from *Grey's Anatomy*, and anyone she wanted to be.

From that point on, she rode over most of the other students and only came in second to a squirrely white boy who everyone knew was the school's resident super genius.

* * *

In the aftermath of Science Bowl, most of the student audience members fled the building, while the parents and contenders and friends hung out for punch and cookies. Dr. Wade, her wife, and all the sociology students stayed.

From the side of the room, I watched Milo and Mrs. Warren working in concert, without talking to each other. They went from group to group, meeting people from Dr. Wade's classes and introducing them to clumps of students and parents from our high school, staying in the conversation long enough to make sure it really got going and then moving to the next.

I saw two college students standing by the wall, one with a purple-white-green scarf: genderqueer colors. I went over to them. "Hey, I'm Kaz, I go here and Aisha's my girlfriend and I'm nonbinary. Do you want to meet some of the other kids in the gender and sexuality group here?"

"Oh yes!" one said. So I took them over to Meta and Zack.

Once they got talking excitedly about their overlapping geekeries, I pushed up on tip-toes and searched the room for Aisha. I spotted her on the far side of the cookies and punch table having an intense conversation with Mr. Saito, the Physics teacher. Mrs. Warren saw this too and went to join them. From the amount of nodding Mr. Saito was doing, Aisha's independent study for spring was more than handled.

I found Milo sitting with Pops in the front row of chairs and plunked down next to her.

"Looks like it worked," I said, waving in Aisha's direction.

"She did great. He's lucky to have her as a student," Milo said. "But this won't fix everything. She'll still have to fight. We all will."

"Yeah," I said. "But we're superheroes. And now she's got a big team. She's not like Superman, off doing everything alone. That's never been how she likes things. We just needed to have other people to fight with us."

"Kid, always."

CHAPTER TWENTY-NINE

January 2018

Los Angeles

I had an arm around Aisha's shoulders, but that wasn't enough contact, so she took my right hand in hers, pulled it across and played with my fingers. The sun lipped down to the ocean and the air hovered about sixty degrees. I'd taken off my sweatshirt, but Aisha wore a mid-weight jacket.

In Minnesota, the high for the day had been three degrees. Milo faithfully texted me a photo of Wolvie in the snow. They'd gotten four inches in the two days I'd been in L.A.

I'd met two of Aisha's aunts, plus her trans cousin. Darius and his girlfriend drove down from Berkeley. They sat farther down the wall from us, still eating ice cream. Aisha and I had inhaled ours.

Ice cream and a sunset over the ocean in non-freezing weather—Aisha might've been right about California. Not that Minnesota wasn't also great.

She fished in the pocket of her jacket and came out with a small wrapped box, white and silver snowflake paper. She'd gotten me some comics for Christmas but told me she was saving one gift for later. I peeled off the paper and opened the box.

A necklace sat on green tissue paper: one big silver bead with two concentric circles around it, each with two beads. I rubbed my thumb over it, then picked it up, letting the circles dangle from the silver chain.

"That's a carbon atom," Aisha said.

"You remembered my pronouns. From the way the trees use carbon to communicate all pronouns at once."

"Kaz, life itself. You feel like that to me."

"You are too," I told her. "We do all start out the same for the first few weeks of our lives. Maybe that's why the feeling of my body changes, shifts from male to female to both to something else, because all bodies contain that original similarity and I feel it more than most."

"But we're not the same," Aisha said. "Our differences should be strengths, like superheroes. They don't have all the same powers, but they learn to use all their powers together to be greater than they can be alone."

I put on the necklace, looped my arm over her shoulders again, and pulled her close. She rested her head on my shoulder and played with the necklace where it rested on top of my T-shirt.

"You were right about California," I said.

"It's the best."

"One of the best. This summer I'll show you everything great about the family lake cabin and the lake itself. And Wolvie will show Mr. Pickles around. He'll love it."

She nodded. I caught the flash of her grin. "We should invite Riq, he *loves* camping."

Her mom had paused the house-buying, moving-to-L.A. project for now. I'd turn sixteen in a week and in May Aisha would too, which meant that for junior year she could pick any high school within driving distance of our Minnesota town. And

I could go with her because the Warrens were staying in the big, bright house across the alley from mine. Or we could take some classes at our high school, some online, and maybe Aisha would take some college classes.

Long term, the answer isn't Minnesota or California—it's not binary like that—it's California *and* Minnesota. It's all the genders. It's people getting what they need without feeling they've got to take it from anyone else. And it's whole bunch of things we haven't imagined yet: living a present that understands our past but is dreamed from our future.

Author's Note

In terms of race, this is a story about a white person learning to be an ally. There are many great books by black and African American authors about the experiences of black teens, with more being published every day. Read them!

Rather than list the books I read to research this novel and those I recommend, you can find that list on my website at https://rachelgold.com/silences/ along with links to reading lists with more recommendations. On my website, you can also find gender-related reading recommendations and some comic books that I love.

You can also visit:

http://queerbooksforteens.com/find-books/ to find many young adult novels searchable by race/ethnicity and gender of the main characters, and much more.

https://www.glsen.org/article/supporting-black-lgbtq-students for resources to combat stereotype threat.

https://www.translifeline.org/ for support around gender identity and transition.

More than ever, we're not alone. If you're not part of a team of superheroes yet, today is a good day to start gathering your allies and become a hero.

Bella Books, Inc.

Women. Books. Even Better Together.

P.O. Box 10543
Tallahassee, FL 32302

Phone: 800-729-4992
www.bellabooks.com